Bad Widow

·

Bad Widow

Jennifer Hart Shaw

Bad Widow

Published in the United States of America
ISBN 10: 1981338349
ISBN-13: 978-1981338344

Women's Fiction, Contemporary Romance

This book is dedicated
to all the beautiful women I know
who have remained strong and courageous
through life's difficult challenges.

~ ~ ~

I want to especially thank my mother, Sue,
and my husband, Darren, for being first readers,
and Janet, for your editorial input and encouragement.

CHAPTER 1

"All the art of living lies in a fine mingling of letting go and holding on." – Havelock Ellis

Early morning light from the window filters into my room, telling me to get out of bed, but I stubbornly resist. Instead, I snuggle down further into the warm and heavy covers, hoping to drift back into the deep sleep I had been enjoying. As is often the case, though, once my mind is quiet, I begin to fill it up with thoughts and plans for the day. I decide to spend time writing in the morning and then do a little shopping in the afternoon. I think about our old brown paisley curtains and decide that today is the day I will buy new ones. I've been meaning to do it for a long time. I'll see if I can bribe Lauren to go with me. It would be more fun to go with someone, and I'll buy her something new for her apartment while we're out. I wonder if Joseph would like to go out to dinner tonight. We could try that new restaurant he read about in the paper. I'll time my shopping around meeting him after work. Content with my plan, I settle back into my pillow for a few more minutes of rest before I have to get up.

I've just started drifting back to sleep when all at once everything comes back to me like a kick in the gut. Frantic, I push off the blanket that a moment ago was such a comfort, but is now suffocating. I sit up in bed and tell myself to breathe in and out. In and out. I can't have another panic attack. A few more deep breaths and the vise on my chest loosens its grip. I can't believe I forgot all that's happened to me in the last three months. I must be losing my mind. The pain and disappointment is too much for me, so with a heavy heart, I close my eyes, slip under the blanket, and ease back into nothingness for a little while longer.

An hour later, I wake up again. This time my thoughts are crystal clear. I know my husband is dead and I am a widow, which still surprises me. Surely, I'm not old enough to be a widow. The depressing and lonely day is before me, and I don't care at all about my earlier plans. I lay very still with my eyes closed, hoping to fall back into a world where I know nothing. However, my hungry stomach demands to be fed, and I cannot ignore the ache it's causing. I can't remember when I last ate. When I was a normal person I never missed a meal, but the widow in me has no appetite, and I frequently have to be reminded by my growling stomach to eat something. I crawl out of bed, holding on to the nightstand to steady myself as I feel for my slippers. Each step to the kitchen is painful as my body works out the ache that comes from lying in the same place too long. Neglecting my usual morning ritual of a cup of coffee before eating, I open the fridge and pantry, only to be hugely disappointed that I have nothing breakfast-like to eat. My rumbling stomach demands food– any food –so I pull out a container of mystery casserole that my neighbor, Susan Gardner, brought over a week ago. Poking my fork into the dish, my nose involuntarily scrunches up as I sniff it. Ordinarily, I would have tossed it out, but hunger, laziness, and general apathy prompt me to put the dish into the microwave and heat it up. I don't care what it is or how old it is, as long as it's edible. I make a mental grocery list while I wait for the microwave to beep, already deciding to head to the store right after I eat. Since breakfast is all I can think about, my list consists of eggs, orange juice, bacon, muffin mix, bananas, cereal, and raisin bread–BEEP,

BEEP–the microwave interrupts my shopping list and diverts my attention from images of breakfast to focusing on the process of chewing and swallowing whatever is in the container. I try to think of something, but all I can think of is that it's hard to think of anything. Since Joseph's death, I have a difficult time focusing on more than one thing at a time. All of my prior multitasking skills are gone, buried with my love. All I can manage to focus on are the basic necessities of life, like when I'll eat, sleep, and if I'll take a shower or bath each day. Focusing on only one thing at a time is working pretty well for me. I haven't had any big meltdowns in at least two weeks.

A peculiar aftertaste from the casserole is beginning to turn my stomach so I throw out the rest. Now that the hunger isn't screaming so loud, I can focus on getting dressed. Sweatpants, t-shirt, ponytail, and tennis shoes. My new widow's uniform is as practical as it is comfortable, and I'm thankful that I am no longer expected to look good.

The grocery store lot is crowded, and as I wait for a blue Honda to back out of the space I want, I try very hard to remember what day it is. It's disorienting not knowing something so basic and simple. It isn't Sunday because Lauren always calls me on Saturday to see if I am going to church. I think she does this in part to remind me of what day it is, and in part, because she isn't going to go to church if I don't go. It isn't Monday or Tuesday because I didn't go to church just yesterday or the day before. Other than knowing it isn't Sunday, Monday, or Tuesday, I really have no idea what day it is, and truthfully, it doesn't matter. The thought troubles me for a second but is gone as soon as I pull into the parking space.

As I get close to the entrance, I realize the mistake I've made. Since Joseph's death, I have been driving a few extra miles to the Randall's down the road, but now I find myself back at our usual store, H.E.B. I have not been back here since that terrible day. I have also not been back to my yoga class. These two mundane activities have become reminders of the day I lost him. The day I was too busy to answer his calls.

Approaching the door, my heart begins pounding and I will myself to calm down. Taking big breaths in and out, I forge ahead, grab a cart and bravely walk toward the produce section. Joseph loved the produce section. On the days when he would shop with me, we would divide the grocery list, and he would predictably request the produce and meat items. He took time to find the best of everything: apples with no bruises, lettuce with no wilt, equal sized baking potatoes, and just-right ripe bananas. I would often finish all the other shopping before he would complete his half of the list. Today, I quickly grab three bananas and a carton of strawberries. I do not check for bruises or ripeness.

I follow my list, moving down the aisles without really looking around me. I am working hard to keep my emotions under control, determined not to cry in the grocery store. When I get to the cereal aisle, I pick up my box of Honey Nut Cheerios and then reach for the Frosted Flakes. I have them in my cart and I'm walking away before I realize that I don't like Frosted Flakes. Joseph liked Frosted Flakes. Joseph ate them almost every day, if not for breakfast, then for a late night snack. They belonged to him. The room shrinks and everything starts swimming around me. To steady myself, I lean against my cart. It's getting harder to breathe, so I rest my head on the handle and take big steadying breaths in and out. I close my eyes and suddenly Joseph is in front of me at our round kitchen table. He looks up and grins as he shovels a spoonful of cereal into his mouth. His eyes twinkle and he winks at me. His mouth is too full and his cheeks bulge as he chews. Crunch, crunch, crunch.

I think I'm going to fall down.

"Miss? Miss?" I feel a gentle touch on my arm. "Are you alright?"

Slowly, the kitchen fades, and I am aware of the fluorescent lights, tile floors, and the voices of strangers all around me. When I look up, a very kind, plump face is staring directly into my eyes.

"Are you okay? Do you need anything?"

"I, um, I'm sorry," I mumble and start moving my cart down the aisle.

"It's okay. You don't have to be sorry," she says behind me, as I move further away from her.

If I stay, I will cry.

Suddenly, I don't care about buying everything on my list. I just want out of here. I consider leaving my groceries in the basket, but then I'd have nothing. And I don't want to have nothing. I check out as quickly as I can and push my cart to the car.

I fully intend to drive home and crawl back into bed, but for some reason, I don't turn toward home. For some reason, I take an exit I never take, the exit where they found Joseph's car. I drive slowly when I get close to where I imagine it happened. I never saw it myself. A tow truck took his car to an impound lot. Joseph's brother picked it up for me, and at my request, sold it. I never saw it again. Up ahead I see an inlet on the side of the road. Immediately, I think this is a place to stop your car and have a heart attack. I cross over the adjacent lane, ignoring the blast from the horn behind me and park my car. For the third time this morning, I tell myself to breathe in and out. The traffic races by me, occasionally shaking my little car. Every jostle sends my heart racing again and I start over with my focused breathing. Eventually, I feel relaxed enough to move. I reach to the back seat, putting my hand in the grocery bags and fumble around until I feel the large rectangle box of Frosted Flakes. I get out of the car and stand between it and the ditch, away from the road. I open the box, tearing into the plastic bag. Then I turn it upside down and pour all the flakes onto the ground, covering the grass and dirt. The traffic noise that seemed so loud only a moment ago, is now a soft hum in the distance. All I hear are the flakes tumbling out of the box, chiming. For reasons I can't possibly explain, this makes me feel better.

When I get home, I carry in my two bags and put everything away, including the empty box of Frosted Flakes. It goes in the pantry right next to my Cheerios. Looking around my kitchen I think of all the times Joseph and I sat around our breakfast table talking about the day ahead or the day behind. Sometimes he would sit, waiting, as I cooked at the stove. On a few occasions, I had asked him if he wanted to cook with me or maybe take a couples cooking class. Joseph always seemed to have an excuse.

"The kitchen's too small for us to both cook."

"I'd just mess it up. You're already so good at it."

"I like to read the paper while you cook. It relaxes me."

"If you want to take a class, go ahead. Maybe you could take Lauren."

Of course. Maybe I should ask Lauren. It was a dumb idea anyway.

It is only 10 a.m. when I get home from shopping and I'm already tired. My trip to the store, emotional trip down the aisle, and neurotic trip on the side of the road, has worn me out. My stomach rumbles and I remember the reason I went to the store in the first place. I don't feel up to cooking anymore, so I just pour my cereal and carry it to the couch, where I sit for the next couple of hours and watch a Lifetime movie. I have no idea what it is about. Since Joseph's death, my memory and ability to attend to things just isn't there anymore. I can sit and watch TV for hours and have no memory of what I've just watched. I can also talk to someone, have a complete conversation, then not remember anything we've said. It's becoming such a common occurrence that it should worry me, but worrying about it is so exhausting.

After the movie is over, I sit on my couch until I feel the hunger pangs again. This time I make the breakfast I really want–eggs, toast with red plum jam, and fresh strawberries. I also pour my third cup of coffee. As I sit down at the table to eat, I'm again reminded of all the times I shared with Joseph in this same spot and a sudden sense of peace washes over me. It isn't happiness, but the darkness lifts, and for the moment, I'm content. Most of my days begin with a darkness hanging over them, but at some point during the day, the heaviness lifts and is replaced with something else. Sometimes it's peace, and other times it's just an indifferent emptiness. The empty feeling scares me, I hate it. I have to find a way to escape it, so I go on walks. The walks usually turn into runs. Feeling empty sitting inside my house is sad and depressing, but when I'm outside moving around, I feel inspired and hopeful.

Running saves me from a lot of despair and quickens my healing. It's like muscle recovery for my soul. I don't intend to lose weight. My personal appearance is, for once, not a focus at all. I just have to run, and it's very difficult for me to eat, so the natural result is rapid weight loss. I wish I could appreciate it more, but the price I pay for it is too high.

Still, intentional or not, losing weight of any amount is so unusual for me that I make an appointment with my doctor, sure that I have some disease that will leave my poor children orphaned. I insist that he run a multitude of test to check for any possible problem. At my follow-up appointment he comes in carrying the papers that hold my fate.

"How bad is it?" I ask, fear clenching my heart.

"Well," he says, with a grin that I do not appreciate, "there is absolutely nothing wrong with you."

"I knew it. What should we do?" I blurt, before his words sink in. "Oh, wait...are you sure?"

"I'm sure, Alison. Listen, you've gone through a very difficult and stressful situation. It is not uncommon to lose weight in times of extreme stress."

"Yeah, I know. But thirty pounds in less than three months?" I raise an eyebrow and fold my arms over my now flat stomach.

He clears his throat and sits down. "Well, you did say you had been running a lot more."

I look down and nod.

"I think the reduced appetite and increased exercise just came together at the right time. I truly believe that you are healthy and there is nothing wrong. In fact with your weight loss, you are now in a healthier weight bracket than you were before." He smiles and pats me on the knee before standing up.

I make an effort not to scowl. "Okay, thank you Dr. Roberts."

"If anything else comes up, make an appointment. Oh—do you think you might need some antidepressants? You know...to help you deal with everything?"

I smile tightly. "No, thank you. I'm managing on my own." I have no intention of taking any drug. Running is better therapy for me than any pill will be.

I leave the doctor's office, unsettled and annoyed. I need a distraction, and since the mall is on my way home, I make an impulse decision to pull in. None of my clothes fit my new physique and since I won't be dying anytime soon, I decide to buy some new jeans. I have no idea what size I am anymore and so I carry back an armful of different sizes and styles into the dressing room. The fluorescent lights feel harsh and the two women in the adjoining room are annoying me with their shallow gossip about celebrities. Don't they know some people have real problems and don't want to listen to their trite conversations? My mood isn't made any better by trying on jeans, which in my opinion is almost as bad as swimsuits when it comes to finding a pair that actually look good. I try on my first pair and find that they are too big. I pull them off without unzipping them. Must be sized wrong, I think. I slip on the next pair one size smaller and still they feel too big. This can't be right. Surely I haven't lost that much weight. I venture back out into the store and reluctantly pick up two more pair in sizes that can't possibly fit me. I pull on the first pair and gasp. Can it be? I double check the size. Eight. I can fit into a size eight! Twelve has been my magic number for so many years, I didn't ever think I'd buy an eight again. The eights are a little loose, but I can't possibly be a six. I don't even try them on. For a moment I forget about the pain that led me to the eights, and do a little victory dance in the dressing room. I immediately feel guilty.

Good widows do not rejoice in the mall.

As I leave the dressing room, I pass through the formal wear department and see a little black dress that reminds me of one I used to have. It seems like a million years ago that I had come to this same mall and bought my first nice outfit, the one I wore to Joseph's college graduation dinner. The night that changed my whole life.

He picked me up a little early, wearing a new suit and a sheepish grin. I wore my new dress. It was off the shoulder, form fitting, and was the sexiest dress I had ever put on my body. I was just a month away from my twentieth birthday and felt very grown up. On the drive over to the restaurant, Joseph took a detour and parked at Mount Bonnell. It was a favorite place of ours; a romantic spot overlooking the large, expensive houses sitting on Lake Austin. We dreamed of owning one of those houses someday. In order to get the best view of the lake, we got out, and hiked to the top of the mount, careful not to mess up our nice, grown-up clothes. At the top he got on bended knee and asked me to share his life with him. I said yes and broke into tears. I loved him so much. A small group of teens nearby erupted in applause as Joseph hugged and kissed me. Could I have been any happier?

Our first year was good, despite the usual struggles of settling into jobs and figuring out how to budget money. We rarely fought, and if we did, we never stayed mad for long, just long enough for the make-up sex to mean something. After one quick year I found myself pregnant. I was shocked and worried when the two pink lines appeared on the pregnancy test, but Joseph was elated. Grinning like a mad man, he spun me around and smothered me with kisses. I knew everything would be all right and was confident Joseph would forever take care of both our baby and me. We soon found out however, the baby would be babies. Seven and a half months later I gave birth to our son, Paul, and our daughter, Lauren. It was an amazing, miraculous day. The children totally changed our world and solidified our marriage. I never worried about Joseph leaving me. He was so enamored with our children and loved them with an incredible passion. He was very protective and nurturing, and unlike other dads, Joseph actually spent quality time with the kids when they were little. I remember many times smiling fondly at him as he donned floppy hats and fake jewelry while having a tea party at Lauren's tiny, little pink table with his legs all scrunched up. In the next moment he was wearing a Superman cape and shooting Nerf darts at imaginary villains as he and Paul, once again, saved the world. As the kids grew up, Joseph grew with them. He often understood what they needed better than I did. When they were upset, it was typical to find Joseph sitting in their rooms, talking and listening as they worked out their problems together. He was not only a great husband and father, he was the full package—a great man. Not a moment has gone by these last three months that I have not missed him with a deep longing. Not a week has passed that the kids have not called to reminisce and cry over the loss of their dad. He was the man who always loved them, but would never walk them down the aisle or meet their future children.

CHAPTER 2

Grief is not as heavy as guilt, but it takes more away from you." – Veronica Roth

I have a special flat wooden box that I put my mail in. I usually keep it on my kitchen counter, but lately it's been overflowing and spilling out. Seeing it there is causing me stress so I move the growing pile to a bigger box and relocate it to my bedroom on the small desk I have in the corner. I can see the box from my bed if I lift my head just right and look over to the left. I try not to do that very often. The first month, I was on auto pilot, worried that I would crash if I didn't stay on top of everything, so I paid all the bills and read every sympathy note. But after three months of paying bills, our existing bank account is greatly depleted and I'm scared to death. Now, the bills and condolence cards are mounting up unopened and ignored. When Joseph died we had about seven-thousand in savings, eight-thousand in checking, and two investments I shouldn't touch for ten more years. We have only fifty-thousand left on our mortgage, no credit card debt, and a car that is totally paid for. We seemed financially stable when his monthly paycheck was coming in, but the situation is different now. I have no income, and the money I have compiled won't last me very long. If I could have foreseen the future, perhaps I wouldn't have quit my job two years ago to stay home and focus on my writing. Pursuing my dream has yielded two articles in *Women's World,* and one completed manuscript. When Joseph died I had my full manuscript out to two agents. I have been waiting on their reply for months, hoping for an offer of representation, but I can't hold out much longer. I have to get a full time job soon or potentially lose our home.

I hate that I'm in this situation. I hate that my life has changed without my consent. The taunting box has become a dark space on my desk and I'm tempted to pick it up and throw it in the garbage without looking at it. But I don't. Instead, I carry it to my kitchen table, and arm myself with a full coffee mug, a chocolate bar, and a box of tissues, knowing I will need them at some point during the process. I pick up the first bill and hold it carefully in my hands, unable to open it. As I sit, avoiding the inevitable, the phone rings and startles me.

"Hello. Can I speak to Mrs. Collins?" says a deep male voice.

"This is she."

"This is Bert, from Liberty Financial. I'm calling to discuss your husband's life insurance policy."

"Umm. My husband didn't have any life insurance." I am embarrassed to say this, as I assume most responsible adults have a policy. I can't explain why we don't have one, but in hindsight, it obviously would have been a good idea. Anyway, it's a sore spot given my circumstances and I'm feeling rather defensive about it.

"Well, actually, he did have a policy through his employer. The policy was paid for by the company and was issued for all employees at his level."

"Oh. I didn't know. Are you sure? He never mentioned it to me."

"Yes, ma'am. I'm sure. I have the policy right here in front of me. Your husband, Joseph Collins, signed it. We just need some information from you before we can release your funds."

I'm not sure if I should believe him. I've been warned

about all the scams that target widows. It's been over three months since Joseph died, so why haven't I heard about this before? Yet, the bill I'm holding and the large pile in front of me increase my need to believe in this stranger on the phone.

"Okay. Um, can I ask how much the policy is for?" I assume if there really is some insurance, that it's probably the traditional ten-thousand dollar policy common with many employers.

"Yes. It is for four-hundred-fifty thousand. I just need some bank information from you so we can proceed with a funds transfer."

I gulp and don't say anything for a moment. Can this be real? Please God, please let this be real.

"Ma'am? Are you there?"

"Yes, sorry. Can I call you back? I just want to verify this with my husband's employer first." I say, sounding much more competent and secure than I feel.

I hang up and call Joseph's old boss right away. As I'm waiting to be connected to him, I remember the last time I called Mr. Furney—the day Joseph didn't come home. My hand trembles briefly, but then Mr. Furney picks up and his soothing and gentle voice calms me. I've always liked the older man who mentored Joseph. He has always been good to us, and I'm hoping that he'll come through this one last time.

"Alison! Hello dear, how can I help you?"

"Hello, Mr. Furney. I have a question..."

Mr. Furney confirms the policy and apologizes that it took so long for someone to contact me. Apparently, a new secretary had forgotten to send in the death certificate and file the claim. I can't believe it! As soon as we hang up I put my head down on the table and cry tears of joy, gratitude, and grief. Joseph came through for me once again, even after death.

Over the next two days, I complete the necessary paperwork via phone and fax, all the while, disbelieving that everything will really be okay. The money comes in and I decide to pay off our mortgage first. I know there will still be plenty of money left over to sock away, invest, and cushion my checking account to get me through the rest of the year. Since, I've never had this much money, I figure it will be wise to consult a financial adviser who can help me figure out the smartest way to distribute my new wealth. I'm still hoping my writing career will take off and supplement any income I'll need. Even though four-hundred-fifty-thousand dollars seems like an enormous amount of money, in reality, I know it's not enough to last me for the rest of my life.

I decide to give each of my children ten-thousand dollars. Although money can't ease the pain they're dealing with, it can ease some of the stress. Lauren and Paul are both supporting themselves, but Joseph and I often helped them out financially as many parents do when their kids first get out of college. They were both good students and had graduated with honors. Lauren quickly found a job after college with an advertising agency as a public relations assistant. She lives alone, has a cat, and seems to enjoy her job. Lauren has several long term, loyal friends whom I approve of, and has been dating the same young man for a year and a half. She still meets me at church most Sunday mornings and calls twice a week, even more now that Joseph has passed. She is a model daughter and I'm proud of her. It pleases me to do something so tangible for her.

Paul, however, has had more trouble finding a job, or more accurately, deciding what he wants to do with his life. Finding a job is not the issue because he is incredibly smart and capable. He actually had companies pursuing him before he even walked the stage to accept his diploma with Summa Cum Laude honors. Paul earned a Masters Degree in Civil Engineering from The University of Texas. He is über smart. The problem is he wants to be a rock star. Fortunately for him, his brain fires on both sides. He's multi-talented and a naturally gifted musician. Eventually he'll fall in love and get married, and he'll be able to provide for a family with a stable engineering career. Once he does these things, he will most likely do them for the rest of his life. He is a man of honor, like his father. So, I'm very proud of the choice he's making to not get an engineering job right away, to not get seriously involved with a woman at this time, and to work hard at getting his band off the ground. Paul isn't a slacker and with the options he has, he'll be okay.

I'm really excited to tell the kids about the money, not only about my portion, but that I'll be sharing part of it with them. When you live a fairly frugal life, it's thrilling to have the opportunity to give away so much money. Again, I know ten-thousand dollars, or even four-hundred-fifty-thousand dollars, might not seem like a lot to some people, but to me, it's an enormous amount. I picture how I will tell them and how they will respond. I invite them over to dinner for the following Sunday. Having this bit of good news puts me in better spirits for the few days leading up to the dinner. I'm almost happy. I feel terrible letting money make me happy, when I have so much to be sad about, but I guess that's the way money is.

Sunday finally arrives and I prepare my first real meal since Joseph died. I have so many donated dishes from well-wishers that anytime someone comes over I just pull out a frozen dish. Most of the time, it's just me and I don't care to cook for myself anymore. I'm tempted to make lasagna for the kids since it's their favorite, but I just can't bring myself to do it. Lasagna is the dish I made for

Joseph on that terrible day. It was intended to be a make-up dinner, apologizing for the fight we had gotten into the night before. Instead, it got cold on the stove while I sat in a hospital room hearing from a stranger that my husband was dead. I don't know if I can ever make lasagna again.

When the kids come over we don't waste much time before eating. I make chicken enchiladas and I'm pleased with how they turn out. I realize that I miss cooking. Afterwards, I get out dessert (apple pie and Blue Bell ice cream), make some decaf coffee, and tell the kids I have an announcement.

"What is it, Mom?" Lauren asks, suspiciously. She cast a sideways glance at Paul, who's sitting next to her at the table.

"Well, it's pretty exciting! A man called me last week..."

Paul interrupts. "Oh, God! Please don't tell me you're dating already."

"What? No, I..."

"Oh my gosh, Mom. I couldn't handle that right now. Don't you think it's too soon?" Lauren questions, wide-eyed.

"Wait a minute–I'm not dating anyone, and yes, I do think it's too soon."

"You think it's too soon? So that means you plan on dating again later?" Paul's mouth hangs open, waiting for my response.

"Maybe. I don't know. Wait! Can you two please let me finish!"

"Sorry," they reply in unison.

"Like I was saying, I got a call from a man–not anyone I know–and he informed me that Dad had a life insurance policy through work. As it turns out, I got four-hundred-fifty-thousand dollars!" I wait for the cheers and look at them expectantly. I don't get any reaction. Maybe they don't understand what I said.

"I said that I got four-hundred-fifty-thousand dollars. Isn't that great? I didn't know Dad had a policy, so it's really good news."

Still nothing.

"And...I'm giving you each ten-thousand!"

More silence.

"I think it would be a good idea to save most of it for the future. Although, you could use some to get caught up on bills or whatever right now. I trust you to make a good decision with the money."

"Oh, my god," Lauren says first. She looks at Paul. He looks down at his hands.

"I know. Isn't it great?" I say with a smile, totally confused. Why are they acting so strangely? Are they in shock?

Lauren leans in to talk to Paul. They exchange a few secret-language sentences that I can't hear or understand. When you have twins, these kinds of conversations are pretty normal. They usually discuss most things together, and then come to me with a unified response. In this case, I'm at a loss as to what needs to be discussed. Finally, they both look up at me. Lauren seems stricken. Paul speaks first.

"It's good news, Mom. I mean we're happy that you won't have to worry about bills and stuff. It's just that it feels kind of wrong, you know?"

"No. I don't know. What feels wrong about it? I honestly don't understand."

"It's like death money!" Lauren blurts.

"What in the world...death money?"

"Mom, how can you not see it? How can we get excited about money that came in because Dad died!"

"Oh, good grief."

They both stare at me with sick, forlorn expressions.

"I think it would have been better if you had been dating," Paul says.

Lauren nods in agreement. "I just don't see how you can spend any of it, Mom."

They leave soon after that and go to Lauren's house to watch a comfort movie. I'm glad they're going because I can't trust myself to not tell them how utterly ridiculous they're being. I am trying to be sensitive to their feelings, but give me a break! How can they not see this as fantastic news? What twenty-three year old wouldn't be happy about receiving ten-thousand dollars? Can't they see that this is Joseph's final way of providing for them?

Even though I feel so sure about this, as the night goes on, I begin to question myself. They are, after all, really upset. Maybe they're right. Probably most widows would be conflicted about spending "death money." I don't know what to think because I've never been a widow before. All I know is that I'm happy because I don't have to run out and get a job, and can instead, continue to focus on healing and on my writing. Maybe I really am a bad widow.

I lay down in bed after cleaning up the kitchen, confused and heavy. I replay Paul and Lauren's reaction in my head, all the joy from giving the monetary gift gone. I'm not sure what part is more upsetting–their reaction to the idea of me dating or how guilty they made me feel with my new financial situation. I really need to hash this out with someone–someone who isn't also grieving the loss of Joseph and can talk with me from an honest and unbiased perspective. I make a mental note to call my best friend, Janet, the next day, and make lunch plans.

CHAPTER 3

"Guilt is perhaps the most painful companion to death."– Elisabeth Kubler-Ross

Janet and I have been friends for ten years and have been going to lunch once a month for almost as long. We would meet more often, but she lives about thirty minutes away in the suburbs and works a full time job. She also has two school-aged children who keep her very busy. Even though we're the same age, we're at different stages in life. Janet was Paul's fifth grade teacher. We met when I attended the fall parent conference, and had begun to apologize that Joseph couldn't be there with us. All of the sudden, she broke down in tears. I quickly handed her a tissue and waited for her to compose herself. She apologized profusely, and I asked if she wanted to talk about what was wrong. She said she had recently (the summer before school started) lost her husband, also named Joseph, in an auto accident. They didn't have any children and had only been married two years, but I still couldn't imagine the grief she was feeling. After that moment, we became fast friends. I volunteered to be the homeroom mom and spent more time than was necessary at the school. I helped with reading groups, making copies, planning teacher appreciations, and class parties. Janet continued to cope with her loss. Eventually, two years later, she married a wonderful man named Steve and now they have two children, ages five and seven.

"Oh, my god! Alison, you look fantastic!" Janet exclaims, after I sit down across from her in our favorite café.

One of the reasons we're such good friends is because she always says just the right thing to me. I blush and reply, "Actually, I've lost some weight. I've been running a lot. So, you can tell, huh?"

"What do you mean, can I tell? You look amazing. I was such a wreck after my Joseph died. I gained about twenty pounds and looked a mess for months."

"See? I knew it. I'm such a bad widow. I should be gaining weight or acting depressed," I say gloomily.

Janet looks at me like I'm crazy. "Hold that thought," she says. Our server is waiting for our drink order. After Janet orders iced tea and I order a coffee, she continues.

"Did you just say bad widow? How in the hell can you be a bad widow?"

"Well, like you said, I've lost weight and I don't look depressed. I'm doing it all wrong," I whine.

Janet laughs aloud. "You are so crazy sometimes. There is no wrong or right way to act when someone you love dies."

"Well, that's not entirely true. Don't you ever watch Ricki Lake? Oh, never mind, of course you don't. You're gainfully employed and probably never sit around in your PJ's all day, eating cold casserole from a giant pan, watching really trashy daytime TV."

Janet pats me on the arm and tries to suppress a smile. "Oh, honey, I wouldn't worry about it. You must be a good widow because that is the saddest thing I've ever heard. Maybe you shouldn't look so damn hot when you go out though."

"Yeah, whatever. It would take more than losing some weight for me to look hot," I say, while looking at the menu. What should I have? I could have a salad, but all this talk is making me want a big greasy, gonna-regret-it-later burger, and maybe some pie. I order my indulgent meal when the waiter comes back.

"So tell me, what's behind this crazy concern over being a bad widow?" she asks.

I think for a moment, wanting to explain myself correctly. "I am devastated over losing Joseph…"

She squeezes my hand. "I know you are. You two truly loved each other."

"We did. I miss him so much. The other day I had a complete breakdown in the grocery store."

Janet nods. "What happened? Did something trigger a memory?"

I sigh and relax a little. Janet has been through this before, so I feel less nutty explaining these kinds of things to her. "I accidentally picked up his cereal."

"Oh, yeah. That would do it."

"It was surreal what it did to me. There I was, standing in the cereal aisle, holding a box of Frosted Flakes, when the room started spinning. I had to put my head down on the handle and take big breaths. People were staring, and then this poor lady asked if I was okay. I just looked at her all dazed with tears in my eyes and then practically ran away." I glance up at her. "I still bought the cereal, Janet."

"That's okay." She pats my hand gently. "Why do you think you did that, though?"

"I don't know. It just felt wrong to put it back. Joseph used to eat a bowl of Frosted Flakes every damn day. If we were out, I would run up to the store to buy more. Isn't that crazy? It was a kids cereal! I hated buying Frosted Flakes. I don't know why I did it again."

"I guess it just felt right."

"But that's not the crazy part! Guess what I did after I bought it?"

"What?"

"I drove to the place that I think his car was found on

the Interstate…" I pause while the waiter brings out our orders. The big, greasy burger doesn't look good to me anymore. My stomach turns and I push the plate away.

"Why? What did you do?" Janet asks leaning forward in her seat.

I glance around, hoping no one else can hear me. "I dumped out the whole box on the side of the road and just watched as all the flakes fell to the ground. Then I took the box back home and put it next to my Cheerios."

"But, it was empty, right?" she asks, fork in mid-air, and eyebrows furrowed.

"Yes." I pick at a French fry.

Janet leans back in her seat and takes a drink. "Hmmm…" she says.

"Please, don't judge me…I can't explain it myself. Sometimes I think I'm losing my mind, but honestly? It made me feel better to pour the cereal on the side of the road and put an empty box in my pantry. Ughhh. Do you think I need to see a shrink?" I ask, flopping back against my seat. Tears threaten to pour out any second, but I do my best to hold them in.

Janet looks sympathetic. "Honey, I love you. I am not going to judge you. I remember feeling and doing crazy things, too, when my Joseph died. I think it is completely normal to be abnormal right now."

I sniff. "You do?"

"Yes, absolutely. What I don't understand though, is why you think you're a bad widow? You sound like a perfectly normal widow to me."

I look down, shuffling my food around for a minute. "I'm not sad all the time. Some days I feel okay. I mean I have plenty of terrible days when I don't get off my couch, change my clothes, or even answer my phone. Then I have days where I go on a run and feel great, or I want to go shopping just to see how things might look on me now. Or days when I get so into my work that I forget that Joseph won't be coming home for dinner. Those are the days I feel good," I admit reluctantly.

"I think that's good, Alison."

"You do?" I look up, surprised.

"Of course. You can't stay in a perpetual state of grief. It would kill you. You're supposed to be adjusting. That means you will have some good days and some bad days." She smiles slightly, and tilts her head to the side. "I don't think you should worry about it."

"Did I tell you what the kids said?" I ask, looking down at my uneaten plate.

"What? Do you mean about the death money?"

"Well, yeah that, and about me dating."

"No! What did they say?" she asks protectively.

"Well, they set up accounts with the money I gave them. They don't plan on touching it until at least the year anniversary of his death. They also asked me to consider not dating until the year is up." I look at her closely, trying to gauge her reaction. I'm not sure how I'm supposed to feel about all this, and I want a sane person's perspective.

"Well, they can do whatever they want with their money, I guess, although it's totally ridiculous. But they should not be giving you dating rules! When, and if you date, is your choice, not theirs. You know that, right?"

I nod. I do know that, but it doesn't really matter, because I have no intention of dating.

"I guess one year is supposed to be the acceptable finish line for mourners," I say with a smile.

She smiles back. "I guess so."

I steer the conversation away from me for the rest of lunch, asking about her kids and work. I appreciate her support and her comments make sense to me, but I still can't shake the feeling that I'm missing something-something important.

CHAPTER 4

"They that love beyond the world cannot be separated by it. Death is but crossing the world, as friends do the seas; they live in one another still." -William Penn

I've been thinking a lot lately about time and how little meaning it carries for me on a daily basis. It wasn't always like that. In fact, I remember when time was the most valuable commodity I could think of. When our children were young, time seemed to zoom by with alarming speed. We were so busy racing between soccer practice, dance lessons, church outings, and business dinners, that I barely had time for friendships and showers. There were also periods in my life when time seemed to pass like a crawl, and I would be driven mad with anticipation or impatience as I waited for something to arrive, such as the birth of my children, a bonus check, or a call from a literary agent. But when you live alone with only memories, and have little to look forward to, time doesn't race *or* crawl, it just seems to stands still.

The first months after Joseph's death I was in survival mode. I had so much to do: prepare for a funeral, help my children cope with the loss of their father, sort through paperwork, and try to make sense of Joseph's business affairs. There were tons of concerned family and friends dropping by to visit or simply calling to check on me. The truth is, I actually felt busy in my first month as a new widow. There was so much to do, in fact, there was no time for real contemplation of what was going to happen next. However, after the second month, my status as a new widow lost its shine. I was suddenly expected to not only be comfortable with my new role, but was also supposed to know how to behave and what to do next. The problem is that I actually have no idea how to do any of those things. There is no "widow's handbook" to reference. My only option is on-the-job training, and it's not easy. In fact I feel like I'm failing all the time.

It's past the third month now. I'm trying to figure out how to spend my days, so that I don't go completely mad. When not running, crying, or managing money, I try to spend my time writing. If I can just get a book sale before the next year rolls around, I can justify my writing career and hold off even longer on getting a real job. I know Joseph would want this for me. He was my biggest cheerleader when it came to me being a writer. Since the manuscript I sent out still hasn't yielded any returns, I begin working on my next novel. During a long day plugging away at the computer, I get that very important call all wanna-be writers dream about.

"Can I speak to Alison Collins, please?" says a pleasant voice on the other end of the line. The caller ID shows the number is from New York, which makes my heart jump.

"This is she."

"Hello, Ms. Collins, this is Kendall Leigh with Lewis Literary Agency."

"Yes?" I can't believe it, this is my top pick agent!

"I've reviewed your manuscript, *Watching Over Me*, and I would love the opportunity to represent you and your work."

"I...I would love that! Thank you." In the back of my mind I hear a voice telling me to play it cool. I don't want to blow this and part of an agent's call is seeing if you have any chemistry together.

We discuss her terms, the prospective publishers she would pitch to, and her predictions about the book. She asks me a few personal questions to get a feel for my personality. I ask her a few also. Thank goodness I remember the article I read last month: "What to ask your agent." The conversation goes really well. She says she'll keep me posted on her progress and we hang up. Viola! I have an agent!

After getting off the phone, I do a little dance and cheer in the kitchen, then look around expectantly for someone to tell. That's when it hits me. Hard. No one is here, and most importantly, I can't tell Joseph. I can't share this moment with the man that I have loved and shared everything with for most of my life. He would have swooped me up in his arms, whooping and hollering, rejoicing with me. He would have called our friends to brag on me, and then he would have taken me out for a fancy celebratory dinner and told our waiter with pride that his wife was a writer. Where moments before I had been elated beyond measure, I am now staring at the very silent walls of our home and filled with grief. More than any other time since Joseph died, I realize how alone I am, and how very much I miss him. I can't control the sorrow that quickly overtakes me and suddenly I'm sobbing. Not just quiet, controlled sobbing, but full, out-loud, wailing, sobbing. The kind where snot runs down your face and your eyes swell shut. The kind where you have to lay down because your grief has left you crippled, and you can no longer stand. My extreme emotional shift from complete elation to overwhelming sadness, in the span of thirty seconds, has caused a severe headache that leaves me curled up on my bed and in the dark for the next few hours. If my kids could see me now, they'd be so proud. I am finally being a good widow.

~~~

About three weeks later, my new agent calls. She's already close to procuring a deal with a publisher. I am actually going to sell my book. I can hardly believe it! It feels very surreal, and made even more so, by not having Joseph to share it with. Does anything really happen without him? If your book sells when your husband is dead, and he doesn't know it, does it really sell? This feels like a big dividing line between my old life and my new life. I mean, obviously being widowed is the true dividing line, but my husband dying happened *to* me, getting published is happening *because* of me. It defines me, as a real author. I guess the other thing defines me too, as a sad, lonely, tragic, widow. I am so happy, but I feel so guilty for being happy. Being a widow stinks.

Even though I am beyond excited about getting an agent, I haven't told anyone but Janet, my news. She's thrilled, of course and understands how hard it is to even get this far in the book business. She asks me what the kids reactions were, and I admit I haven't told them yet. I'm worried they will be upset that my life is moving forward, and if they are, I know I'll be mad at them for taking away my joy. It seems easier to wait and see if I actually get published before I start celebrating. What will other people think about my success so soon after Joseph's death? Maybe they'll think I've just gotten really busy and really creative with all the time I now have on my hands. Maybe they'll think I'm not sad enough over the loss of my husband since I'm able to start a brand new career in the face of his death.

They don't know that I wrote the book and sent it out to agents before he died. They don't know that I could never have written this book without him. Joseph was absolutely instrumental in my dream becoming a reality.

He was the one who would encourage me when I felt like giving up. He would read pages that I wrote and exclaim how amazing it was, how talented I was, how I could not deny the world a chance to read my book. He was more excited about it than I was half of the time.

About a year and a half ago, I had terrible writer's block at a crucial place on my manuscript. I dreaded going into my small office every day, dreaded the blinking taunt from the cursor on my computer screen, and dreaded reading the uninspired dribble I was writing. Unwilling to admit my own failure, I convinced myself and Joseph that my stale location and old, slow computer were the problem. I was only venting because I knew we didn't have the money for a new computer.

One morning, Joseph had already gone to work and I woke up feeling particularly uninspired. I had poured a cup of coffee and was making myself head into the office to write. I was still in my PJ's and slippers, hadn't combed my hair, or even brushed my teeth. I dreaded walking into that room and turning on the computer. I had absolutely nothing to say. My main character had come to a standstill and so had I.

I walked in with my head down. I first noticed the light spilling in from the window casting rays onto the carpet where I was standing. I wondered why the blinds were left open all night. My gaze slowly moved up to the desk. Sitting in the place of my decrepit old desktop was a brand new beautiful laptop. It was open and a Word document was displayed. In awe, I moved closer and read it; "Merry early Christmas my darling, amazing, beautiful and talented wife. I love you so much! Now you can take your writing out of these four walls. I can't wait to read what inspires you!"

Tears fell from my eyes and rolled down on my face. I knew what a sacrifice this meant to us financially. Once I had dried my tears, I noticed an envelope on the desk with my name on it. Inside was a reservation to a bed and breakfast about an hour away. It was for two days later in the week. A note from Joseph was inside.

"I thought a get-away might help to re-inspire you. Please don't question it, just go, and write! I know you can do this, Alison. You were born to be a writer. All my love, Your Joseph."

It was exactly what I needed to get me out of my slump. I wrote more in those two days than I had in months and got the idea for a plot twist that absolutely improved my book and made it publishable. On the second night, Joseph showed up and surprised me. He knocked on my door and as soon as I opened it, grabbed me in a passionate kiss and pushed me deeper into the room, closing the door with a kick. That night was exactly what we, as a couple, needed also. Our love life had been in a similar, uninspiring slump, and Joseph brought us back to the passion we had been desperately missing.

My God, how I miss him.

Nobody else knows how involved Joseph had been with this book. If I make a big deal about being published, all anyone will see, is that I'm moving forward when I should be grieving. After all, it's only been four months since he died. According to my children, I still have at least eight months to go before I can show any happiness, have any success, spend any money, or God forbid, date anyone.

Date? The idea is so foreign. First of all, who would I date, even if I wanted to? I can't imagine myself with anyone other than Joseph. It would feel like an affair. Just thinking of the word "affair" makes my cheeks go hot. Only one time in all our years together has another person even come close to causing problems in our marriage. It was my fault, my indiscretion, my almost affair.

Every summer when I was growing up, I attended a sleep-away camp at Camp Crest for four weeks. The camp is located about an hour away from the city, and is on the outskirts of a small town. It rests on a lake, is surrounded by the Texas hill country, and was my favorite place in the whole world. I loved it so much, in fact, that after I turned eighteen, I continued to go there as an employee. It was a perfect summer job. I worked for three summers before we got married and afterward I still went back for two weeks in the summer until I got pregnant with the twins. I wish we could have sent our kids to Camp Crest but we never had the money. They spent their summers like most kids; going on free trips to the community pool, library, and park.

Many of the kids and counselors at Camp Crest came back year after year, and over time we all became good friends. Most of us went to different schools, so we didn't talk much during the actual school year, but once July rolled around, as soon as we unloaded our cars and found our cabins, it was like a family reunion. The only thing that ever created a dread about going to camp rather than an anticipation was summer love. Since we spent our whole summers together, any romances we experienced, usually happened between those of us a camp. It was so simple when we were just kids, but once we became teenagers, everything changed. Many of us had our first kisses or first sexual experiences (listed in the brochure as a fun alternative to rock climbing) at camp. Although it was very exciting to mix the sexes, sometimes it became uncomfortable. This was especially true if two friends decided they liked each other, messed around, and then later broke up. It would interfere with the whole group's dynamic. Usually, by the time the next summer rolled around again, we would put the embarrassment behind us and pretend like nothing had happened. There were exceptions, of course, and my relationship with Jeremiah was one of them.

Jeremiah and I had known each other since we were eight. We had first started camp the same summer and our moms discovered we lived in the same city. It didn't matter to us that we were from the same city, or that our moms had hit it off. All we cared about was what happened once it became summertime and we could go back to camp to play with our friends.

Everything changed though the summer before our junior year. Jeremiah had come to camp that July completely transformed. Just the year before, he had been skinny, short, and obnoxious. I'm sure he thought I looked just as bad. I was flat chested, pimply, and had a mouth full of braces. However, sophomore year had been good to us both. My braces came off, my skin cleared up and I had developed a few curves in the right places. He had grown about six inches, and was now a little over six feet tall. His muscles were bigger and more defined, and he had lost his annoying, smart-aleck mouth.

My friend, Denise, and I had arrived around the same time and were waiting for our cabin assignment to be announced. We watched from the sidelines and commented as cars drove into the circular drop-off and unloaded our friends. A black Volvo with dark windows pulled up and we couldn't see who was inside. Finally, the front door opened and out stepped Jeremiah. His tossed his mom the keys as she climbed out of the passenger side. He then popped open the trunk and quickly grabbed his bags. Before we could close our hanging mouths, his mom had driven off and left this young, handsome man behind. He walked right passed us, brushing my shoulder as he did, and smoothly said, "Ladies," with a slight tip of his head. If I hadn't been so shocked, his confidence would have annoyed me. Denise and I turned to each other, eyes wide and mouths agape. "Oh, my god! Did you see him? He is gorgeous!" Denise loudly whispered. I still couldn't believe how much Jeremiah had changed in one year. I also couldn't believe how seeing him had just flipped my insides every which way. "Damn," I said in my most grown up voice. "It's gonna be a good summer!"

It was a good summer, and so was the next one, but by the time we graduated camp, Jeremiah and I avoided each other at all cost. For him, that meant rarely coming to one of the camper reunions, nor keeping up with any of our old gang. Nobody blamed me directly, but everyone knew why Jeremiah never came around anymore. I often wondered if I was worth it. Jeremiah had been very popular and just about everyone loved him. I was liked, but I'm sure the males would have picked one of their own over me any day. The women would have picked him, too. After all, Jeremiah was incredibly handsome, had gone to a good college, and was one of the nicest guys around. He would have been a welcome addition to our gatherings. Especially for the single women.

Jeremiah, and our summer romance, occasionally haunted my dreams and thoughts, but for the most part I kept him hidden in the recesses of my heart. I had, after all, married an amazing man whom I had met just months after my last encounter with Jeremiah. Joseph stole my heart and healed the heartache caused by all other men. He was all I needed and all I cared about. I didn't even think it was possible to feel anything for another man when I was so in love with Joseph. I felt that way for years, until the day that I didn't.

That day came about five years after I graduated from high school. We had finally all moved on in our adult lives but were starting to miss seeing each other again. A mini-reunion was in order and I, along with a few others, was roped into planning the gathering. There were thirty of us who graduated in '88 or '89 and had always attended the July session—a total of fourteen boys and sixteen girls. We had started out as homesick eight-year-olds and ended our camper experience at the adventurous age of eighteen. For our reunion, we planned a simple dinner at a restaurant in the small town close to camp. Afterwards, we would head over to the camp for a bonfire and roast some s'mores. It was off season and the director had given us permission to use the facility for a few hours. It was my idea to do the bonfire and I was proud when everyone expressed their excitement about the plans. Someone else was in charge of finding and notifying everyone of the event. Most of the people still lived in Texas, so we figured there would be a good turnout. Two days before the reunion, the list was faxed over to me so I could get a head count in order to plan for the s'mores. As I was scanning the list, I realized I may not be over Jeremiah as much as I thought. His name jumped out at me and I would have sworn it was in bold and larger than the rest, but of course it wasn't. I had the terrifying feeling that maybe the bubble Joseph's love had created around me could be popped. Shaking off my sudden feeling of vulnerability, I told myself to stop being silly. We hadn't seen each other in years and our last interaction had been very uncomfortable. He had stayed away from any gatherings since that time, so I had just assumed he wouldn't be coming to this one either. It would be fine though. I was a grown adult, married, and the mother of two children. No way was I immature enough that seeing an old high school boyfriend would bother me. And anyway, Joseph was planning to come with me, so I knew everything would be fine. It always was when I was with Joseph. Unfortunately, when the night of the reunion arrived, Paul came down with a terrible stomach bug. Just an hour before the babysitter was to show up, he threw up all over the kitchen floor and then again once we got him into bed. We decided Joseph should stay home with the kids and I would continue on to the reunion. He didn't understand why I was upset about the change in plans.

"Alison, it's fine. I'll be here to take care of Paul and you'll get to still have fun with your friends," he said definitively.

"I don't have to go. I can call and get Mindy to come by and pick up the stuff for the s'mores and the key to the camp."

"That's crazy, honey. Go. Have a good time. We'll be fine," Joseph assured me.

What he didn't understand was that I wasn't sure I'd be fine. I couldn't possibly tell him I was nervous about seeing Jeremiah. Would the whole night be uncomfortable? Would everyone be whispering about our ugly break-up? Would I feel anything when I saw him? By the time I arrived at the restaurant, everyone else was already there. They had saved me a seat and that seat happened to be right next to Jeremiah. I approached the table with a smile, stopping to greet my closest friends. I leaned down to hug my friend, Denise, and whispered in her ear. "Why did you put me by him?"

She whispered back. "I'm sorry! It was his idea."

My heart stopped for a moment. I suddenly felt very nervous, but was determined to act normal. I took my seat next to Jeremiah and said hello as if I would to any other old friend. I could pretend he had never meant anything to me. I could pretend he wasn't the most handsome man I had ever known. I could pretend I never loved him, but I couldn't pretend I didn't like him. Jeremiah and I had always been friends, always gotten along really well. The only reason we weren't still close was because we had broken each other's heart. It wasn't easy to act friendly with someone who had the ability to break you. You either married them or never spoke to them again.

We started talking through dinner and continued our conversation as we toured the camp and set up the bonfire. We sat together as we roasted s'mores and talked about our lives since we had last seen each other. I found out he had been engaged for four months to a girl named Cindy. Jeremiah said he loved her, but something in him knew she just wasn't the one, so he had broken it off. He said he had always worried that the one he really wanted had gotten away. We drank too much wine out of plastic cups, and our hands brushed against each other way too many times. It was midnight and we had been sitting at the bonfire for three hours. Most everyone had brought a date or spouse with them and all of us had been drinking. The catching up and laughter had died down some, and many were now talking quietly in small groups or whispering intimately to their significant other. With the fire flickering and the stars shining brightly, everything seemed so romantic. Jeremiah asked me if I wanted to go on a walk, and I said yes. As I stood to get up, I stumbled on a tree stump. He quickly put out his hand to steady me and gently took my hand in his. I didn't pull away like I should have. We started walking, holding hands, along the worn path. He felt so big and sturdy next to me. Joseph was a smaller man, and although it had never bothered me before, I was now aware of the contrast between their physical sizes. I liked how Jeremiah made me feel. Admittedly, the wine and my memories were playing a much bigger role that night than they should have been. He stopped along the path and suddenly folded me into his chest, as he wrapped his big arms around me.

"The stars are amazing tonight," he said, as we both looked up, our chins almost touching.

"They really are," I agreed, taking it all in. The beautiful night, the clear sky, the crisp air, his strong arms, his cologne, and the memory of his kisses all those years before. We looked down at the same time and he kissed me. At the moment when our lips touched, I was shaken from the spell. In just a split second, thoughts of Joseph flooded my heart and reminded me of how much I loved him and how I had just betrayed him. I pushed Jeremiah away.

"No, I can't Jeremiah. I'm married... happily."

He looked at me with sadness and longing, a small smile spread across his lips. "I know. I'm sorry. I was out of line."

I couldn't look at him, too afraid of how I would react. We turned, and without holding hands, walked back to the bonfire. It was getting late and a lot of people had already left. Jeremiah helped me load up the items I had brought and walked me to my car. Before I got in, he said, "Alison, I'm sorry. I hope you won't hold all this against me. Joseph is a lucky man to have you. I hope you have a good life and a good marriage."

I dared to look him in the eyes. "Thank you, Jeremiah. I hope you find the one soon."

"Yeah, me too. Promise me something, though," he said, as he reached for my hand and held it a moment, "if anything ever happens and you find yourself single, will you come find me? Give me a chance?"

I was embarrassed and surprised by his request, so I tried to make light of it. "Yeah right. You'll be happily married in no time."

He smiled and kissed me on the cheek. "Goodbye, Alison."

"Goodbye, Jeremiah."

That was the last time I saw Jeremiah. I kept up with him some over the years however, through mutual friends. I thought of him often, especially during the rough patches Joseph and I occasionally went through. He emailed me once shortly after the reunion and asked if we could get together and have lunch. I told him that it wasn't a good idea. I didn't completely trust myself not to get emotionally involved again with him. Jeremiah was a fire I knew I shouldn't play with. I didn't have the courage to tell Joseph about the kiss, so I was glad he was already asleep when I got home that night. I stayed awake almost all night, drifting off to sleep about the time he woke up. The next day, Lauren also came down with the stomach bug. We spent the day cleaning up after and comforting sick babies. By the time he asked me how the reunion went, I told him it was fine and everyone had fun. That was the end of the conversation. When another ten years rolled around and the next reunion was planned, I made sure Jeremiah wasn't going before I RSVP'd.

I thought about Jeremiah's last request to me many times. At the time, I was young and practically a newlywed. The thought of ever finding myself alone was completely stupefying. I knew Joseph and I would never divorce. Him asking to call if I was ever single seemed like a silly romantic notion, especially since it was coming from a guy who was lonely and thought he had let *the one* get away. Either way, I vowed to never let myself get tangled up in an affair. Jeremiah was the only man I could ever imagine having the potential to cause problems in my marriage. For that reason, I stayed far away from him.

CHAPTER 5

"It takes strength to make your way through grief, to grab hold of life and let it pull you forward. " – Patti Davis

Since Joseph's death, I have really only communicated with my family and my best friends, Janet and Denise. I've known Denise since I was a child at camp, and although we are complete opposites, she is still the one I tell my secrets to. She calls frequently to check up on me and try to get me out of the house.

"Hey, friend, how's it shakin' today?" she asks as soon as I answer the phone.

"It's shaking, I guess. I don't know..."

"Well, have you checked your email?" I hear Denise turning water on somewhere, then a couple of loud unfamiliar voices in the background.

"No, not lately. Where are you?"

A door creaks and more unfamiliar voices. "Oh, I'm on a date. We're at Matt's El Rancho–the wait's forever."

"Who's your date?" I ask, feeling incredibly removed from the reality of Denise's life. I wouldn't be out at a crowded restaurant for a million bucks, especially with a date.

"Oh, it's this guy from work. Not worth bringing you up to date...get it? Up to date? Anyway, he's waiting outside. So, your email? You should check it. There's an invite for the camp reunion."

"Really? Didn't we just do that a few years ago?"

"I think it's been like five years. It'll be good. I want you to go." Her voice is heading into whine mode.

"I don't know, Denise. I don't know what I would say to anyone."

"You'd say 'how the hell are you and don't ask me a damn thing about my dead husband,' then we'd drink a little and have fun with old friends. Come on—it'd be good for you to get out, and you know we all love you."

I laugh at her suggestion. She knows I would never say anything like that. "I'll think about it."

"Okay, think about it. I'll call you tomorrow for your answer. Oh, I gotta go. I think our table is ready...finally! Bye!"

I hang up and reluctantly go over to my computer. I know Denise will call tomorrow and will expect an answer. I typically avoid my computer unless I'm working on my writing. It's a portal to the outside world that I don't really want to know about. I went to a coffee shop a few days ago and every person there was sitting in front of a computer. The soft, subtle glow of their screens cast a golden hue, like artificial sunlight, on their faces. Some appeared happy with what they saw on the screen and others appeared to be in deep concentration. The smiling ones freaked me out. What were they seeing? Who or what had touched them enough to make them involuntarily smile into a screen? The intangible world had invaded their space and affected their soul. I can't take a chance of that happening to me, even if the information I receive is good. What's waiting for me in those unsolicited emails or unpredictable social media sites? I'm fragile and it takes very little to send me into states of sadness, depression, hopelessness, or dismay. The news is completely off limits right now. In fact I even canceled my cable TV subscription, opting instead for a Netflix account. With Netflix, I'm never surprised because I have complete control over what I watch. No commercials or breaking news will bombard me with unsolicited trauma or sentiment.

I open my email account and quickly scroll down the subject line, deleting all emails I know I will never read. I stop scrolling when I see the one with the subject: *Camp Reunion woohoo!* When Brad Shugline's wife died five years ago, the reunion committee thought it best not to send him an invite to the upcoming gathering. I'm not sure if we did that because we were worried about offending him by having fun in the face of his misery or if maybe we were just too chicken to face someone who was going through such grief. Either way, Brad was offended he wasn't invited and several of us wrote emails apologizing for our insensitivity. I guess a lesson was learned because I received my invite email just like everyone else. I'm usually part of the planning committee, but thankfully someone had enough sense not to ask the new widow to organize the party. I'm not sure that I want to attend though. How can I be myself when I feel like everyone will be expecting me to somehow act different? Even my kids, who know me better than anyone, and love me even more, seem disappointed in my behavior. What will these people, who only know me casually, expect of me?

Denise calls me the next day and tries to convince me that attending this event will greatly contribute to my being normal again. Although I'm unconvinced, I reluctantly agree to go. Now that the day of the reunion has arrived, I regret my decision. I park outside of the Punch Bowl Social and stare at the door, wishing I had driven with Denise so we could walk in together, rather than brave an entrance by myself. It has been almost five years since I last saw this crowd, and even though there is a special bond among us, we actually know very little about each other's personal lives. The last time we were together, Joseph had been with me. As usual, he was a hit and loved by everyone. In fact, at the end of the night, more people asked for Joseph's number and vowed to keep in touch, than they did mine. He was that kind of guy. I never felt uncomfortable with Joseph next to me. I used to believe it was because I was such a people person, but the truth was that Joseph put everyone, including myself, at ease. He was witty, thoughtful, intelligent, and the life of a party. I'm not sure I'm fun enough on my own to make up for him being gone.

I check my face in the visor mirror before going inside. I look pretty good for someone who cried for forty-five solid minutes just a few hours ago. In fact, I think I look better than I did at our last reunion. This morning Denise insisted we go for facials, manicures, and a new haircut. My hair is now shoulder-length with shimmery copper highlights. We also went to the mall to buy something to wear. I haven't bought any new clothes since I started running except that one pair of jeans and she's right to say that all my clothes look saggy and frumpy on me. Still, I worry that buying new clothes will imply that I'm trying to make myself look good, and what in the world (or who in the world, as my kids would question), do I need to look good for?

Being persistent as she always is, though, Denise talked me into buying an outfit I would never have considered on my own. It's cute and it makes me feel good. I'm wearing dark "skinny" jeans (size six), and a thin long sleeved V-neck t-shirt. It isn't just any t-shirt, it fits perfectly, accentuates all the right curves and is ultra soft. I'm also wearing new ballet flats with a touch of bling. I finish off my outfit with a dainty, silver chain and some silver hoop earrings. I really do feel great about how I look. That is, until the guilt kicks in right as I get out of my car. What am I doing looking so good? These people will expect a mourning Alison, not someone who looks like she's having the time of her life.

As soon as I open the doors, I feel out of place. Quite a few people turn to stare. I see a few subtle whispers and lots of plastered smiles. Everyone already knows about my new status as a widow. Denise said she received a separate email addressed to the whole group telling them about Joseph's death. I assume this was done with good intentions, but I feel like a piece of gossip. I worry that everyone will act strange around me or worse yet, scrutinize my every move. And tonight I really just want to be 'Alison, the old friend from camp,' and not 'Alison, the poor woman who lost her husband.'

I ignore all the looks and glance around at the layout of the room. There are a few old-fashioned bowling lanes to the left, anchored by half-moon leather couches and a coffee table. In the middle of the room is the bar, and the restaurant tables are on the right. The music and lights are perfect for a party. Since our group is waiting for bowling lanes to open up, they're all congregating between the bar and lanes, drinks in hand, catching up. There are about fifteen campers so far. Two of the women, Christy and Jill, quickly accost me and lead me toward the bar. I look around for Denise to save me as I am being pulled along, but she is nowhere to be found.

Christy asks me what I want to drink and I tell her I don't want anything. She seems disappointed by this and I almost reconsider just to make her happy. She's a nice enough woman, but her cheerfulness and tendency to try and fix everything is irritating. I don't want to be her special project tonight. She puts her hand gently on my upper arm and leans in to tell me something when suddenly Jeremiah and Todd appear behind her. Todd makes a face that she can't see and I snicker. Christy turns, sees the men, squeals with delight and promptly lets go of my arm so she can give them hugs. I take the moment to breathe in and compose myself. I didn't expect to see Jeremiah. Of course, I knew it was a possibility he would be here, but since he hasn't been at our gatherings in so long, I didn't think he would show up to this one. It really shouldn't matter, but it does.

Someone more interesting comes through the door, and Christy and Jill leave to go and greet them. I'm left standing alone with Jeremiah and Todd. I feel like a fish on dry land. I shouldn't be here, I have nothing to say to anyone. This is a party and I am not ready to party. And worse yet, seeing Jeremiah has caused a physical response in me that I am not emotionally stable enough to deal with.

Jeremiah speaks first. "Hi, Alison, It's good to see you," he says while leaning down to give me a hug.

I smile. "You too. It's been a long time." I feel my cheeks flush and tighten. Thank God it's dim in here.

"Can I get you something to drink?"

"Sure. I'll take a Guinness." He nods and leaves for the bar.

Todd turns to me and quietly asks, "So, how are you Alison? Are you doing okay?"

Todd is a good friend and we stayed in contact over the years, even when not having an official reunion. He and Joseph got along well, and Todd and his wife were sweet enough to come to his funeral.

I look up at him and smile slightly, nodding, "Not too bad. It's been hard, but it's getting better. Thanks again for coming to the funeral."

He hugs me. "Of course. Wendy couldn't come tonight, but she wanted me to tell you hi. Joseph was a good man. We'll all miss him."

Tears push against the back of my eyes, and although I appreciate his kindness, I wish I could have a night out without crying.

Jeremiah comes back and hands me my drink. I feel

guilty when our hands touch.

"Thanks. What do I owe you?" He waves me off.

The three of us stand there awkwardly until Denise comes over and makes it all better. She can put any person at ease with her thoughtful questions and genuine laugh. I'm grateful she is still my friend after all these years. It's not that I can't make my own conversation with Todd and Jeremiah, it's just that my mind is a complete blank. I have nothing to say that won't seem too trite for a person who is mourning, and I assume the men have no idea what to say to someone in my condition. Being a widow is like having a disease that no one wants to mention in public. It's kind of like leprosy. People are afraid to touch you for fear you might fall apart, or worse, that they might catch your bad luck.

After a few minutes of chit chat, the rest of the group arrives. Of the thirty campers invited, twenty-three came along with about fifteen of their spouses. I wonder about Jeremiah's wife, as I heard he married ten years ago. I don't have the courage to ask though, fearing he'll ask me about Joseph. I'm fragile, and one heartfelt question or token of sympathy will send me over the edge. I especially don't want sympathy from Jeremiah.

They soon announce our bowling lanes are available and everyone meanders over, claiming a spot on a couch or picking up shoes from the desk. Todd, Jeremiah, Denise and I decide to get our shoes first, so by the time we get to the lanes, there is only one corner of the couch available. Denise and I sit while the men stand behind us.

I hear all the voices catching up and laughing. Sometimes I'm aware of who is doing the talking, but mostly I feel like I'm in a bubble. I smile, feign interest in what's going on, and wait for someone to tell me it's my turn to bowl. I'm guarded and afraid I will be asked how I'm doing as a widow. I am overly aware of Jeremiah standing behind me talking with old friends. His laugh is hearty and warm. I wonder why his wife isn't here.

"Alison," I hear Denise call. The bubble breaks, voices are louder and lights are brighter. "It's your turn to bowl," she says.

I get up, find the ball I think I can manage, and suddenly remember the last time I bowled. Joseph had an annoying, yet endearing, way of coaching me after every turn, telling me if my hand was turned in or I released too early. He did it lovingly, of course, but I don't want any coaching tonight so I do my very best. The ball races and each pin falls with a crash. I turn back to the group with my fist in the air and a silly grin on my face. Strike!

"Awesome! Great bowl!" Jeremiah comes out and gives me a high-five.

"Thanks! It was luck, trust me," I say, despite my foolish grin.

Jeremiah bowls next and instead of returning to my seat I stand with Todd behind the couch. Todd bowls, and when he's done, sits down next to Denise on the couch, leaving Jeremiah and I to stand alone. Did I plan this? I must have, for I'm pleased it worked out this way. I feel a stab of guilt wondering if Joseph is watching from heaven and is disappointed in my interest to talk to an old boyfriend. Jeremiah and I stand close, our arms slightly touching. He leans down and quietly says, "I'm sorry about your husband. Todd told me about it and said he was a real stand-up guy."

I look up into his eyes. "Thank you. He was a great man. The kids and I miss him."

He nods. "I can't imagine going through that. If you ever want to talk about it..."

How strange that I would talk to him, a man I hadn't seen in so many years, a man I really barely know. Yet, it seems right. Other than Denise and maybe Todd, he is the only other person at the reunion that I would talk to about it.

I smile and nod. "Thanks, Jeremiah. I appreciate it. Tonight though, I just don't want to think about it, ya know?"

"Sure, I understand. Believe me, I understand."

"What do you mean? Is it about your wife? I was wondering..." I trail off, embarrassed.

He sighs, and turns away from the couch and listening ears. "Claire and I are getting a divorce. We've been separated for six months."

"Oh, I'm sorry Jeremiah. I really am. I can't imagine how difficult that would be."

He looks confused. "Sure you can. Having your husband die is pretty difficult."

I think about it for a second. "It's different though. Joseph and I never went through all the fighting. We never broke each other's hearts. Divorce is drawn-out pain and disappointment. It's bitter. Death is just sad."

"Well.. now I'm depressed," he says.

I laugh. "Sorry. Maybe you should hang out with someone else. I may bring on sudden and unexpected depression."

"I'll take my chances. Hanging out with you is the only reason I came tonight."

I look down to hide my smile. About the same time, I notice Jill and Christy watching us. We make eye contact and they turn away, whispering. I can guess what they're saying. Hasn't my husband only been dead a few months? Look how I'm flirting with an old boyfriend, and he's technically still married. I bet if their husbands had just died, they'd still be home crying, not out bowling and laughing. I hate to agree with what I assume they're saying, but maybe they're right. It is too soon. I still have months to go before my kids can give me the green dating light.

After my next turn to bowl, I resume my spot on the couch like a good little widow and don't flirt with the tall, handsome, ex-boyfriend anymore.

~~~

The next morning I wake up, and for the first time since Joseph's death, I don't greet the day with despair. In fact I'm not thinking of Joseph at all. Instead, I'm thinking about a peaceful dream I had where I'm in a big empty field with Jeremiah. His hand is around my shoulder and we're watching the clouds drift by. Nothing else really happens, but the dream is so peaceful and lucid that even after waking up, I can still feel his arm around me. The dream is wonderful, but it makes me feel guilty, and I wish I could have had a happy dream about Joseph instead. I want to recapture a little more of the peace I feel, but just as I determine to try and go back to sleep, my phone rings. The caller ID says Lauren's name. Although I don't feel like talking, I pick up quickly. Since the day Joseph died, I never miss a call from one of my kids.

"Mom," I hear Lauren's strained voice, "it's over!" She erupts into sobs.

My poor baby! I can't bear to hear her cry. I can only assume that her boyfriend, Dan, has dumped her.

"Do you want me to come over?" I'm already out of bed and getting dressed.

"Yes, please," she whispers.

It is common in our family to appear in person if one of us is in need. We don't feel the phone is an adequate way to communicate when you're upset. I stop at a bakery on the way to buy kolaches and donuts. It's another Collins tradition. I wonder if she's called Paul. Although the twins are very close, this seems to be more of a girl conversation. Paul will only get angry and offer to beat up Dan. When I arrive at Lauren's place, I don't see Paul's car, and am somewhat relieved.

Lauren comes to the door quickly after I knock and I embrace her as soon as I get inside. She starts crying all over again. I lead her to the couch so we can sit down side by side then I gently push her bangs out of her face.

"Tell me what happened, sweetie."

"Oh, Mom, I don't really know! He came over last night. We made dinner and watched a movie. I thought everything was fine." She stops to blow her nose then starts crying again.

I wait patiently for her to continue. I know there's more to the story than what she's telling. Lauren is notoriously private and will likely keep many of the details from me.

"I don't know how you're doing it, Mom," she says, with her face in her hands.

"What do you mean?" I say while rubbing her back.

"I mean, losing Dad! How are you handling it? I feel like dying and we weren't even married!"

How am I handling it? Sometimes I do feel like dying. It usually hits me worse at night, when the house is so empty and quiet. When I lay down to sleep, I remember that I'll never be touched, or loved again, by my sweet Joseph. I may never be loved again by any man, for that matter. Those are the moments I feel like dying. But, morning always dawns, and with it, a renewed desire to live. I have my kids to think of, and my writing gives me a goal, something to distract me.

"Sometimes I feel that way too, honey, but it's not how Dad would have wanted me to live. No matter how sad you feel now, life does go on. Do you want to tell me about it? Why did you two break up?"

Lauren gets up at that point and goes to the kitchen to get a donut. "Do you want any coffee?" she asks. I say yes, and follow her in to make my cup. I know better than to push her. She is incredibly stubborn and private. Paul is the only person she confides in without hesitation. However, this must be too personal even for him. We sit at her little kitchen table and miracle of miracles, she begins to open up to me.

"Dan says I close him out, but I don't see it, Mom." She takes a huge bite of her donut and looks down with teary eyes while she chews.

"Well," I proceed with caution, not wanting to disturb the delicate balance and cause her to shut down, "why do you think he feels that way?"

Lauren finishes chewing and just as I think she is about to tell me why, she burst into sobs.

"I guess because I probably do!" she wails.

"Oh, sweetie!" I scoot over and wrap my arms around her. She buries her head in my shoulder, crying uncontrollably. She cries like that for several minutes.

I feel strangely victorious. My daughter is confiding in me, not Joseph or Paul. She does need me.

"I miss Dad so much!" She looks at me with her big eyes, pleading for me to somehow bring him back.

"I know honey, I do too. I'm glad you called me though. You know I'll always be here for you."

"Thanks, Mom. Paul didn't answer and with Dad gone, I just didn't know who to call. I knew you would be home, and you were! Thanks again for coming."

My short lived victory is suddenly less sweet. Maybe I'm not so mad at Dan, after all. I mean, really, if the girl can't warm up to her own mother....

~~~

With Lauren's break up and the revisions my editor wants

me to do on my manuscript, I barely have time to think about how I brushed Jeremiah off at the reunion. I feel bad about it, but I don't owe Jeremiah anything. I have enough to worry about without adding his feelings to the list.

I shouldn't be thinking about him anyway. According to Lauren, I should be focused on not wanting to die. I'm having a hard time dealing with her theatrics. Joseph would have had a better idea about how to help Lauren through this difficult time. I'm pretty mad at her boyfriend for breaking up with her so soon after Joseph's death, however, it takes a strong man to be in a relationship with Lauren. Her reserved, yet intense nature, coupled with her extremely close relationship with her brother, makes it hard for any man to get very close. Joseph had an amazing way of questioning her in just the right way. She always ended up confiding without even realizing it was happening. He would take her to lunch or the museum and they would be gone for hours. I'll admit it made me a little jealous at times since I thought daughters were supposed to confide in their mother first. Paul is so independent and stable, he rarely seems to need me, either. I feel parents should not burden their children with adult problems, so as a result, the kids and I don't ever get extremely personal with each other. We do have fun together, though. Our favorite thing to do is cook special meals with a full-blown theme, elaborate menu, and a perfect movie to complement our event. It's been awhile since we've done that. Every time the kids have come over since the funeral, everything always ends up very serious, with all of us in tears. I decide I will call them later to plan a dinner/movie night. What we need is to have fun again. I figure enough time has passed for that. I know Joseph will love watching us be happy from his heavenly position. It's the kids I'll need to convince.

CHAPTER 6

"There is a land of the living and a land of the dead and the bridge is love, the only survival, the only meaning." – Thornton Wilder

With Joseph gone, I often feel the silence around me, and it's not unusual for a whole day to pass without speaking to anyone else. Janet is my best friend and we try to stay close, but her life is so filled with her young children, husband, and job that we only see each other a couple of times a month. We try to keep up by phone though and knowing about the reunion, she calls me a few days later to see how it went. I've never told her about Jeremiah but suddenly feel the need to talk to her about him.

"Okay, let me get this straight," Janet says. "The only other man you've ever loved, besides Joseph, has just resurfaced...and he's about to be divorced? And he flirted with you... but you felt guilty so you rudely brushed him off?"

"Yeah, that sounds about right. But I don't think it's fair to put him in the same category as Joseph as far as me loving him. We were teens for god's-sake! And I wasn't that rude."

"Okay. So he doesn't compare with Joseph, that's fair, but you definitely had strong feelings for him at one point?"

"Definitely."

"And you think he's interested in seeing more of you?"

"Seemed that way. He did say talking to me was the

only reason he showed up," I admit.

"Wow. That's bold. How long since you've seen him?"

"Gosh, let me think. It was at a reunion when the kids were little, so about twenty-one or twenty-two years." Saying it out loud makes me feel so old. I can't believe it's been that long.

"Twenty-two years and the man shows up right after your husband dies, and he's getting a divorce?"

"So? What does one have to do with the other?"

"I just think it's interesting. Have you thought that maybe he's getting a divorce because you're now available?"

"No. That's crazy! He doesn't know if we'd be good together, or even if I would be interested in seeing him. Besides, he said they had been separated for six months and it's only been five months since Joseph died." Only five months and I'm talking to my best friend about another man. I deserve an award for Worst Widow.

"Okay, so maybe it's not planned, but I do wonder if you being available makes it easier for him to get a divorce?"

"I think that's a stretch. I mean we need some perspective here. I barely know him anymore! Anyway, it doesn't really matter, I guess, because I probably won't see him again anytime soon. Besides, I still have seven months before I'm cleared to date."

"Oh yeah...the kids' rules, huh? That's ridiculous, by the way. You know that, right? You have to decide for yourself when, and if, you want to date. Your kids don't get to determine that."

"I know. It just seemed easier to agree with them than argue about it. Besides, I don't want to date yet. I mean, it *is* too soon. I cry almost every night over Joseph. I don't think it would go over very well if I started crying when out on a date. I just wish I had run into Jeremiah a year from now. I would have more time to really see how I feel about him."

"Well there's nothing that says you need to decide now. You'll still be a widow in a year, and he'll still be divorced," she says.

"Or not. I mean he may not wait around for me to reach my grief expiration date before he goes out and finds a new Mrs."

"Maybe not, but that's not your problem. You have to do what's right for you. If he really wants to see more of you, he'll wait until you're both ready. I mean, he's not even divorced yet!"

"That's true. I don't want to get mixed up in his divorce, so if he calls, I'll just keep it all very friendly. No flirting."

Talking to Janet helps me find perspective. I don't need to worry about Jeremiah right now. All that has really happened is that I talked to an old friend. It's not like he asked me out, or we're involved in any way. I mean, I was happily married for twenty-four years. Dating is the last thing on my mind.

~~~

Over the next two weeks, things start looking up in my life. I'm making progress on my book revisions, Lauren and I are growing closer, and I've gone three nights in a row without crying over Joseph. I feel good. I still miss him terribly, but I'm getting used to being alone at night. The silence isn't as big and loud as it was before.

Talking with Lauren has surprisingly helped. Although our relationships can't be compared in the big scheme of things, the advice I'm giving her to deal with her breakup with Dan, is also helping me with my loss. Lauren is very keen on talking about Joseph and our love for each other, but it doesn't upset me. On the contrary, it helps me to appreciate all we had and to remember I will always have him through our memories and through our children.

One morning, Lauren and I go to the Blanton Art Museum on the University of Texas campus. We walk around, admiring the new art display downstairs and marveling at the beautiful classic art upstairs. Occasionally, we talk about Joseph or Dan, but mostly we just try to enjoy the moment. It feels wonderful and makes me wonder if the closeness of her relationship with Joseph somehow hindered her relationship with me. My feelings of frustration with her began to intensify after Joseph died, making me realize that he had been a buffer between us when our personalities would clash. She depended so much on him that she and I never really had to work on our own relationship very much. I wish that it had not taken the loss of Joseph to bring us closer, but at the same time, I'm happy that at least one good thing has come out of all this. Having these few intimate and personal times with Lauren is helping to improve my overall mood.

It isn't long before I truly feel like I'm turning a page in my life and doing pretty well. So well, in fact, that I accept an invitation for all the camp crew for the following Friday. The invitation says we will all go out for drinks and dinner at a restaurant called Fados, here in Austin. In the past we have longer time periods between our gatherings. However, at the last one, everyone expressed their feelings of wanting to hang out together more, especially those who live in the Austin area. Had Joseph been alive, and I had a real life, I probably would have declined and said I was too busy. But, since my alternative was to sit on my couch and watch a not-so-great movie on Netflix, I decide that getting out more is a good idea.

I don't know if Jeremiah will be there. Part of me hopes he won't be. I feel ready to get out in public and socialize, but I don't think I'm ready to be around someone who affects me so much. I want to prove that I can carry on conversations without Joseph, and that I am interesting enough on my own to develop relationships with other people. What I don't want, however, is a repeat of our last get together where I shamelessly flirt with my ex-boyfriend and attract whispers from my old friends.

A few days before the dinner, I decide to check the email thread to see who will be coming. About ten of my old camp-mates will be there, along with several of their spouses. The last confirmation is from Jeremiah. I have mixed feelings about seeing him, but mostly I'm just nervous. The night before our gathering, I call Janet.

"You're seeing him tomorrow night? What are you wearing?"

"What am I wearing? I don't know. I hadn't even thought about it."

"Well, why not? You only have that one nice outfit that fits, right? And he's already seen you in it."

"It doesn't matter what I wear because I'm not trying to impress him."

"Okay, but you also don't want to not impress him, and no offense, but your baggy old clothes don't look so hot."

"Well, thanks a lot. I don't think my clothes are that bad." I look down at my sweatpants and stick my finger in the hole that is growing on my thigh. "I guess I could go shopping tomorrow."

"Get something sexy."

"No! You are not helping. I need you to tell me this is not a big deal. This is not a date and I don't need to worry about how I look."

"It's kind of a date though. At least a group date.

What are you afraid of?"

"I'm afraid of having fun. I'm afraid I'll end up flirting with him. I'm afraid this is all happening too fast and I'm not ready! And, even if I do like him, it's too soon for that! I'm afraid of being the worst widow in the world. Joseph could be looking down at me with shame and sadness, and think I don't love him if I fall for someone else so soon! That's what I'm afraid of!"

"Is that all?"

"No. I'm also afraid that the first time another man touches me, holds me, or kisses me, I'll either freeze up or fall apart."

"I do understand, Alison. I worried about those things too, when my Joseph died. I know it's not the same..." she trails off.

"Well, it's not that different. What did you do when you started seeing Steve?"

"It helped that I didn't meet him until the year mark had passed. I felt somewhat ready by then."

"So, my kids were right? I should wait a year." I sigh and fall back on my bed.

"It's not the same. You already know this guy. Besides, you said yourself, it's not a date, and no one is pressuring you to move too fast. It's just old friends getting together for dinner. Right?"

"Yeah, I guess so. Thanks, that helps. I just need to remember that and not make it bigger than it is," I say.

I go to the mall the next morning. Without meaning to, I buy a very nice and a little bit sexy outfit. I put it on an hour before I'm supposed to be at the restaurant. I can't help but look at myself in the mirror. Who is this woman wearing skinny pants and heels? Certainly not the same frumpy mother and wife I had been the last twenty-four years. Certainly not a respectable woman who was widowed only five and a half months ago. I almost change my clothes, I really do. I mean, even I can admit I look really good. Is this the image I'm trying to project? If I believe this is a casual dinner among old friends and nothing more, why am I looking this hot? What will Joseph think?

I plan to get downtown early enough to get a good parking spot in a lot close to the restaurant. But, by the time I get there, the lot is full and I have to park in a garage and walk an extra block. I've been to Fados only once before, with Joseph. We met one of his co-workers there about a year ago. The man had been recently divorced and brought along his girlfriend. She was quiet, somewhat rude, and the whole evening had been uncomfortable. The place had been nearly empty and the four of us had sat at a corner table making awkward conversation. That experience tainted my idea about the Irish bar, so I'm not expecting to walk in and find it loud, full, and bustling with energy. I spot my group immediately, sitting on the stools around the center bar. Denise sees me walk in and waves me over. I'm grateful that she's already here. As independent as I am trying to be, I need an anchor at public places, or I start feeling a little lost. Joseph had always been my anchor.

"Hi, friend." I greet her with a hug.

"Hey. I'm so glad you came!" She pulls away and looks me up and down with her eyebrows raised. "You look amazing! Wow. Are you hoping to see a certain someone?"

"What? No! Of course not. I just had to buy some new clothes," I say, feeling self-conscious.

"Why? Because you're so damn skinny now? Honestly, if I didn't love you, I'd be jealous."

Jealous? "Well, I'm skinnier because I'm incredibly depressed, so you really shouldn't be too jealous," I say.

She looks at me and frowns slightly, "I know. I'm

sorry. I didn't mean I was jealous of your life right now. But you do look beautiful."

"Well, thanks. I guess it's better than being sad *and* ugly." I smile and squeeze her hand to show I'm not really upset.

A waitress walks up and asks me if I'd like a drink. I order a Carlsberg then look around to see who else is here. A few old friends, Christy and Wendy, give me hugs and stand to chat a bit. The waitress brings me my drink and we continue to catch up and make small talk. I do wonder if Jeremiah is still coming, and the fact that Denise calls me on it so easily, frustrates me. I don't want to want him to come. I want to be a respectable widow, hesitantly venturing out in public and seeking solace from my friends. But here I am. Looking good. In a bar. Waiting for my old boyfriend.

After about twenty minutes, we're told that our table is ready. Before sitting down, I excuse myself to go to the bathroom. When I come back out everyone is already seated in their places, and there is only one empty chair left. It's right next to Jeremiah. When did he get here? He grins at me and scoots my chair out.

"Are you saving this for me?" I ask with a smile.

"Who else?"

"I wasn't sure you were coming."

"I wasn't going to, but I checked my email and saw that you'd be here," he says.

"Well," I say, hoping the blush in my cheeks doesn't show, "I hope you won't be sorry. I'm not the best company."

"I don't think I'll regret it, if that's what you mean." He winks at me and turns his attention to the menu.

I stare at him for a second, noticing that the hair around his temple is turning grey. He squints his eyes to read the small print better, and I smile. It's strange, and yet very endearing, to see that he's older. We're older. If I wasn't consciously looking for signs of age, he would look the same to me as he had when we were eighteen. I wonder what he sees when he looks at me. Age is a funny thing. I never noticed Joseph aging either. Not until I looked down on him in that coffin. Then he not only looked much older, with the life stolen from him, but also like another person. They said he was my husband, but I barely recognized him. I realized that the life within us identifies us so much more than physical features do. Joseph didn't look like Joseph when his soul wasn't looking back at me through his eyes. Jeremiah doesn't look any different now because it's the same man inside his physical frame that looked at me when we were eighteen. This knowledge comforts me.

He looks up at me, can probably feel my eyes on him. He smiles, and I smile back.

"You look really beautiful tonight."

"Thank you. You're looking nice, yourself," I say. The woman sitting across from him looks up at me just then. She doesn't exactly frown, but I get the message. I look down at the menu, kicking myself for being so obvious. Why am I flirting with him? Is it right to lead Jeremiah on? He clearly is interested in me, and I'm acting as if I'm interested, too. Is that fair, when the truth is, I am in no way ready to date?

He catches the subtle look from the other lady, and to my relief, turns his attention on her for a moment, asking about her family and job. This makes me feel better and seems to do the trick She actually smiles at me, and asked how my kids are and what have I been up to lately. The three of us continue talking for a few more moments. Even though Jeremiah politely talks to all nearby equally, every time I glance at him, he's looking at me.

I order bangers and hash, at the waiter's

recommendation, and it's delicious. The combination of Irish comfort food, the warm glow of the bar and the security of eating with people I've known for most of my life, relaxes me more than I expect. Soon, I'm actually laughing at the jokes of others and even contributing to some of the banter. I don't feel sad, lonely, or guilty. It's wonderful. At one point, Tom tells a particularly funny story and we all burst out laughing. Jeremiah puts his hand on my knee under the table and I freeze. I don't think anyone notices me suddenly getting quiet but Jeremiah does. He looks over at me and then seems to take notice of where his hand is. He quickly removes it, aware of my stiffness.

"I'm sorry. I didn't mean to do that," he says quietly, leaning toward me.

"It's fine," I reassure him, "it's no big deal." I smile, but he isn't buying it.

"No, really," he whispers, "I can tell it isn't fine. I apologize."

I notice a couple of people looking our way, so I say, "Let's just talk later, okay?"

He nods and sparks up a conversation with a male friend of ours a few seats down. I just sit here trying to figure out why it freaked me out so bad. Is it just being touched by another man? Is it because part of me likes that he touched me so personally? Is it the secrecy of it happening under the table? Aren't we already being secretive? There's a lot of good tension between us, but we're both trying our damnedest to appear normal and act like everyone at the table is equally as important to the two of us as we are to each other. We both know it isn't so. Is it obvious to anyone else? A wave of guilt washes over me. I feel like a child reprimanded in public. I don't want to look anyone in the eyes.

Dinner is coming to a close, our plates are cleared, the

bill is separated, and people begin saying their goodbyes. Although I mostly had a good time, I'm relieved the night is over. It's hard to be a good widow around Jeremiah. The effort has exhausted me emotionally. Before he has a chance to talk to me again, I stand up and say a general goodbye to the table, give Denise and Wendy a hug, and then excuse myself. As I reach the door, Jeremiah catches up to me.

"Alison, wait!"

I turn and smile politely. "It was nice to see you Jeremiah, but I need to go."

"Okay," he says, resting his hand on my arm. "I'm sorry again if I made it weird."

I shake my head. "No, you didn't do anything. I had a nice time. I just have a headache and want to get home before it gets worse."

He furrows his brows and looks a bit confused. "Okay. Well... feel better. I hope I get to see you again soon."

"I'm sure we will. Thanks, Jeremiah, and um....okay. Bye." I fumble with my words and clumsily turn away without giving him the hug I know he expects.

I walk back quickly to my car and notice a few men turning to look at me as I pass by. The attention feels unwelcome and intrusive. I can't wait to get home, shed my new clothes and put on my old frumpy sweatshirt. The one that makes me feel safe, secure, and sad. I want to curl up on the couch, watch a movie and behave in a way that does not bring on guilt or whispers from others. From now on, I vow to be a good widow.

CHAPTER 7

"Be reverent before the dawning day. Do not think of what will be in a year, or in ten years. Think of today." – Romain Rolland

My doorbell rings, and I literally jump up from my place on the couch. I'm not dressed and there are tissues and dishes strewn around the house. I want to cry. I stand frozen in my living room hoping that if I don't make a sound, whoever is there will go away. When I don't hear anything else for another minute, I slowly and quietly make my way to the door and tentatively look out through the peep hole. No one is there, so I open the door. At my feet is a small Fed Ex box. My eyebrows shoot up and a thrill courses through my body. I love surprises. I carry the box back to the couch and begin opening it with childlike anticipation. I don't know what I'm expecting or why it's so thrilling to receive something unexpected in the mail, but it is. I tug at the packaging tape and rip through the paper to pull out a little book entitled, *Grief 101*. There is a note taped to the front from my Aunt Emily. I stare at the cover for a moment wondering why she sent it to me. What am I supposed to do with it? Then I realize that I'm actually the perfect recipient of this book. I'm supposed to be grieving and obviously have no idea how to do it correctly. Other grievers probably have many books to help them along the way. Maybe even some go to a class. No wonder I'm failing so miserably. I didn't have a course book until now. I'm suddenly very grateful to Aunt Emily for the guidebook that will help me pass the test. Clearly this is what I've been missing. Armed with the hope of knowledge, I take my book to the couch and begin studying. The first chapter deals with the individual stages of grief: denial/isolation, anger, bargaining, depression, and acceptance. Before detailing the individual stages, the book assures me that everyone goes through them at different times and with varying levels of severity. So, acceptance might be easier for me than, let's say, anger. I'm not sure I agree with the five stages. I mean surely I've already gone through them all. I accept Joseph's death. It happened. What is there to deny? I know he died. I don't expect him to come walking back through the door. I know that I will never see him alive again. Sure, I was angry at first. I had a right to be angry. Joseph wasn't some old man who had lived a long life. He also wasn't a man who didn't take care of himself and was just asking for early death. Joseph was healthy, loving, and giving. He deserved to live a long life. Would I have bargained for his life had I been given a chance? Sure, I definitely would have! What does that mean anyway? I guess I'll find out later. Depression. Well that one seems obvious. I understand it. Who wouldn't get a bit depressed when a loved one dies? These nice compact categories don't resonate a whole lot with me, and suddenly I'm not so thankful for the book. In fact, I'm a little insulted that the author can so easily compartmentalize my very real, mixed up, and complex emotions relating to the death of my husband. Who the hell are they to tell me my grief has five nice little stages I have to go through before I'm over it? I sigh. Clearly though, I do need help. I put the book aside, promising to pick it up again soon. I'm just not in the right state of mind to read it now. I don't really believe it can help me. Or maybe, I don't want the help it promises. Letting a book guide me feels like cheating on a big exam. Shouldn't I be learning about all this as I go along, instead of following stages outlined in a book? I mean, why read about grief when I'm living it, day and night?

Getting over Joseph's death feels not only impossible, but also wrong. Although I'm learning to handle it pretty well, I don't think I'll ever be "over it." Some days I still can't leave my house. I wake up with good intentions, such as planning to go outside and run, have lunch with a friend, or work hard on my new book. But my intentions are like a blooming flower, choked out by the weeds of despair I still have growing in my heart. On these days, I find myself in my closet holding on to the few shirts of Joseph's I've kept. I wrap them around my body and regret that I haven't kept all of his clothes, so that I can bury myself in them. Or, I end up sitting in a pile of photographs, with memories strewn all around me. Every photo or old card is like a clamp around my lungs, squeezing tighter with every remembrance until I can't breathe anymore. Other days I don't even have the energy to grieve. I just lug my body from bed to couch and watch TV all day long, ignoring phone calls and pushing off any thoughts of hope for my future.

Thankfully, these days are few and far between, but they're still there. Six months after his death and I still have some pretty bad days... I guess I need to accept that maybe I'll always have some days that are worse than others. After all, no matter how much time passes, I will always miss Joseph. I will always wish we had grown old together. I will never think that it is okay that he died.

The idea of getting over his death is ridiculous. I might get used to it. I might learn to control my emotions. I might figure out how to navigate through life without him. But I will never get over it.

That being said, I don't want to live my life in a state

of grief. I want my life to have meaning and lately I've been more aware that something is missing–something less obvious than my husband. I try to keep busy running, working on my book revisions, and spending time with my children, but it's not enough. I'm missing companionship with non-grieving adults who live regular lives. The problem is there are only a handful of people I'm comfortable with right now– Janet, whom I love and appreciate, but who is very busy with her young children; Denise, my loyal and long time friend, but who has a very large personality and is sometimes hard to be around; and Todd and Wendy, who always make me feel relaxed when I am with them, but who I don't know all that well. Still, Todd and Wendy stick out in my mind as they live close and I'd like to expand my relationships beyond my two best friends. I email Wendy and ask her about getting together sometime. She quickly replies with an invitation to their house for dinner.

The day before our dinner I call Wendy to see if I can bring anything.

"No, I've got it all taken care of. I'm so happy you're coming over!"

"Me, too. Thank you so much for asking me."

"Oh, I hope you don't mind. Todd invited Jeremiah over, too. Is that okay? You two are friends, right?"

Wendy didn't go to camp with us, and likely doesn't know about my past relationship with Jeremiah. Todd may have told her, but I doubt it. Men don't talk about that kind of thing much.

"Um, yeah. Of course. Of course, that's fine," I say hoping the hesitation in my voice isn't obvious.

"Poor guy. He's been coming over about once a week lately. This divorce is pretty tough on him. I think he just needs some friends, and you know he and Todd are pretty close."

"Of course! No problem. I'll see you tomorrow!"

I get off the phone quickly and put my head in my hands. I've proven that I can't be near Jeremiah and still behave appropriately. And even though I'm worried about getting through the night without embarrassing myself, I'm also ashamed to admit that I'm excited Jeremiah is going to be there. I wonder if I didn't seek out Todd and Wendy subconsciously knowing the two men are such good friends.

On the night of the dinner, I take extra care with my clothes and make-up, and ignore the nagging voice in my head. I continue to tell myself I need more friends and that I have no intention of dating Jeremiah. I arrive at Wendy and Todd's a few minutes late and see Jeremiah's truck in the driveway. I'm suddenly very nervous. The last time I saw him, I felt both excited and guilty, all at the same time. Although feeling excited is nice, I can't enjoy it without the nagging guilt.

"Alison! I'm so glad you could come," says Wendy, as she hugs me at the door.

"Thanks for having me, Wendy," I reply with a smile.

Their home is warm and inviting, and Wendy is a natural hostess. I'm put at ease almost immediately.

"I'm so sorry about everything, Alison. If you ever want to talk or hang out, I'd love it," she says quietly in my ear.

"Thanks, Wendy. I'm doing pretty well, although some days are definitely harder than others."

She squeezes my arm and leads me into the living room. Todd and Jeremiah are discussing the football game on TV.

"Hey guys, Alison's here!" Wendy announces.

The men turn around and Todd comes over to give me a hug. I can see Jeremiah over his shoulder. He smiles at me and I smile back. Todd excuses himself to help

Wendy in the kitchen, leaving us alone. Two old lovers, both newly damaged adults, staring awkwardly at each other. Finally, Jeremiah motions toward the back patio door and asks if I'd like to go outside for a minute. I nod and follow him out.

"I want to apologize about Fados," I say.

"What about?"

"I think I was kind of rude. I mean, I was having a great time talking to you and everything...it's just, I guess I started feeling a little guilty. I still haven't figured out how to have a nice time when I'm supposed to be mourning."

I've been looking down while I say all this and when I look up, Jeremiah has a soft, tender expression on his face.

"I can't imagine how hard it must be. I think it's different with a divorce. Everyone expects you to be a little angry, or depressed, but they also seem to think it's okay to get back out there and have a little fun. It's different when someone dies. No one wants to see a widower flirting or having fun. That just seems wrong, I guess."

"So, you do understand." I smile at him. "I'm having a hard time figuring it all out. I miss Joseph terribly, and if I could have him back here, I would do it in a heartbeat. But, I also have this strange peace about it. I don't know...maybe I'm still in the wrong phase of grief. My kids expect me to be a crying, devastated mess, but that's not how I am, and that's not how Joseph and I handled things. I feel him with me all the time. Maybe he's helping me be strong."

"What do you mean, you feel him with you?"

"I don't know. How do you separate yourself from your husband after being one with him for twenty-four years? I guess I don't think of death as completely final. We aren't physically together anymore, but that doesn't mean he hasn't helped to shape who I am, and that he's not still in my head, you know?"

Jeremiah looks down for a minute, thinking. "I get what you're saying, but I don't really know, first hand," he answers solemnly.

A shift in our mood becomes apparent. I can practically feel the invisible wall come down between us. I reach out and touch his arm.

"Did I upset you?"

"No, you didn't do anything. I just realized that I don't know if I ever had that level of relationship with my wife and I wonder why. It sounds like you two had something really special."

Jeremiah starts walking back into the house, while I linger on the patio.

"Yeah, we did," I say quietly, before following him inside.

When I step back in, I smell a mixture of garlic and onion that instantly reminds me of home. Almost every meal I used to make began with sautéed garlic and onion. It's been awhile since I've actually cooked anything tasty for myself. Lately, I just fix a sandwich or eat a bowl of cereal. I don't see the point of cooking when no one will be appreciating it, myself included. I hear laughter coming from the kitchen, and discreetly make my way toward the sound and watch as Todd holds something out of Wendy's reach. She tickles him to make him drop it, and he wraps his arms around her pinning her hands down her sides. He kisses her. They look so intimate that I feel wrong watching them. I look around for Jeremiah, but don't see him. I wouldn't be surprised if I drove him off, talking about my dead husband being with me all the time. I sigh and am about to go sit back in the living room by myself when he comes out of the bathroom.

"Pretty annoying, huh?" He smiles and winks at me.

"Don't they know who they invited over?"

Wendy and Todd look over, grinning. I laugh, relieved that he's joking with me.

"No kidding. The soon-to-be divorced man and the recent widow are not so impressed by public displays of affection."

"Sorry guys," says Todd, kissing Wendy again. "You're just gonna have to deal with it, cause I love to kiss my wife!"

Wendy punches him on the arm playfully. "Dinner's almost ready. Anyone want wine?"

We sit at a round dinner table, adorned with fresh flowers and lit candles. There are also two bottles of wine on the table, both of which are quickly being emptied. Wendy has prepared an amazing meal and my taste buds are very grateful for the change in my diet. I catch myself groaning in approval more than once. I look up from my plate and blush as they all laugh at me.

"I'm glad you like it," Wendy says.

I almost cry. Everything is so nice. These old friends are nice; their house is nice; the food is nice; the pretty flowers on the table are nice. All of it is perfect. I'm sitting with other adults, conversing about real life issues, and they want my opinion about things. Suddenly, it dawns on me that my opinion counts, all on its own, and I can make my own decisions without consulting Joseph on everything. I can determine when I'm going home, what my plans will be the next day, and where my life is headed, in general. It's equally terrifying and liberating to realize this. Why I suddenly realize it between bites of Chicken Marsala, I don't know. Nonetheless, it makes me tear up.

The men exchange quick glances and Wendy puts her hand on mine. "Are you alright, Alison?"

I nod and take another bite of chicken with my free

hand, staring at her with big, wet eyes. I'm sure I look pretty pathetic. I can't bring myself to look at the men so I keep my eyes on Wendy, and continue to chew. Finally, I speak, "It's all so nice." I then start crying for real. Nothing too awful, but there are still, big fat tears I have to wipe off with my cloth napkin, and of course I smear black mascara all over it.

"Excuse me." I get up, napkin to my eyes, and quickly walk to the bathroom to compose myself. I look in the mirror. The woman looking back is pretty, but tired. Her eyes are red and her face is streaked with tears. She doesn't reflect the confidence and independence I thought I had begun to feel. Maybe my inner self knows better; knows that no amount of exercise, or shopping, or success can hide the fact that my husband died six months ago.

After several minutes, I tentatively come back out. I worry that I may have ruined Wendy's lovely dinner and created a very awkward situation. When I return to the table, the dinner dishes are cleared and replaced with cheesecake and cups of coffee. The three of them are discussing Wendy's plans for a new garden shed. The men debate about the lumber Todd will need and it sounds like Jeremiah has volunteered to help. Nobody says anything about my episode.

"So, Alison, I hope you were done eating, because Todd gave all the scraps to Pete."

"Sorry. You said you were getting dessert so I thought we were done. Besides, Pete was hungry, weren't you boy?" Todd reaches under the table to give their old and spoiled mutt a good scratching.

"It's fine," I say with a smile. "This looks delicious."

Jeremiah winks at me from across the table. "Wendy makes the best cheesecake I've ever had. Last time I was here I think I ate at least half the cake by myself."

"I didn't realize you guys had stayed in touch."

"Well, I ran into Todd not long after Claire and I separated. I was pretty depressed and when Todd asked how I had been, I let it all out. He felt sorry for me and invited me over for dinner. I've been mooching off of their hospitality ever since." Jeremiah says with a sheepish grin. "Sorry, guys."

Wendy pats his hand. "You're welcome here anytime, Jeremiah. At least you appreciate my cooking."

"Hey, I appreciate your cooking. I appreciate your everything, honey," Todd says, with a wink.

I laugh. These generous and warm people diffuse the uncomfortable situation I almost created, and I already love them for it. I pick up my fork and hover it above the cheesecake.

"Okay if I eat this now?"

"Dig in, everyone!" Wendy says.

After dessert, coffee, and small talk, I notice Todd looking at his watch a couple of times. I remember that their teenage daughter is out on a date, and it looks like she's late getting home. Wendy gets a phone call and excuses herself to the other room. She then calls to Todd to join her. He sighs, gets up from his chair, and follows Wendy. Soon, I hear a frustrated, one-sided conversation.

"I remember those days. I'm sure glad my kids are grown." I smile at Jeremiah, who looks confused.

"You know what that's about?"

"Oh, yeah. That's a kid calling to see if she can stay out later than her curfew."

Todd's voice escalates. "And Todd sounds like a man who is pretty annoyed with his daughter."

Jeremiah shakes his head. "So, maybe I dodged a bullet by never having kids, huh?"

"Having children is equally the most amazing and most difficult thing you could ever do." I smile softly at him. "Maybe we should head out soon, what do you think?"

"I think we should head out together. I'm not ready to tell you goodnight," he says.

"Me neither," I admit. I'm not sure what I want, but I know I don't want to miss this chance to be near Jeremiah. Jeremiah, with his dark hair and green eyes. Jeremiah, six feet tall and broad shouldered. Jeremiah, whose eyes crinkle when he smiles at me. Jeremiah, whose kisses I barely remember.

Todd and Wendy come back in the room a minute later, looking tired. Jeremiah stands up and stretches.

"Hey guys, tonight was awesome, but I think Alison and I are gonna head out and give you guys some family time."

"You don't have to leave yet. That was just Makenzie pulling one of her tricks," Wendy says.

"I remember those all too well. Lauren was queen of changing the rules, once she was out. You'll need to deal with her when she gets here and won't need an audience. We had a great time, but it's getting late." I take Wendy's hand in mine. "I can't thank you enough for such a nice evening. I really needed it." We hug and she whispers in my ear that I can come over anytime or call.

Todd pats Jeremiah on the back and I hear him quietly tell him, "Be good, man."

Jeremiah and I walk out and before we reach our cars, he asks if I'd like to come over to his place. With pretty much no persuasion, I follow him a few miles down the road to a new apartment complex. A perfect place for a man going through a divorce. A perfect place for a widow to hide.

We walk up the stairs to his second story unit, all the while saying things like what a nice night it is, how nice and bright the stars are, and how nice his place seems to be. I'm getting tired of the nice. Jeremiah opens the door letting me walk in first. He then shuts the door and turns on a lamp. His place is clean and warm. It's obvious he bought new furniture. It all matches and is very un-lived in. I'm glad Claire got all of *their* things. I'm also glad we came here and not my house. My house is very much mine and Joseph's house. I haven't changed anything since he died. Not even our bedroom.

I remove my shoes and walk around the small living room, trailing my hand over the back of his couch and chair. I turn to look at him, standing over by the kitchen.

"It's nice."

He keeps his eyes fixed on mine in the two steps it takes him to reach me. His arms wrap around my waist, pulling me in close. His lips meet mine, and they're gentle and soft. I'm lost in his size and I love it.

"Alison, I..."

"Jeremiah, can we just please....not talk?" I whisper into his neck. I don't want him to question what I so badly want to do...the same thing I wanted to do at camp twenty-two years ago under the stars with the heat from the bonfire against our skin. I don't want to question the wisdom in it or if we're ready. I just want what I want.

He kisses me passionately. It should feel weird with another man touching and kissing me, after being with the same man for twenty-four years, but it doesn't. It just feels right.

~~~

Several hours later, I crawl into my own bed, despite Jeremiah's urging for me to stay at his place. We made love. Usually, I don't like it when people use those words when in fact, there is no love involved, just sex. But, I can honestly say, Jeremiah and I made love. I don't know if it was new love or the old feelings of love we let go of prematurely over twenty years ago. I'm guessing it was old love. Either way, it was exhilarating, terrifying, magical, and raw. It was what my body needed, yet now my heart feels extremely conflicted. I try not to think too much about it as I lay in bed. I'm so tired. I wish I could fall into that warm, deep, post-coital sleep, but all I can think about is how disappointed Joseph would be, how disappointed everyone would be, if they knew what a bad widow I was.

CHAPTER 8

"When the heart weeps for what it has lost, the
soul laughs for what it has found."
– an old Sufi aphorism

Jeremiah, being the gentleman that he is, calls me the
next morning. I let it go to voicemail, and instead of
returning his call, I go on a long run. Am I scared?
Maybe. However, I have other things I need to worry
about. I signed up to run my first 10K race last week. The
exciting thing is, I will actually be able to run it now, and
not just walk along. I've been steadily increasing my speed
and distance the last few months. What is the best therapy
for a sad, lonely, widow? For me, it's spending hours
outside, hitting the pavement running past the same
streets, over and over again, in my small neighborhood.
It's adding a thousand songs to my iPod so I never get
bored, and spending two hundred dollars on running
shoes, because everyone knows red shoes make you run
faster. It means avoiding running by my house because it
reminds me that someone is missing in there. Even with
the new shoes and iPod, running to me is far cheaper, and
more effective, than any shrink could ever be right now.

I use the alone time and the repetition that comes
with running, to work through some things. For instance,
am I okay with the changes my editor wants me to make
to my book? They're fairly minor, but one change in
particular is really bothering me. She wants me to change
some elements about my leading man, the character
pretty strongly modeled after Joseph. He wasn't Joseph,
of course, but the things she wants changed really remind

me of him. It feels wrong to wipe him out of my book. Joseph was so instrumental in my even writing the book. Plus, he deserves to be in print, even in a small way. Joseph was a real-life, leading man. The real deal.

Another issue troubling me is my children. They seem to have switched places. Lauren, my responsible, reserved daughter, who normally handles crises by propelling herself into work, reorganizing her entire apartment, or maybe watching an endless stream of sad movies with her brother, is now partying with a new friend from work almost every night. She's getting home late, and showing up late for work. How do I know this? Her boss actually called me. Lauren's been late to work on several occasions recently and looking hung over when she arrives. This is so out of character for her, that her boss of three years felt I should know about it. I almost laugh when she calls. Lauren is a grown woman, and when I was her age, I was already married and expecting twins. I certainly felt like an independent adult then and would not have wanted anyone calling my mom about me. I should be grateful, though, that her boss cares so much about her. I assure her Lauren is just going through a rough time with the loss of her dad, and her boyfriend, but in reality, I'm not so convinced.

Soon after I hear from Lauren's boss, Paul calls and tells me he's looking for a real job. He wants to make more money and get a place of his own. While this sounds great, I worry that he'll get stuck in the boring corporate world too soon. I also don't want him to make these decisions when he's dealing with such a big loss. Joseph and I always agreed that important life choices shouldn't be made in the middle of stress. I don't know though, maybe it's normal to act out of character when you're dealing with grief. Like staying out too late with friends, or getting a new job, or sleeping with a man who's not your husband.

I avoid Jeremiah's calls for four days. On Saturday and Sunday, he leaves sweet messages, telling me what a great time he had on Friday. He says he's happy we found each other again, he wants to see me soon and maybe go out to dinner. By Monday, it has deteriorated into, "What is going on Alison? Can we please talk about this?"

I feel bad, I really do, but I don't know what to say. I'm dealing with a lot. My editor called on Sunday and wants to fly me to New York on Thursday. She wants to work face-to-face on some of the revisions we've discussed. Actually, they just want me to comply with their ideas, it's me who insists on a personal meeting, and me who's footing my own airfare, to do it. However, that's beside the point. The point is, with my book issues, Lauren and Paul making huge lifestyle changes in the middle of stress, and my race looming so soon, I just don't have time to deal with a romance I never should have started to begin with. I do care about Jeremiah, though, and I acknowledge that I'm treating him poorly. I would feel horrible if he were doing the same thing to me, especially after the amazing night we shared. I just don't know what to do or say. Should I tell him that it feels like we we're rushing it? That I'm not ready? Yes. I should and I will.

"Jeremiah? It's Alison," I cradle the phone with my eyes shut tight, hoping he won't hang up on me. It is now Wednesday afternoon, and he hasn't called me since Monday morning.

"Hi," he responds with an indifferent tone that makes me want to cry.

"Hi. I'm really sorry."

"What the hell, Alison? We're not teenagers," he says. "Why are you treating me like a one-night stand?"

Oh God, I have treated him that way. "I'm so sorry.

You're right, I've been terrible," I say, willing myself not to cry. "I don't know why I haven't called."

"I thought Friday night was pretty amazing."

"It was," I whisper. "Too amazing."

"What do you mean?"

"I don't know. Can I see you?"

He sighs and pauses long enough for me to realize how badly I don't want him to say no.

"Of course. Do you want to have dinner tomorrow night?" He doesn't sound too excited about it, but at least he doesn't say no.

"Actually, I can't tomorrow. I'm going to New York in the morning to meet with my editor and agent."

"That's great, Alison. I'm really happy for you."

"Thanks, but I'm going there to fight for my main character. They want to make some changes I'm not happy about. Is there any way we can get together tonight for dinner?" I literally cross my fingers.

"Well, tonight might not work. I have dinner plans with Claire."

"Oh." My heart drops to the floor when he says her name. What an idiot I am.

"It's not what you think. She just wants me to sign a paper saying I won't fight her for certain things that are hers."

"And you need to have dinner for that?" I say with an edge in my voice, that I instantly regret.

"Look Alison, I've been calling you for days. You're the one who hasn't called me back. Not that I need to explain, but Claire is part of my life. I'm not in love with her anymore, but that doesn't mean I'll never see her again. You're the one I wanted to see this week, but as far as I knew you didn't want to see me. So yeah, when Claire asked about dinner, I accepted."

"I know, Jeremiah. I'm sorry. Look maybe we should

just plan to talk in a few days. I've said I'm sorry a lot already, and if we keep talking, I'll probably stick my foot in my mouth and have to apologize again. I hope you have a nice dinner, and I mean that, sincerely. I'll call you in a few days."

"Yeah, I'll talk to you later. Have a good trip."

As soon as I hang up I burst into tears. What is going on? This is exactly why I don't want to get involved with him. I can't be crying over two men at the same time. It's just wrong.

Hours later, I'm in full out sympathy mode, eating ice cream in in my PJ's and fuzzy socks, with a towel around my head, watching *You've Got Mail*. I just love Tom Hanks and Meg Ryan. They're so happy in the movie, even when nothing is working out, and their business is failing, and they break up with their significant other. Even then, they act so happy and wonderful, and I want to be their friend.

I hear something, so I turn down the volume. There it is, definitely a knock. Who's stopping by this late? It must be one of the kids, although why they wouldn't just use their key, I don't know. I pull myself up. "Hold on, I'm coming," I call as I approach the door. Just to be safe I look through the peep-hole. Not one of my kids. Big, tall and handsome. Why does Jeremiah have to show up tonight? I'm a mess! I quickly tear off my towel, slip out of my fuzzy Christmas socks, shake out my hair, and then reluctantly open the door. He's grinning at me in a way that makes me want to slap him and kiss him at the same time.

"Hey Alison." I open the door wider and he steps in.

"Jeremiah, what are you doing here? I thought you were out with Claire."

"I was, it was just dinner. I really wanted to see you."

He puts his hands on my hips and pulls me into him. "I felt bad how our phone call went."

It suddenly dawns on me that he's never been here.

"How did you know where I lived?"

"It's a secret. Don't worry, I'm not a crazy stalker."

"I'm not so sure."

I assess my foyer for any signs of Joseph. All clear. A few weeks ago, I had at least moved his shoes, coat and keys that usually occupy the entryway into a box in the garage. I can't have Jeremiah here. It feels too weird. I'm about to tell him so, but then he bends down and kisses me. Not nice and quick, but a slow, deep kiss. The kind of kiss that tells me he doesn't care if I'm in my PJ's, or that my hair is wet. He doesn't care that he's uninvited and unexpected, and doesn't care that my dead husband's things might still be lying around somewhere.

"I have to catch a flight early tomorrow," I whisper, with my head against his chest.

"I know. I'm not staying. I just had to see you and kiss you. I had to know that last Friday wasn't a dream." He gently cups my chin in his hand and tilts it upward so I'm looking in his eyes. "It wasn't, was it?"

I shake my head, then wrap my arms around him, tight. I can't find the voice to tell him I can't see him anymore, that I'm not ready and that Joseph would not approve. I can't push this man out of my life. Not when I need him so badly.

CHAPTER 9

"Grief can be a burden, but also an anchor. You get used to the weight, how it holds you in place." – Sarah Dressen

I wake up early after a restless night and look to my left instinctively, only to be slightly surprised that no one is there. I've been waking up next to the same man for twenty-four years. For the last six months, I've woken up to an empty bed. This morning when I open my eyes, I half expect to find another man altogether next to me. Jeremiah left soon after he came over, never even venturing beyond my foyer, but still, he followed me to bed and stayed in my dreams, however restless they might have been.

My flight leaves at 8 a.m. so I get up, shower, dress, and make my coffee. My pre-packed suitcase is by the door, and I'm waiting for Lauren to pick me up to take me to the airport. I keep glancing anxiously at the hall clock. Where is she? With all the security at the airport, I planned to get there by 6:30 a.m. It's a twenty minute drive at least, and it is now 6:10 a.m. Lauren is already ten minutes late. I call her cell phone and it goes directly into voicemail. I text her with several exclamation points and all caps. Still nothing. At 6:20 a.m. I call Paul. He answers in a groggy voice. To a musician, 6:20 a.m. is the middle of the night. While I'm trying to explain my dilemma to him, Jeremiah beeps in. I get off quickly with Paul.

"Jeremiah, I'm sorry, but I can't talk right now. I need to call a cab," I sigh. If I miss my flight, I'll wring a neck or two.

"A cab? Do you need a ride?"

"Are you serious?"

"Of course. I'm just walking out the door. I can be there in less than ten minutes and it will be quicker than a cab."

"Oh, my gosh! Thank you so much! That would be fantastic. Lauren was supposed to come and get me, but she never showed and she isn't answering her phone."

"No problem. Be there soon. Bye."

"Bye," I whisper into the phone.

He arrives, grabs my bags, and has me on the road in no time. It isn't until I'm comfortably settled that he asks, "Do you think everything is alright with Lauren?"

I hadn't even thought about that. I was so frustrated that it never occurred to me there might be a bad reason she hadn't shown up. What kind of mother am I? I dial her phone again and get the same response. "I'm sure everything is fine," I say with feigned confidence.

"Is this something she would typically do?" He seems concerned, which I appreciate.

"Actually, it's not something she would have ever done a few months ago, but now? Yeah, I think now, it's not that surprising."

I recount the phone call from her boss and the instances when she was late to work or didn't show up at all. Saying it out loud makes it sound somewhat alarming. I feel tears arise and I try to wipe them away before he sees. Too late.

"Hey," he says, while gently touching my arm, "it'll be okay. Would you like me to go by her house later and check on her?"

What? And have my kids thinking I have a new boyfriend trying to play dad?

"No. Thank you, though. I'll call her work later. If

nothing else, I'll have Paul go check on her. I'm sure everything's fine."

"Okay. If you're sure. I don't mind, though."

"The truth is, Jeremiah, that I don't think Lauren would appreciate it if you stopped by. My kids seem to think I shouldn't date anyone until the one year mark after Joseph's death, and I'm just not ready to explain who you are."

I feel like a wimp. I'm always trying to please everyone else. Well, what about me? I hate how I let my kids opinion about how I should live my life affect me. I am more willing to worry about Lauren than accept this gracious man's offer. When will I feel like I'm in charge of myself? When will my life really be my life? I have an impulsive and insane thought.

"Do you want to come with me?" I ask boldly.

"Come with you? You mean right now, to New York?" He seems very surprised, but is smiling.

"Why not? It could be fun!" I say, then immediately begin doubting myself. How I wish I could be spontaneous without regret. I always have buyers remorse, second-guessing my decisions.

Jeremiah thinks about it for a minute, a pensive expression on his face. I pretend that I'm not holding my breath, and I fiddle with the visor.

"I don't think I can, Alison. As much as part of me really wants to," he says, without further explanation. He reaches over and puts his hand on mine.

"Sure, I understand. I mean, it's crazy anyway. I don't know what I was thinking. I think I'm just a little nervous. I've actually never traveled alone. Isn't that pathetic?"

We've reached the airport, and are pulling up to my gate. He stops the car in the loading and unloading zone, and shuts the engine off. Turning to look at me, he says, "You're gonna be great, Alison. I have no doubt you will handle New York with ease. Call me when you get there... and any other time you want to talk."

"I will."

He pops the trunk open and has my bags out in a second. "I'm sorry I can't go," he whispers, leaning into me. "You make it very tempting, believe me."

I sigh and fall into him, resting for a moment in his size and sturdiness. He's like an anchor and I'm a boat, foolishly detaching itself before heading into deep, unknown waters.

~~~

Six hours later, I open the shades in my room at the W Hotel on Lexington Avenue, and look out over the city I've heard so much about. I've never been so proud of myself. Not only did I plan this trip on a whim, to take a stand for my work, I also manage just fine at the airports, and I get to my hotel without incident. I'm a forty-four year old widow with two adult children, and I've proven I can travel all by myself. Does this mean I'm finally a real grown up?

I call my agent's office and confirm our appointment for the next day. I then call Paul and Lauren to tell them I made it safely to my hotel, but have to leave messages on both their phones. I unpack my small bag and sit on the edge of my bed, staring at the wall.

What was I thinking? I don't want to be in New York City by myself. I should be here with Joseph. We always talked about coming together, but it was one of those trips we never got around to. What was the rush? We'd have plenty of time and money once the kids were grown and out of college. But the reality is that we never had any extra money because I quit my job to pursue writing, and Joseph never had the time because he was always working. Then, well... he had to go and die, so now we'd never go to New York together. I'm so mad at him! He ruined everything. I look for something to throw, but these damn modern rooms are so minimalist, there isn't even a Bible on the nightstand to chunk. That's what I'm looking for. That way I can be mad at Joseph and God. I'll show them!

Right before I start to cry, my phone rings. It's Jeremiah. I forgot to call him.

"Hi Jeremiah," I say, hardly hiding the sadness in my voice.

"Hey. How's your room?"

"How do you know I made it to my room?"

"I just know. You did, right?"

"Yes. It's nice actually. Way over-priced though."

"Well, I think that's just New York. So, what are you gonna do your first night there?"

"I have no idea. I didn't plan this very well."

"What about a Broadway show? I hear Chicago is great."

"I'm sure it is, but I doubt I could get tickets this late. Besides, I wouldn't want to go alone," I say, sounding more and more pitiful.

"How about going with me?"

"Ha. Not very funny at the moment."

"I'm not kidding,"

I hear a knock at the door. "Someone's knocking...can you hold on a minute?" I walk across the tiny room to the door and look through the peep hole. I drop my phone as I fumble with the bar lock and the dead bolt. I swing the door open and Jeremiah catches me in his arms and squeezes tight.

"What are you doing here?" I bang once on his chest and keep my hands there. My eyes are big and my mouth hangs open in wonder.

He starts laughing. "I'm so glad you're happy. On the

way up the elevator, I started having serious doubts." He walks in the room and closes the door.

"Why? I asked you, remember?"

"I know, but that was just on a whim." He moves closer to me, wrapping his arms around my back while we talk. "I don't want you to think I'm stalking you."

"Aren't you?"

"A little bit." He kisses me tenderly on the lips.

I look up at him with a silly grin that I can't hold back. "I'm so happy you're here. I was just thinking how un-fun it was to come to New York by myself, and now you're here. How did you get here so fast?"

"As soon as you went inside I checked available flights and United had one that left at ten, with no layovers. I rushed home and back. My plane landed about forty-five minutes after yours," he says proudly. "And, I already bought tickets for Chicago tonight. Not the best seats, but not too bad."

"I can't believe it! You are amazing. I don't think I brought anything to wear though."

"Well, let's take care of that. What time is it?" He looks down at his watch. "How about we get some coffee, and then go get you a dress for tonight. Should leave us plenty of time to come back and change before dinner. The show starts at eight."

I look up at him in awe. He's taking care of everything. Part of me wants to make this trip all on my own, but a bigger part of me is so grateful and impressed that he's done this huge, expensive, spontaneous thing, for me.

"Sounds fantastic." I look around him. "Don't you have a suitcase or something?"

"Oh, yeah. I left it downstairs with the front desk. I wasn't sure if you would want me to get a separate room. If you do, I'm totally fine with it."

Do I want him to get his own room? On the one hand, it would probably be the right thing to do. I appreciate his sensitivity, because despite us already sleeping together, I'm not sure I want to make that the expectation. I mean having sex one time is one thing, but if he stays with me won't we be going from crazy fling to dating status? According to just about everyone I know, I've not waited long enough to get involved with someone. This will definitely seal my bad widow image. On the other hand, who really has to know? Isn't that the beauty of being in a different city? I can enjoy these two days and still make it clear to Jeremiah that I'm not ready to get too serious.

"I'm fine with you staying here. In fact, I'd like you to," I say, kissing him gently on the lips. He pulls me in tight and upgrades my kiss a few notches.

"Good. I was hoping you'd say that." He lets me go and dials the front desk, asking them to bring up his bag.

Soon, we have our Starbucks drinks in hand, and are walking the three blocks to Saks 5th Avenue. Since my decision to let Jeremiah stay in my room, makes me the worst widow ever, I decide to break another big no-no. I'll use some "death money" to buy myself something extra nice to wear tonight. I mean, how often am I ever at Saks 5th Ave.? It's wrong to be in New York City and have an incredibly handsome, kind man surprise me with Broadway tickets, and then wear something from Kohls, which is where I buy most of my wardrobe. I also plan to pick up some pretty underwear, since I had not planned on anyone seeing my supportive, practical, and now baggy, undergarments.

We arrive at Saks, and I'm stunned by all the beautiful clothes on the dazzling displays. I turn around in circles, mouth agape, trying to decide where to go first.

Jeremiah's phone rings. He looks at it, and says,

"Sorry, Alison, but I need to take this." I nod as he walks back to the entrance and out the door.

A saleslady approaches, and asks if I need help. "I'm looking for something to wear to a show tonight," I say, feeling strangely like I'm on the set of *Pretty Woman*. I blush and she smiles warmly back at me. She's in her mid-50's, with salt and pepper hair that is cut in an expensive bob. Her clothes look pricey, and her shoes are very sensible, but feminine. I bet if she were a widow, she'd be a good one.

"Would you like a cocktail dress?" she asks, while leading me to the escalator. I really don't know what I want. I just know that neither the boring business suit, nor the jeans and blouse I packed, will be appropriate for a Broadway show.

"What do you think I should wear? I've actually never been to a Broadway show."

"I think people wear a variety of things. Some dress up quite formally and others might wear slacks and a simple blouse. It's up to you. Are the going with someone?"

"Um, yes. He's just a friend though. I mean a little more than a friend, I guess. I'm recently widowed and it hasn't been a year yet..." I blurt out defensively, sounding like a loon.

"Oh, okay. Well, I was just asking because perhaps you'd like to dress in a similar fashion. It might be uncomfortable if you wear a gown and he shows up in jeans." She smiles reassuringly at me, and pats my arm gently. "It's hard, I know. I was widowed three years ago."

"Really? Did you start dating after six months, too?" I ask, hopefully.

"Oh, no. I still don't think I'm ready," she says, then notices my stricken face. "But don't worry, dear, everyone is different."

I knew it. I just knew she'd be a good widow. I sigh and look around for Jeremiah. He's still outside the door on his phone. "I think a cocktail dress would be nice, just not too dressy. I imagine my date is just wearing slacks and maybe a dinner jacket."

She leads me up to the right department and suddenly, I'm surrounded by beautiful, classy dresses. The kind I always see and say, *Where would I ever wear that?* Well, now I know. You wear it in New York City to a Broadway show with a handsome ex-boyfriend. I try on several that are a size eight, but they're all too big. The good-widow saleslady then brings me more in a size six. I can hardly believe they fit. Every dress I try on looks good, but I'm having a hard time enjoying the process of finding the right one. You need a friend or doting husband with you when you're trying on pretty dresses. Someone to *ohh* and *ahh* over them. I step out of the dressing room to get a better look in the three-way mirror of the dress I like best. Jeremiah appears out of nowhere and whistles at me. He comes up from behind and wraps his arms around my waist, nuzzling his lips in my neck.

"You are gorgeous," he whispers.

I feel like I should be uncomfortable with this level of intimacy and familiarity, considering we've just recently gotten reacquainted after twenty-five years apart. The problem though, or maybe it isn't a problem, is that it feels fine. Better than fine, actually. I spin around to show off the dress, then ask, "What are you wearing?"

"I brought a white dress shirt and black slacks. Forgot my tie though, so I'll get one here to match what you're wearing. That's the dress you're getting, I hope," he says, eyeing me up and down with an appreciative smile.

"I think so." I blush. "I need to get a few other things real quick," I say, wondering how I can buy some sexier undergarments without feeling too silly in front of him.

He seems to guess what I want to do because he just smiles and says he'll be down in the men's department (getting a tie to match my very beautiful Badgley Mischka red silk dress). The saleslady says she'll get the dress bagged up while I look at lingerie.

Saks is proud of their undergarments, displaying bras, panties, slips and bustiers as elegantly as they do their evening gowns. I run my hand over delicate lace and ultra-soft silk, wanting to be seen and touched in all of it. I blush again, even though no one is watching me. Suddenly, I realize I care very much what Jeremiah would like to see on me. I don't have much lingerie at home. Joseph and I were so young when we married and there was no need to dress up the package. We were just thrilled to be anywhere near each other when we got in the mood, and any extra clothing always seemed to come off without a second glance. Seduction was not necessary. He never seemed to care if I had any sexy lingerie and I always felt silly trying to wear it anyway. But, tonight...tonight I know there will be a moment when Jeremiah slips my very beautiful, silky dress over my head, and when he looks down at me, I want to be wearing something he remembers.

CHAPTER 10

"You can clutch the past so tightly to your chest that it leaves your arms too full to embrace the present." – Jan Glidewell

Chicago is an exhilarating show. I imagine any show on Broadway is great, considering the high standards and caliber of performer that exist here. However, Chicago is the right show to see on a spontaneous trip to New York City. Especially if you are with the handsome ex-boyfriend you'll be having sex with later, in your very nice, albeit small and over-priced, New York City hotel room. All through the show, I can feel the sexual tension between us. Seats R22 and R23 are super-charged. I remember feeling this way early on in my marriage. There were times that Joseph and I would flirt and tease all day, and I knew what we'd be doing once the kids went to bed. It was exciting and fun, and always seemed to make sex a little more special, more purposeful. Sex with Joseph was also really exciting when I wasn't expecting it. Sometimes he would suddenly surprise me when I was reading and toss my book aside, put his hands all over me, and his mouth would be passionate and hot as he kissed me. Either way, sex with my husband was mostly good, sometimes great, and rarely bad. But, I don't know if I've ever been quite so worked up about a future sexual encounter, as I am on this night. Maybe it's the spontaneity and sacrifice that Jeremiah made to be here. Maybe it's the shopping and the way the silky dress and sexy underwear feel on me. Maybe it's the "wrongness" of it all. Whatever it is, I'm very much anticipating the after-show.

When the curtains come down, I'm ready to get back to our room quickly, but Jeremiah doesn't seem to be in any rush. He stands up, stretches, and says, "That was great. I really liked it. Better than the movie, for sure." He grins and takes my hand as we exit the theater. "How about some coffee?"

"Coffee? Um, okay I guess. Or we could order some coffee and dessert from room service," I suggest not too subtly.

It's already 10:30 p.m. and the appointment with my agent is at 9 a.m. the next morning. Not to seem too old, but I need my sleep. I want us to get this show on the road. It suddenly occurs to me that maybe Jeremiah isn't thinking the same way I am. Maybe he isn't assuming that we're going to hop into bed together. Or worse, maybe he does think that, but isn't planning on it being anything special or worthy of allotted time. We walk out hand in hand, and Jeremiah hails one of the many cabs waiting for the show to end. We climb in, and to my relief, he says, "The W on Lexington, please." I smile and ease back into the seat. His hand rests on my knee.

"Thank you for taking me. It was a fantastic night," I say, with genuine appreciation.

"You're very welcome. Did you have a favorite part?"

"Of the show or the night?"

"The show. The night's not over yet. You can tell me tomorrow about your other favorite parts." He teases me. I can't see his eyes, but I imagine they're twinkling. I feel my stomach flip over, and I smile.

"Well, my favorite part in the show was with the puppets. I could relate."

"Really? Well, let's talk about that, but maybe just not tonight?"

I laugh. "No need to talk about it, anytime, actually."

We arrive at the hotel quickly. Jeremiah pays the cabbie, as I wait under the hotel awning. He leads me into the bar. We place a late dessert order, and request it be sent up to our room. On the way up, he holds my hand. It feels so comfortable and normal, which would surprise me if I allowed myself to think about it. How did we so quickly and easily slipped into this couple mode? Just two days ago, I was about to tell him that our liaison was a mistake and that I was not ready to date. Just two months ago, I hadn't seen him in over twenty years. Just seven months ago, I had been holding Joseph's hand, and I had done that for a very long time. Technically, Jeremiah and I are just on a second date and if I were to really analyze each date, I would see that we were sleeping together on both of them. I never thought of myself as a woman that would sleep with a man on a first and/or second date. Am I acting just as crazy and out of character as Lauren? Or, is it different with Jeremiah and I? After all, we've known each other longer than Joseph and I had. We were best friends and lovers once before. It isn't like he's a stranger...right? All of these thoughts linger lightly in my subconscious. So lightly, in fact, that I'm able to push them away with very little guilt or remorse. I'm in a different city, after all. I'm not married and therefore am not cheating. I'm a grown woman, capable of making my own decisions. I want, no need, to be loved and held by this generous, kind, spontaneous, and handsome man.

By the time we enter our room, I have given myself over completely to the night and whatever it holds. I excuse myself to the restroom and when I come out, Jeremiah goes in. I take a moment to check my phone, which is a mistake. I have four messages. Two from Lauren, one from my agent, and one from Paul.

Lauren's voice is both frantic and remorseful. "Mom!

I am sooo sorry! I went out last night with Jen and left my phone in her car! I slept in this morning. I thought your flight was tomorrow! Are you sure it was today because I had it written down for tomorrow. Jen just brought my phone over and I saw all your messages. I am so sorry! Call me!"

Message 2: "Mom, I just talked to Paul and he said he thought your flight was tomorrow too. Are you sure it was today? Call me. I can take you in the morning if you still need a ride."

Is she for real? How is it my kids think I can even manage to live on my own? Didn't I already call her and tell her I had gotten here safely, and she still thinks my flight is tomorrow?

Jeremiah comes out of the bathroom, tie off, and shirt unbuttoned a few notches. I'm sitting on the edge of the bed with the phone to my ear. I signal to him by holding up my finger, that I'll be a minute. I must look as annoyed as I feel, because he asks, "Everything okay?"

Paul's message only further serves to exasperate me with my two children; "Mom? Hey- Lauren said you had a flight today. I thought it was tomorrow. Is that why you called this morning? Sorry, but man, that was early! I could barely keep my eyes open. So, do you need anything? Everything good now? Okay talk to you later." Grrrr. I know kids by nature are pretty self-absorbed, but come on!

Jeremiah slips off his shoes and bends down to remove mine, as well. I listen to the message from my agent asking if we can move the meeting back to 10 a.m. I look down at the top of Jeremiah's head, as he carefully removes my shoes and begins to massage my feet. I smile, and quickly text my agent that, yes, the change in time is fine. I decide not to respond to my kids' messages, and to remove all thoughts of them from my mind for the time being. I toss my phone aside, and meet Jeremiah's eyes with a smile. He traces the curve of my feet with his thumbs, applying pressure in a way that instantly relaxes me. I lean back on my elbow and let my head fall back. His hand cups my heels, his fingers gently move their way up my calves, as he massages my tense muscles. He rises slightly, and I fall back completely, closing my eyes and relaxing my arms. His hands move up my thighs, under my dress. The red silk still rests lightly against my skin, his hands roaming freely underneath it. I feel both covered, yet completely exposed. I'm surprised when his lips kiss my inner thigh and cry out. He chuckles, and I turn my head to look at him. His eyes meet mine, tender and hungry for me.

"You are so beautiful, Alison." He comes up to kiss my lips. He rests his weight on one elbow, freeing up one hand that continues to stroke the length of my body. He kisses and lightly bites my lips. To my extreme shock and disappointment, a memory of Joseph kissing me assaults my senses, and tears spring to my eyes. It is so sudden, strong, and unexpected that I can't even cover it up. Jeremiah stops kissing me, sensing something has changed. He looks at me with concern and confusion, "What is it? Are you okay?" he asks gently.

I can't reply, afraid that I'll cry. What's happening? The feeling of Joseph is so strong, I wonder if his spirit is in the room with us. If I worried that it was too soon to be doing this, I definitely have my answer, at least as far as Joseph is concerned. I'm fine with it. I want it, need it, and crave it. Once again, I feel bitter that my life isn't just my own. Seeing the look on my face, Jeremiah leans back and removes his hand from my upper thigh. He moves the hair back off my face and gently traces the outline of my cheek.

"What is it? Too soon?"

I nod, my eyes pleading with him to forgive me. I'm still afraid to speak; I know I will cry. He kisses my forehead, still hovering right above me.

"It's okay," he whispers, "come here."

He lays back, pulling me into him until my head rests on his chest. I wrap my arm across his stomach. His head leans atop mine and his hand lightly brushes the hair off my face.

"Do you want to talk about it? Did I do something wrong?"

I find my voice and whisper, "No. It's not you. You were perfect. I wanted this, too." As I speak, the feeling of Joseph is leaving, and I begin to feel like maybe it is just me and Jeremiah in the room after all. I owe him an explanation. "It's just that all of a sudden, I felt Joseph's presence really strong, like he was here or something." Jeremiah raises his head and looks around the room in mock seriousness. I giggle and playfully hit him on the chest. "Stop. I know it sounds crazy, but it felt so real. I thought I was ready. But, I just don't know."

"Were you thinking about him?"

"No. I wasn't," I answer honestly. "That's what made it so weird."

There is a knock on the door. He moves away from me, the spell obviously broken. Room service has delivered our desserts and coffee. Jeremiah pulls over a small end table to put the coffee on.

"These look good," he says, opening the boxes and revealing cheesecake and chocolate cake.

We sit, cross-legged on the bed, eating out of both dishes. If we were passionate lovers a few minutes ago, we are now like college roommates, spilling our secrets. I am sorely disappointed.

"Tell me something about Joseph," he says.

I'm not convinced he really wants to know, and I'm

not sure I want to talk about Joseph anymore. I don't want it to interfere with our night more than it already has. But, since the romantic mood seems to have been put on hold, I begin...

"Well, Joseph was pretty great. He adored the kids and always took care of us," I say, noting how generic it sounds.

"I'm sure he was a great dad and husband. But what was it that attracted you to him?"

"Hmmm. Well, we were really young, so part of it was just the excitement of falling in love. I always felt very safe with Joseph. He was really nurturing and a little bit controlling. I know that sounds bad, but when I was young, it made me feel protected and cared for. He made most of the decisions for us, and basically took care of almost everything."

"And you liked that?" He furrows his brow and looks down as he uses his fork to cut into the cheesecake.

I think for a minute. "A lot of times I did like it, but of course there were times when I didn't. As I got older I found I had some strong opinions and ideas about things. Although Joseph was never condescending, I felt like he didn't always take me seriously. The worst thing was, I started noticing that the kids basically acted like they thought I didn't know anything. They would always go to Joseph with their problems or questions. Sometimes I felt like an outsider in my own family."

"But, you're so smart! How could anyone think you weren't capable? I mean, look at you, you wrote a book and you're in New York meeting with your agent. That's pretty smart stuff."

"Thanks. You're sweet. I've wanted to be a writer for a long time, and Joseph always encouraged me to follow my dream. It just took me a while to believe in myself enough to make it happen. Joseph was good, and I was happy with him…"

"But?"

"But, I think I was too dependent on him."

"Huh. That's interesting you say that."

"Why?"

"Well you don't seem like a woman who would live in anyone's shadows, or rely on a husband for everything. You seem really independent to me. Very strong and capable. You're not a typical widow."

I frown. I understand he's complimenting me, but it isn't what I want to hear. "You're right. I'm not a typical widow. I'm a terrible widow."

Jeremiah grins and then he starts to laugh. "You are not a terrible widow!"

"Yes, I am! Look at me! My husband has been dead only six months, and here I am sitting on a bed, in a hotel room, with another man." I bury my face in my hands.

Jeremiah is still laughing. "Yeah, but, like you said, we're sitting. Not doing what I hoped we'd be doing, only because, you *are* a good widow. You felt so guilty, that you conjured up the spirit of your dead husband to come in and sabotage my night." He playfully punches me in the arm.

I really don't like where this is going. I'm wearing my beautiful, red silk dress and my new sexy underwear, on a bed next to a handsome, if not gorgeous, man who wants and desires me…and here we are, talking about my deceased husband. Good grief! I wasn't looking for a counselor when I invited him to join me. I doubt he changed his plans and spent all this money, so he could surprise me in New York, just to become my therapist. Right or wrong, I want this man. I want this night to be better than this. I lost Joseph, and there was nothing I could do about it. I don't want to lose Jeremiah, too- especially not when I can do something about it.

"I didn't conjure him up," I sulk.

Jeremiah smiles slightly, then brushes the hair off my face again. His hand lingers lightly over my ear. I slowly move in closer. His hand pulls me towards him as his lips gently touch mine. Something inside me stirs and flips, and suddenly my tongue is in his mouth, my body pushes up against him. He responds in turn, and soon I'm on my back again, with his hands under my dress, moving urgently over my thighs, hips, navel, then circling my breasts. The beautiful silk dress slips off easily and I have the look I want. He leans away from me, his eyes taking in the way my new lingerie accentuates my body. I see through him, how sexy and beautiful he finds me, and I love it. There are no more thoughts of Joseph, Claire, or anything else for that matter. There is just Jeremiah and me, our bodies intertwined, our hearts healing.

The next morning, I wake up with a strong, hairy, arm wrapped around my shoulders and a low, soft snore rumbling in my ear. The light is streaming in through the curtains we forgot to close all the way, and the morning sun makes me feel warm all over. I have a big, content smile on my face. There is something incredibly satisfying about my relationship with Jeremiah. For starters, it isn't really a relationship. Since his divorce is not final yet, I feel like it gives us a little wiggle room so that there isn't any premature talks of marriage between us. One does not jump into marriage so soon after a death or a divorce.

Another plus with us is how well we get along. It's easy to be with Jeremiah. He's fun, light-hearted, and kind. We also have sexual chemistry, which to me, is a very big deal. Truthfully, the sexual chemistry is the main reason we're together on this trip. I doubt I would have asked him to come along if he didn't affect me this way.

I carefully slip out from under his arm, then start getting ready for my appointment. After my shower, I re-enter the room in my towel and am greeted by a warm, naked, hug from Jeremiah. He seems very happy to see me and is pulling me toward the bed, but I firmly protest.

"No way, mister, I can't be late for this meeting, I am barely going to make it as it is."

"Aww, don't go, Alison," he pouts, nuzzling his face in my hair.

I push him away playfully. "My meeting should be over in time for a late lunch. Do you want me to call you when it's almost done, and we can meet up?"

He smiles, kisses the tops of my hands, and says, "Sounds great. I'm gonna explore a bit. You take your time, call me when you're ready, and I'll show you around the city as if I live here."

"Sounds perfect. Thank you for being so wonderful to me."

"How else would I be?" He winks and goes into the bathroom for a shower, leaving me with a nice view to remember him by.

I take a cab to my agent's office. It's located in a converted Brownstone in an old neighborhood. Several buildings appear to have been made into offices for various professions such as, lawyers, homeopathic doctors, talent agencies, etc... My stomach is full of butterflies as I walk up the steps.

I cannot blow this.

I am well aware that the competition is fierce, and any number of manuscripts can replace mine, especially if I prove to be a pain in the butt. Maybe I have it all wrong anyway, and I'm fighting for something in my book that I need to let go of. These women are professionals, they know better what makes a book successful. I'm hoping a good compromise between us can be made. The changes my editor is suggesting converts my leading man into someone that reminds me more of Jeremiah, than Joseph.

I just don't want to do that. I already feel like I'm betraying Joseph in my bedroom and I don't want to do it permanently in print. My fling with Jeremiah is, after all, temporary. My book will be forever.

~~~

Three hours later, I leave my agent's office, close the door, and slowly walk down the steps of the Brownstone. Despite the bustle of the city, this particular block seems deserted and strangely quiet. I look back over my shoulder, although I know no one is following me, in practice or thought. As soon as I turned the knob on the office door and made to leave, my agent diverted her attention back to the call she had on hold and to the numerous other clients she has. Clients who are, perhaps, easier to work with and who haven't written into their main character, twenty-four years of their own memories and six months of grief and guilt. Clients who aren't torn between their past and their future.

I saw in her eyes, apprehension about me as soon as I walked through the door and introduced myself. The novice writer who, so quickly into the process, stubbornly dug her heels in. The writer who put on a fake smile and used too high of a voice; who pretended to have flown all the way to New York for a little vacation when both of us know my impromptu trip reeks of desperation and despair. I am surely labeled as "too emotionally attached." She's right, I am too attached, but why shouldn't I be?

I feel myself start to crumble and realize if I don't sit down soon, I might fall over. I spot a little bench just a few steps away. A pocket park. I slowly walk over and sit down. I need to think. In the back of my mind, I know Jeremiah is waiting for my call, but I can't face him just yet. I have to sort it all out. What am I really doing here? I thought I was protecting my rights as an author, showing integrity by fighting for my characters and myself. But now, I feel that I'm on a very small ledge, and at any moment, I could fall off, losing everything. The truth is, getting what I think I want, isn't worth losing everything over. I'm not even sure that I know what's best. I'm trying to hold on to Joseph in my work, yet I seem very hell-bent on letting him go in my private life. Maybe I have it all backwards. Joseph would be very disappointed if I let my dream slip through my fingers, just because I'm being stubborn and difficult to work with. I wish so badly that he was here to help me. Joseph always had an answer, always knew what was best. I bury my head in my hands and sob. I don't care that I'm just feet from my agents door, or that people are starting to walk by and are giving me weird looks. I don't care that Jeremiah is waiting for my call, or even that Jeremiah is waiting at all. I don't care that I'm wearing a size six, or that I am in the best city in the world. I just care that I am alone.

I cry until I'm empty, then sit slumped on my bench, staring into nothing. I'm vaguely aware of my phone buzzing and of the sky changing colors, but really have little notion of how much time has passed. Suddenly, I'm startled to hear my name called.

"Alison?" A voice calls from down the block. I turn toward it and see the silhouetted form of a tall man walking toward me. It takes me just a second to register that it's Jeremiah, and in a moment, come to the realization that I've left him waiting and worrying for hours. I do not deserve him.

"Are you okay?" he says softly, gently reaching down to touch my shoulder. I look up into his worried and beautiful face, and nod like a fool.

"I'm fine. I'm so sorry."

He sits down next to me on the bench and puts his

arm around my shoulder. "What happened? Did something go wrong in your meeting?"

"Kind of," I say quietly. I look down at the folded hands in my lap. They don't seem to belong to me.

He sighs, unwraps his arm from around my shoulders, and finds my hand instead.

"Tell me about it." He lifts my fingers to his lips, and kisses them.

"I have to do something first." I get up and Jeremiah follows me back up the stairs to my agent's door.

She looks up, slightly startled, when I walk into her office. Jeremiah lingers behind, waiting patiently.

"I came back to apologize," I say contritely, hoping for the best. She smiles, and motions for me to sit down. I turn back to look at Jeremiah, and he indicates he'll wait for me in the lobby.

"So, how did it go?" he asks, as I walk up to him twenty minutes later. "That was pretty quick."

"Well, it doesn't take long to throw yourself on the altar and beg for mercy."

"Threw yourself on the altar, did you?" He takes my hand and we walk out the door.

I grin. "Not exactly, but I did have to apologize and convince her that I wouldn't be a total pain-in-the-butt to work with."

"And she believed you? Did you have to lie much?" He chuckles.

I playfully hit him on the arm. "Shut-up."

We walk down the street, hand in hand, as I retell the events of the afternoon. When I get to the part about my breakdown in the park, I hesitate, wondering if I should tell him about Joseph and how much I miss him. I decide to let it go for now. I've already ruined much of our day. I don't want to make it worse by getting into a long sob story about how it stinks to be a widow and how I'm doing it all wrong.

"Anyway, I'm sorry I left you waiting so long. I had a mini-breakdown and just needed some time to get my head together."

"Is that all? Because you looked pretty lost when I found you. Is it about Joseph?" he asks with an incredible amount of kindness and patience.

I can hardly stand how easy Jeremiah is making it for me to fall for him, and how hard he's making it for me to leave Joseph out of our trip.

"It might have been, a little. Honestly, Jeremiah, almost everything is a little about Joseph, or at least about me losing him. I could talk about it incessantly, if you wanted me to, but I don't think you do, and I know I don't want to." I look up at him and notice a subtle release in his shoulders.

"You're right, Alison. I don't really want to talk about him. I'm jealous as hell of him, even though I know I don't have the right to be, and I just want to enjoy the little bit of time we have left here."

"I agree. What's on the agenda?" I am determined to perk up. If he isn't already, Jeremiah might soon be wishing he hadn't come to New York after me.

"I had a few things planned, but we're running out of time to do it all," he says, looking at his watch.

"I'm sorry."

"Hey, no worries. Let's get a coffee and head over to Central Park."

I agree, and we begin our day together, late in the afternoon. Two new lovers, two old friends, and two broken people trying to move forward. I ignore the small nagging voice asking me why I can't be alone, because as much as I want to move forward by myself, I feel I need someone to hold my hand and help me right now. I think Jeremiah needs me too, although, he rarely talks about his soon to be ex-wife with me. I should probably tell him that I'm not ready to be in a relationship and I'm not over Joseph, but I'm afraid of letting him go. I may never be over Joseph. That doesn't mean I want to be alone forever with just my ghost and memories of him. What I need is someone to tell Joseph how I feel. Some heavenly mediator to explain to him, that while I will always love him, he can not, under any circumstances, come visit me while I'm in a hotel room with another man. Ever again. Someone to explain to him that my career will have to move ahead, with, or without, his character in my books. Some heavenly counselor to encourage him to visit the kids and help out a little more with their troubles. I can't do everything!

CHAPTER 11

"My grief and pain are mine. I have earned them. They are part of me. Only in feeling them do I open myself to the lessons they can teach."
– Anne Wilson Schaff

Being okay with being alone is crucial for any writer. Of course, most writers will tell you they aren't alone, not really, even if no one else is in the room with them. After all, writers have the characters they create. Saying this always freaks out normal people with real jobs, but it's true. I spend the next two weeks, after returning from New York, locked inside my house working on the changes required to turn my manuscript into a real book. As I delete dialogue that sounds like something Joseph would have said, I assure myself I am doing the right thing, and that Joseph would have agreed. It isn't as if I'm erasing him from my life, only from my character. He doesn't need to live on in this book to be remembered. That being said, it doesn't take long as I'm making the revisions to realize my character is becoming less and less like Joseph and more and more like Jeremiah. I feel as if I'm being unfaithful to Joseph. My conscience is constantly nagging me and the voice in my heart and brain keeps saying, "How could you? So soon? Et tu, Alison?"

Nevertheless, I realize that if I am destined to be a bad widow, I can at least be a good author. Being an author might be the only thing I'm good at anymore. I'm certainly not feeling like a good mother. No matter how hard I try, it seems the kids are drifting further and further away from me. I suggest to both of them that we get together for dinner and a movie night. My invitation is met with half-hearted enthusiasm and neither one of them can find the time to set a date. Lauren is spending more time with a new man she's dating. At first, I almost admonish her for dating someone new so soon after her breakup, especially since she was with Dan for such a long time. Hypocrisy, anyone? As for Paul, he's put his band on hold while he searches for what he considers a real job. The disappointment this causes me is hard to explain. After all, wouldn't any parent be glad to hear their son is making such mature decisions? Yet, I'm saddened by whatever is causing him to give up on his dream at what I consider to be a young age.

Not only do I feel like I'm being a lousy mother, but I'm also not being a good girlfriend. Although, to be fair to myself, I have not officially signed up for the title of girlfriend. I've just been given that title from Jeremiah. He calls almost every day. Mostly our conversations are short and friendly, but occasionally we talk for longer periods of time. Tonight he calls around eight, and I'm already in bed. I see who it is and groan out-loud. All I want to do is read my book and be left alone. I know that he and Claire finalized their divorce today, but I don't want to make polite conversation or hear about it. I had a bad day too! I couldn't write anything worth keeping, and both my kids called and insisted on reminding me that it is mine and Joseph's anniversary, as if I don't already know what day it is. I'm actually trying not to think about it. I don't understand why people expect grievers to be more sad on holidays, birthdays, and anniversaries, but want us to act normal every other day. I'm sad all the time because Joseph died. I don't see the need in making our anniversary any worse by hi-lighting my loss.

I try to keep the conversation as light as possible, but since I have little to say and feel very annoyed, I'm not very good at it. In fact I respond pretty terribly to his heartfelt confession that he feels unexpectedly empty after signing the papers.

"It's just hard, you know?" he says, then sighs loudly.

"Yeah, I know," I answer, and roll my eyes. Thank goodness he can't see me.

"And it's not like Claire and I had this amazing relationship either.–not like you and Joseph. I don't want to be back together, but I'm just having a hard time with the finality and coming home to an empty house."

"Yeah, it's hard alright." I'm already exasperated with the conversation.

"You seem to be doing well."

"Yeah, I guess so."

"Maybe you were right. Maybe divorce is harder than death."

"What the hell are you talking about?" I bolt up to a sitting position.

"You told me that at the bowling alley," he says, defensively.

"Are you kidding me? Why would I ever say that? Of course death is harder than divorce. You wanted out! I didn't have a choice!" My voice escalates to near shouting.

"Okay, Alison. Calm down. You win. Death is harder." I can hear the tension and hurt in his voice, but I don't really care at the moment.

"Of course it's harder. I would never have chosen to end my marriage." My voice cracks and I can feel myself slipping toward tears. I don't want to cry. I'm too angry to cry.

"What are you saying?"

"I'm saying that you did this to yourself, you and Claire. Joseph and I didn't have a choice. And you just can't compare it, okay?"

"Yeah, okay." Neither one of us says anything for a minute. I know I should apologize and I'm about to do so, begrudgingly, when he says, "Well, nice talking to you Alison. I gotta go," and hangs up on me.

I flop back down in bed. My lip quivers and tears sting the back of my eyes, but I won't cry over Jeremiah.

Not on my anniversary.

CHAPTER 12

"What we have once enjoyed deeply we can never lose. All that we love deeply becomes a part of us." – Helen Keller

Janet has called me several times since I returned from New York. I've been vague about the details of the trip, and I can tell it's driving her crazy. Instead of our usual lunch date this month, she suggests coming over to the house for dinner and wine. Her attempts to get me to spill the beans are obvious, and a little annoying. I can't say why I'm being so private, but I know I will either have to open up to my friend's questions or come up with a valid reason why I don't feel like talking about it. Since Joseph's death, it seems everywhere I go, and everyone I talk to, asks me how I'm doing. Everyone wants to know the condition of my heart, the thoughts in my head, and the plans for my future. And they want my answers to these questions very quickly and in a concise manner. I imagine how the conversation would go if I were brave enough to say what I'm thinking half the time.

"How are you, Alison? Are you doing okay?"

Well sure! I am now much cuter. Have you noticed my tight little butt and narrow waist line?

"How are you doing financially with no income?"

Well, just great! Thanks for asking! I have a new budding career plus loads of death money. And, thank goodness for the money, because with it, I can travel and take mini-vacations with my new boyfriend!

"Oh, I didn't know you were dating already. Hasn't it

only been seven months?"

Well, yes, but I'm not dating really, just having sex, and boy is it great!

"Oh, my. Well, how are the kids doing?"

Oh, I don't know. I never really see them. They seem to be making huge life changes, though, without consulting with me. Thank goodness for that. I wouldn't want to be too bothered with anyone else's problems.

"Do you see any friends?"

Oh, no. Who has time for friends? Besides, I think they all liked Joseph better than me, and frankly, who can blame them? Yes, yes, he was a much better person. Hmmm? Oh yes, if I had died, I'm sure he would be doing a much better job grieving than I am. He was always better at everything. Oh, really? Is that how you feel? Well, you can go to hell. That's right, you heard me!

While it is very tempting to respond this way, I know that I cannot, so the best course of action is to keep to myself and pretend to be a better widow than I actually am. Of course, Janet, and even Denise, deserve better than that. I don't want to isolate the few people who seem to really care. I'll have to be honest with Janet, and the truth is that I long to talk to her about everything. I am so torn and confused about Jeremiah. Why couldn't he have come along later in my life? I know I'm on shaky ground, and am very close to driving him away, but I just can't be an emotional support to him right now. Everything he says to me in regards to his feelings sounds like whining, and seems childish, compared to how I feel. I'm a horrible, self-centered girlfriend, and I don't think I can change that right now. Why can't he just be available for a distraction now and then? I certainly enjoy the way he distracts me in the bedroom. Geez, even listening to my own thoughts, disappoints me in myself. How would people really feel about me, if they knew all the terrible thoughts I have?

I'm busy in the kitchen making chicken crepes, preparing for my dinner with Janet, when Jeremiah stops by for an impromptu visit. Thinking Janet has arrived early, I don't remove my apron or prepare my heart by the time I open the front door.

"Jeremiah! I wasn't, I mean I didn't…" I fumble for words, flushed to see him. We haven't talked since he hung up on me after our fight. "I wasn't expecting you."

"Clearly," he says, stepping into the foyer and looking around quickly. "That smells great."

"Oh! My crepes. I need to flip them. Come on in!" I motion for him to follow me while I sprint back to the kitchen. I cook them slightly more than I like and I feel frustrated by the inconvenient interruption.

Jeremiah stands on the other side of the open bar, watching me with a frown. I turn to him, laying down my spatula. I have about two minutes before the crepes need to be removed from the pan, so I hold my station at the stove. We stare at one another for a few long seconds. I can't think of anything to say. Although, I'm very aware that that there is much to say between us.

"Are you expecting company?" He's still frowning.

"Um, yes, I am," I answer, and am about to apologize for our previous phone conversation when suddenly, he burst out with, "Are you seeing someone else?"

"What?" I don't understand the question at first, not thinking of Janet as a "someone else." Realization quickly dawns on me and I'm floored! What kind of person does he think I am? Not only is it bad enough that I'm seeing him, just seven months after my beloved husband dies, but now I'm apparently seeing someone else, just days after my new boyfriend makes me mad?

"Are you kidding me? Is that what you think? That I would have two new men in my life? Jeremiah, I'm not even comfortable having you in my life right now. Why in the world would I throw in a second boyfriend?" I feel near hysterics. This was why I don't want a new relationship in the first place. The ridiculous drama that accompanies dating is so much more than I can deal with right now. I sigh, and don't even hide my eye roll. I turn my back and take my crepes off the stove, slowly moving them over to a plate. When I turn back around, Jeremiah has his head in his hands, resting his elbows on the dividing bar. He looks up and I notice the fatigue in his eyes and the stress lines on his face.

"I'm sorry, Alison. I shouldn't have jumped to conclusions. Maybe I don't even have the right to question you about your private life. You told me that you didn't think you were ready for this, and I kind of pushed myself into your life. I'm going to take a big step back and give you some space."

The doorbell rings. I want to reply to him, I really do. As soon as he starts talking, my heart flips. I can't deny that the man moves and captivates me. He is so much of what I want, and even need, but I stay silent and go to open the door.

Janet comes in and when we hug, I whisper, "Jeremiah's here. He dropped by unexpectedly."

"Ooooh," she says, raising her eyebrows, as she moves toward the kitchen. She has never met Jeremiah and I know she's very curious about him. I don't have time to tell her that this is not the best time to come over, that Jeremiah has just broken up with me, that I'm a terrible girlfriend, widow, mother, and probably a terrible friend, too.

Janet practically runs into the kitchen, and in the few seconds that I trail her, she has already introduced herself to Jeremiah. He is polite, of course, and remembers who she is, even though I've only mentioned her briefly a couple of times. I notice the strained expression he holds, obviously bothered by what has just transpired between us. Janet either doesn't notice or pretends not to.

"I hope you're staying for dinner, Jeremiah. I've been wondering when Alison would introduce us." She is charming, I'll give her that.

He looks at me, and I smile reassuringly. What else can I do? Besides, part of me does want him to stay. If he walks out, I'm not sure he'll be coming back. And, although I'm the one doing the pushing away, I'm also not ready to close the door on us completely. I realize this in the few seconds it takes for him to respond.

"I'd love to stay, if it's fine with Alison." They both look at me, with raised eyebrows.

"Of course!" I say, "That would be great. Why didn't I think of it?"

Jeremiah has never even been in my house this long. Will he notice the lingering signs of Joseph everywhere? I quickly glance around, noting all the things that remind me of Joseph and my twenty-four year marriage. There are items everywhere. The wine rack that we bought together in Wimberley on Market Days ten years ago. The painting over the table that we purchased at a street art show. The wall color Joseph wanted that I was never in love with. The picture of us on vacation in Colorado, sitting on the ski lift. The light fixture above the dining room table we both killed ourselves trying to install, and later laughed about what a miserable process it was. The plates we purchased for our fifteenth anniversary because we had never had a proper set before. The stemware his sister gave us for Christmas three years ago. The dish towels his aunt embroidered for me on my last birthday.

I feel panicky for a moment, and then realize that, other than the picture of Joseph and me, no one will know the associations with any of the other items. Only I know. Only I have the memories to attach emotion to the everyday normal things in my house. What Joseph and I shared, and who Joseph and I were, is only known by me. No one else can ever know it, understand it, miss it, protect it, or destroy it. Jeremiah will have the knowledge that Joseph lived here and that we shared this house. He will also likely be sensitive and respectful of that, but he won't see what I see when he looks around. I don't need to stress out. Having Jeremiah here, can not, and will not, take away from all that Joseph and I share. I sigh in relief. Janet and Jeremiah both look at me.

"Everything okay?" he asks.

I smile at him. "Yes. Everything's fine."

He smiles tentatively back. I can tell he isn't ready to fully engage with me. Who can blame him? One minute I'm giving him the brush off and yelling at him, the next, I'm inviting him to dinner and smiling sweetly; poor guy. I'll have to do a lot better than just give him a smile if I want him to stick around long enough for me to get my act together. And no, I'm not talking about sex. I will actually have to start acting emotionally stable. I watch Jeremiah and Janet exchange small talk, and for the first time in a long time, I begin to feel grateful. Grateful that I'm not alone, and grateful that I have people who care about me. Maybe I can do this after all.

"Everything seems to be ready, Alison." Janet jars me from my thoughts when she walks past me carrying a plate to the table. She leans in and whispers, "You okay? Are you mad I asked him to stay?"

I shrug and shake my head. "It's fine. It's probably better this way."

When we're settled and have passed the food around, Janet starts in with the questions. Frankly, I'm surprised she waits until we sit down.

"So, Jeremiah, Alison tells me you're recently divorced." My mouth drops open in disbelief. So much for small talk.

"Yep. It was final about a week ago," he replies, seemingly not bothered.

"How is that working out?"

He stops eating, puts his fork down and looks at Janet. I too, look at Janet. I hope she can feel the daggers I'm shooting her way.

"Well, honestly, it's been harder than I thought it would be. We were separated for a long time, so I didn't think it would bother me like it did when it became final." He resumes eating.

"Do you regret it–the divorce?" I don't know if Janet is just making conversation or is getting at something. Either way, I'm really hoping that all her questions aren't going to make Jeremiah depressed. It annoys me when he starts sounding depressed.

"No. Definitely not. Claire and I weren't right for each other. It was a mistake to get married, and I think we both knew it pretty early on."

"Man, a lot of people get divorced nowadays," Janet observes.

"I know. And, believe me, I'm not saying it's a good thing to do, but at some point you think, do we stay in this marriage because we're supposed to? Or do we give each other a chance to find the right person and live a happy life? Claire and I decided that doing the wrong thing was right for us."

I remain quiet up until now. I probably should continue to be quiet, but I chime in, "If you both wanted this, I don't understand why you're so sad about it."

He looks at me and shakes his head slightly, as if he's disappointed in me. He takes another bite so that his mouth is full. He is probably considering how best to tell me off.

Janet speaks for him. "I understand, I think. It sounds

like you respect the principle of marriage enough to want all it has to offer." Jeremiah nods in agreement. "So, if you feel that way, then you probably want to be married and want to share your life with someone. You just haven't found the right woman. Maybe, you're feeling kinda lonely and wondering if you'll ever have the kind of marriage you really want." Janet smiles and seems proud of her analysis.

Jeremiah points at her. "Bingo. That's exactly right. Thank you for understanding. I couldn't really find the right words for how I feel, but you nailed it."

He smiles at her, she beams back.

I scowl.

CHAPTER 13

"Sorrow makes us all children again - destroys all differences of intellect. The wisest know nothing."- Ralph Waldo Emerson

I have absolutely no idea how to proceed with Jeremiah. I vacillate between feeling overwhelmed and annoyed by his attentions, yet yearn for him so much I ache. Of course, both of these feelings brings on guilt. If he had left when Janet arrived for dinner, I feel fairly certain we wouldn't be talking right now. However, her invitation to dinner and our civil interactions afterwards, puts us in a strange no-man's land. Are we dating, just friends, or broken up? He calls the next day to thank me for dinner, to apologize for over-reacting, and for being too pushy with me. I accept and apologize for my rudeness and schizophrenic behavior in regards to our relationship. He suggests we take a step back and give it some time, and I agree, relieved that he finally is starting to understand what I need. I don't really want to lose Jeremiah, I just want to put everything on hold for a few more months. Despite my friends telling me that I have to decide when to date for myself, the kid's one-year requirement is stuck in my head. And honestly, it seems like a good idea, given my erratic emotional state. I clearly am not ready to have a boyfriend. I am tempted many times to call him over the next few weeks, but I know my heart is fickle, so I resist.

I divert my attention from my own troubles and begin focusing more on my children. I call Lauren every evening. Often she doesn't answer, and even when she does, I get the minimal amount of information out of her. I can tell she's getting exasperated with my questions, so I stop asking them and try hard to just listen to whatever information she shares with me. Sometimes our talks are very brief, but other times she rattles on about her workday, dinner with her friends, a new book she's reading, or a movie she has seen. Never anything too intimate. She stops talking about Dan altogether, and also stops talking about her father. Inexplicably, it bothers me that she is be dealing with his death so well, and not even needing to cry about it anymore. It's only been eight months, after all.

Despite my concerns, Paul is moving forward with the whole corporate job thing. He interviews at three places and is offered jobs by all three. He is now trying to decide which position to accept and is negotiating for the best offer. I should be thrilled, and at the very least, proud, but instead I'm disappointed. He doesn't understand why I feel this way, and in truth, I don't completely understand it either.

I'm beginning to wonder if I need to see a therapist. Maybe we can all go together. I think therapy exists for just about every subject nowadays. Family therapy for recovering grievers. Therapy to deal with guilt about grieving inappropriately. Therapy for mothers who have everything backwards. I'm sure I can find the right group for us as a family, and me, as an individual.

"Hello, my name is Alison."

Hello, Alison.

"I'm a widow, but I'm not very good at it. Can you help me?"

Of course. Let's take a look inside your head.

On second thought....maybe I'll try a little longer on my own. The first thing I need to do is to have some fun with my children. I call the kids and set a date for them to come over for a movie and dinner night. Through a series of phone calls back and forth, we decide to watch *Rear Window* and *The Birds*. Hitchcock has always been a family favorite at our house. We agree that comfort food is appropriate and will have chili, cornbread and ice cream sundaes. Even though it's just my children coming over, and I don't need to impress them with my house, I am still running around the hour before they come, trying to make everything perfect. I feel very disconnected from them and I want to fix that feeling. I want our night together to feel all warm and cozy, and I want them to want to come back and see me more often.

The doorbell rings right on time. I'm in the kitchen stirring the chili and holler out, "Come in!" It rings again. I sigh, lay down my big spoon, and stomp over to the door. I can hear their voices on the other side, apparently in a debate over something.

"You don't have to ring. The door's open," I say, with an edge of annoyance. I mean they're my kids, this is their house.

Lauren glances at Paul, then he says, "We respect your privacy, Mom. It's not like we live here anymore." They both walk in and put their things on the entry table.

"I know you don't live here, but you certainly don't have to ring the bell when I'm expecting you."

Lauren kisses me on the cheek. "Okay, Mom. We won't ring the bell anymore."

"Yeah, next time we'll just barge in and hope you're not naked." Paul smiles, then puts his arm around my shoulder, squeezing affectionately.

I hug him back, happy to have my son at home, even if just for the night. "I will very likely not be walking around naked at any time."

They follow me into the kitchen and Lauren deposits the bottle of wine on the island. "I brought red. I hope that's okay. It seemed fitting for Hitchcock."

"It's great, honey. Good choice. Could you stir the chili? Paul, can you get the bowls down, please? I can't quite reach them," I say, referring to our special chili bowls that are stored on the top shelf. We have special bowls for chili, ice cream, soup, and popcorn. We even have corn on the cob plates curved to hold your cob just right. Joseph liked to have specific items for certain foods. All of the special bowls are labeled. Just try eating ice cream out of the soup bowls when Joseph was around. He would promptly get up and hand the right bowl to you. It's not that he was obsessive, he just thought all the different bowls were fun, and if we had them, we might as well use them. In hindsight, though, maybe he was a little obsessive about it. I mean who cares if you eat soup out of an ice cream bowl?

"On second thought Paul, let's use these other bowls instead." I open the cabinet and reach for the colorful ice cream bowls.

"But what will we eat the sundaes out of?" he asks.

"We'll use the popcorn bowls. They're bigger anyway," I say, matter of fact.

The kids pause and look at each other, then Lauren shrugs. Paul lays out the ice cream bowls, as well as some napkins and spoons. I retrieve the corn bread from the oven and put it on the stove. It smells delicious. I feel strangely victorious for doing things my way, instead of Joseph's. Trying to hide my grin, I bend over the cornbread, cutting it into big squares. I put a piece into each bowl, and then finish it off with a big ladle of chili right on top. Lauren pours us all a glass of wine. Paul puts the first movie in the DVD player and turns down the lights. We carry our food to our usual seats and sit down. I wonder if I am the only one who notices Joseph's seat is empty, despite being the best seat in the room for watching TV. It bothers me for some reason, and I decide to move over into his chair.

"What are you doing, Mom?" Lauren asks.

"What do you mean?"

"It's just....well, that's Dad's chair," she says, quietly.

"Seriously? Honey, I'm either going to use the chair or I'm going to get rid of it, but I'm not going to keep it empty for the rest of my life, like a shrine or something," I say with more of an edge than I intend.

Lauren is quiet.

"Mom's right, Lauren," Paul says gently, "Dad would want one of us to use it. Don't you think?"

Lauren smiles slightly. "You're right, Paul. I'm being silly. It's just that I wish he were here. He would love tonight, watching old movies and eating chili. Of course, if dad were here, we'd be eating out of the right bowls!" She laughs.

I don't think it's that funny.

All through the movie I'm feeling annoyed. I'm an independent woman, not only taking care of my life, but also moving forward successfully with it. I've advanced my career, gotten healthy and in shape, managed my finances and prepared for the future. I have friends who like and respect me, and even have a wonderful man who cares for me. Yet, my kids make me feel like an idiot. Maybe it isn't intentional on their part, but they're always questioning everything I do. Is it normal to see your parents so one-dimensionally? I doubt they would treat Joseph this way if I had been the one to die. I am fairly certain that if given the choice, they would preferred to have Joseph here instead of me. At least Lauren would and I guess that's fine. I can't begrudge them that, especially since they always had a great relationship with their father. I'm thankful they had been so close, however, I'm tired of living in the shadow of a dead person.

CHAPTER 14

"Grief does not change you... It reveals you."- John Green

I'm going on a date tonight. Alone. I've never done it before, and I almost chicken out before I even leave the house. There is a showing of The Shop Around the Corner at the Paramount Theater and I want to go. I could ask Denise, or Janet, or anyone, really, but, I don't, because although I'm nervous about being alone, I don't really want to go with anyone else. I want to go with Joseph. It's the kind of thing he and I would have enjoyed together. We often went to the summer classic films at the old historic theater. It was our thing. Shop Around the Corner isn't my favorite show, but I like it, and have good memories of watching it while snuggling on the couch with Joseph many years ago.

It doesn't seem right to go on a date and just see a movie, so I'm also taking myself out to dinner. I decide to go to Annie's Restaurant, just a few blocks down Congress Avenue from The Paramount. I park in a nearby garage, and walk two blocks to the restaurant. I pull the ornate door open and step inside. The hostess looks up and smiles. She looks around to see who I'm with, a couple has just entered after me.

"Three for dinner?" She grabs three menus.

I glance behind me, "No. Just one."

"Just one?" She raises her eyebrows and suspends the menus in the air.

I force a strained smile, "Yes. Just one for dinner, please."

"Oh," she says, while making a show of putting down two menus. "Would you like to sit at the bar?"

I look to the bar. It is large and rectangular, with a huge mirror on the back wall. It's surrounded by lights and is very impressive, but I'm not interested in sharing my date with Sad Sally and Lonely Larry, not to mention the bartender who flashes me a bright smile while she cleans glasses.

"No, thank you. I'd like a table, please, preferably against the wall."

She seats me at a small two-top between two four-tops. I sit down on the booth side, which runs the length of four tables. I share my seat with a portly middle-aged man on one side, and a pre-teen on the other. Had I someone sitting across from me, I would not have minded the seating arrangements, but as it is, I feel like I'm intruding on two different conversations. My waitress comes and I order the Tuesday Special, which is Steak Frites Béarnaise, with chocolate torte for dessert. It's the second time I will have it. The first was several years ago when Joesph and I came here after touring the Capital grounds. It was a wet and chilly March day and we were huddled together, arm in arm, talking and laughing, as we walked the seven or so blocks down the street looking for a place to eat. Annie's called to us with its friendly awning and pretty window. We were the only two in the restaurant on that early Tuesday evening and even if it had been full, I wouldn't have noticed anyone but Joseph. It had been that kind of day, one of the ones you remember.

As I wait on my food, I try not to listen to the pre-teen telling her parents about why the new boy-band she likes is the "....most amazing thing, like ever!" I also try to ignore the portly man's gripe about his new boss, as his companion listens with bored and exasperated eyes.

When my food arrives, I eat quickly, only slowing to savor the delicious torte that melts in my mouth and tingles my tongue. I close my eyes and imagine for just an instant that Joseph is sitting across from me. As I open them, I catch the eyes of the woman across from the complaining man and smile. She smiles back, and I swear she looks envious of me. It's hard for me to imagine anyone being envious of me, but I can see how being alone can have its perks. I pay my check and head out of the restaurant.

It's early still, so I stroll slowly up Congress Avenue toward the theater. A smiling couple holding hands, passes me. They're about my age, and they could have been Joseph and I, but they aren't. There will never be another time when we will walk down the street holding hands. I tuck this realization into my heart and keep walking.

When I arrive at The Paramount, I hand over my ticket to the man at the door and keep my head held high. There is nothing wrong with seeing a movie alone. I find my seat and settle in, thankful that no one sits down next to me. I do not feel like making polite chitchat or practicing armrest etiquette. It is only when the lights dim that I allow the tears to spill silently down my cheeks, not sure whether they are tears of sadness or joy. Sadness because I would have given almost anything to be out with Joseph just one more time, or joy because despite the tear in my heart and emptiness of my hands, I feel almost whole.

As I leave the theater, I am stronger than I was at the start of the evening. I assumed people would look at me and wonder why I was alone, but the truth is, nobody cares. Before Joseph died, I was often alone, shopping or running errands, and I never felt strange about it. Why I was suddenly self-conscious and insecure, I can't say. It's an adjustment, this being alone. Sometimes it's a comfort, like a warm bath that envelopes me and holds all my crazy together, other times it's like a loud scream stealing my peace and fragmenting my very soul. I don't always know when it will take the form of comfort or despair.

It's been a month since Jeremiah said he would give me space. At first, I was nervous that I would lose him or that it was a mistake to ask for breathing room, but I had to do something. I was always torn between two men. During the times when I was feeling very connected to Joseph and missing him so much it was hard to breathe, all of Jeremiah's attentions seemed like the worst intrusions. I wanted to scream at him or build a thick wall around myself to keep his love out and Joseph's love in. However, when the grief was more manageable and I felt ready to move on, I longed for Jeremiah's company. I wanted to start over, to laugh, and feel new things. I wanted to lay with him and let him discover a new Alison. Sometimes I couldn't tell who I missed more, Joseph or Jeremiah.

The truth is that I am not ready to commit to a new relationship with anyone. I need to figure out if I can be alone and give my heart a chance to heal. At least that's what I read in my Grief 101 book, and it might be the only useful thing I learned so far. That, and also that it's okay to watch movies all day or binge on Mint Chocolate Chip ice cream, as long as I go outside and do something active for a couple of hours. When I think about it, those are both pretty important lessons, so maybe I should be a little more grateful to Aunt Emily after all.

CHAPTER 15

*"So it's true, when all is said and done, grief is
the price we pay for love."*
-E.A. Bucchianeri

My book is coming along well. I'm given an official
release date, which is about two months after the one-year
anniversary of Joseph's death. I'll be required to do some
self-promotion, which I'm nervous to do. My agent says
an easy way to get the word out is through social media,
but I closed my Facebook account after Joseph died. I did
this mostly for the sake of others. Who knows what to
say to the grieving woman who turns up in your chat
feed? Also, it was hard for me, at first, to see everyone's
happy announcements and smiling pictures, when I was
feeling so low. Now things are different and I can handle
more social situations, especially ones like Facebook
where I don't actually have to see people face to face to
tell them about my new book.

One rainy day when I can't go out to run, I reinstate
my Facebook account. I send out lots of friend requests
to family, friends and also to Jeremiah. I then upload a
new profile picture, one that was taken at the camp
reunion while we were bowling. Denise asked me to smile
for the camera right after one of my turns. I'm holding
the ball in front of the lanes and I remember inwardly
wishing she hadn't put so much attention on me. I felt
silly trying to smile and look happy while everyone was
forced to watch. But given how much I had changed over
the last nine months, and how few times I've had my
picture taken recently, it was my best option. I wasn't

about to take a selfie. For my background photo, I choose one of a sunset on the beach that Joseph took me to the last time we had gone to Port Aransas. I complete my Facebook profile by filling in all the interest questions and contact info. I realize as I'm doing it, that this is somehow my way of reaching back out to the world and telling them that I'm ready to be more social again. There are undoubtedly better ways to re-establish relationships, but Facebook makes it so easy. As I finish setting up my account, I receive numerous dings as my notifications box fills up. People are accepting my requests and even posting on my wall.

Lauren: "Hey Mom! Welcome back to the modern world!" Janet: "Hi friend! Miss you!" Todd: with a giant thumbs up picture, and Christy: "Hey girl! We should get together soon!"

Among the numerous acceptances, is Jeremiah, who doesn't post on my wall or send me anything. This doesn't surprise me since we haven't talked in almost six weeks. He is definitely giving me the space I asked for, more than I asked for, actually. I quickly go to his page and scroll down his time-line. He rarely posts anything on his page, and what is there, is not really significant. I examine his photos and see quite a few that look new. Two are of him and a pretty woman, who appears to have been taking a selfie of them. In one picture, they look to be in a restaurant, and in another one they're outside somewhere. I have no idea who she is. She might be his ex, his sister, or a new girlfriend, for all I know. While I'm spying on his page, I notice that he has gotten on Facebook, as the little green light next to his picture is on in my chat feed. I flush and am suddenly embarrassed until I remember that he doesn't know I'm looking at his page. I click on his little profile picture and the chat screen pops up. I type, "Hey there!" and then I wait, and wait. I can see that he's still on, but I get no response. After about five minutes, I feel a little sick and inexplicably embarrassed. I log off quickly, sit back in my chair, and sigh.

Maybe I'm not ready for Facebook.

But, I can't stop thinking of the photos. Who is that woman with her cheek pressed next to my Jeremiah, and why do they look so happy? I feel the sinking feeling of regret, realizing I may have blown it. Although, it wouldn't have been fair to Jeremiah, Joseph, or myself if I had forged ahead with a new relationship that I wasn't ready for. I just hope it isn't too late and I haven't lost him forever. I wish I had a photo of Jeremiah and me together, I don't even have that. Someone else can look at her own photo and stare at his handsome face, and can even see herself having a good time with him. All I can do is look at a picture of him with someone else. To see us together, I have to close my eyes and conjure up an image. Every time I try that my mind flashes to us making love in New York, not exactly the kind of picture I'd post on Facebook. I hope what's-her-face doesn't have a similar mental picture to think about.

I know I will have to brave social media again in order to communicate with all the people in my life who I don't make time for anymore, but I need to take it slowly. If I stretch myself too thin, I'm likely to snap, like a rubber band, or a blown up balloon. The result will be hurt for others and guilt for me. There are certain people in my life that are worth the risk and the effort of playing nice, and those friends I plan to reach out to in person. Soon, very soon. The rest will just have to be my "friends" who "like" my status.

Even if I don't use it for my personal life right now, I recognize that social media is necessary for promoting my book. My limited knowledge ends with Facebook, so I reach out to Lauren and find out about Twitter, Tumblr, Instagram, and Snap-Chat. She tries to set me up on several accounts over the phone.

"Okay, Mom, I think you should set up a screen name that has to do with your book," she advises me.

"Why's that? Shouldn't it be my name?"

"No, I don't think so. I mean you're setting up the accounts to promote your book, right? Not yourself."

"Hmmmm. That's true. But how will people find me? I mean do I send out friend requests like on Facebook?"

Lauren sighs. "No, these other things aren't like Facebook, Mom. Maybe I should set everything up for you, just to get you started. Is that okay?"

"Really? That would be great, if you would do that. It would be so much better if you help. I just don't get it," I admit.

"Sure, Mom." I can tell she's smiling (or laughing) at me. "I don't mind. I can be your publicist, if you want."

Do I want? Of course I want! I don't know why I haven't thought of it before. She is in PR after all. "That would be really great, sweetie. Thank you."

We agree to meet up within the next few weeks after I get more info from my agent about the book's release. I feel like a huge weight has been lifted off my shoulders. I've been so busy trying to be independent and learn how to live on my own that I've almost forgotten that I need other people too. Keeping to myself is so much easier, so it's a big step for me to allow Lauren to help me with this. If no one expects me to be in their life, it's no big deal when I hole up for days at a time, or when I'm not there for them during their own crisis. I'm grieving after all, so people shouldn't expect anything from me. That mindset might have been okay at the beginning. It might have even been encouraged, but the more I heal, the more I realize that I want to contribute to my relationships again.

I don't like the "widow" version of myself.

~~~

It has been over nine months since we buried the love of my life. In the last nine months, personally, I've lost thirty pounds, learned to run, helped my children move forward with their lives, made some positive financial investments, spent some time with old friends, bought a new wardrobe, and gotten my hair cut in a new style. Romantically, I've rekindled my relationship with my ex-boyfriend, slept with him, realized I wasn't ready for a relationship, and then broken up with him. Professionally, I've traveled to New York, met my agent, and succeeded in getting my book approved for publishing.

In the last nine months, more has happened to me than in the past several years combined. I start thinking about other nine-month periods in my life where I had accomplished nothing. One time, when the kids were in third grade, I lost my job. For the next nine months I remained unemployed. During that time, I sat around, moping, watching TV, and reading trashy romance novels. Another time we spent nine months trying to sell Amway. Joseph's brother and his wife had invited us over to dinner (or so we thought), and then spent the whole evening convincing us how our life would change if only we joined this amazing company. We could have all the freedom we wanted: financial freedom, time freedom, lifestyle freedom—all of which we needed in our lives. By the end of the night we had signed up, ordered our first shipment, gone through a training class, and made a list of all the people we were going to convince needed to join us as Amway distributors. For nine months, we attended weekly meetings and did everything we were supposed to. We stared longingly at the successful couples on the Amway monthly magazine covers. It was only a matter of time when we, too, would be making a lot of money and living the high life. Unfortunately, that isn't how it turned out for us. In nine months, we had four fewer friends, an abundance of unused Amway products in our pantry, were worse off financially, and weren't planning to accept another dinner invitation to Joseph's brother's house.

Since Joseph died, nine months ago, I've experienced both the best and the worst times in my life. How is it that something can be awful and amazing at the same time? I'm reminded of a trip I planned for our fifteenth wedding anniversary. We had never taken a proper honeymoon, and even though we couldn't really afford it, we definitely needed a little vacation. The kids were teens and had been driving us crazy. They had insanely busy schedules, and even more insane attitudes. They acted as if everything we did was wrong and had made us start to question our own sanity. Joseph and I had been going through a rocky patch in our marriage, primarily due to the stress of the kids, their activities, and our very busy work schedules. Janet asked me what we were planning to do to celebrate our anniversary and I admitted that we probably weren't doing anything. She insisted that we get away for a while. I didn't think Joesph even remembered our anniversary was coming up and figured I would go ahead and plan something for us. I knew money was tight, as well as time, so I booked two nights at a little bed and breakfast in Fredericksburg. When I told Joseph about it, I expected him to be happy, and at the very least grateful that I had saved him the trouble of having to arrange anything. However, his reaction was not what I expected. He said it was a busy time for him at work and I should have talked to him before making the arrangements. I said he had known about our anniversary for fifteen years, and I didn't know I had to talk to him before surprising him with a fun getaway. He quickly let me know that he didn't think a weekend away would be any fun. My feelings were hurt and he was annoyed. We barely talked for the next two days. As the trip approached, I carried on as if we were going. I assumed he would also be making arrangements to miss one day at work. I planned for the kids to spend the weekend with their grandparents (there was no way in hell I was letting them stay home alone like they wanted). I confirmed our bed and breakfast arrangements, and made a reservation for a special dinner at a well-known German restaurant on our actual anniversary. I also called a near-by vineyard and bought tickets for us to attend two tours and wine-tastings. I didn't discuss these plans with him because I was still mad. Two days before we were to go, I asked him what time he wanted to leave. He put down his paper and looked at me as if I was from another planet. "Leave for what?" he asked, with a blank expression.

"Leave for our anniversary trip in two days," I replied curtly.

"What anniversary trip?"

"Are you kidding me? We talked about this. I told you I made reservations in Fredericksburg!"

"I remember *you* talked about it. I told you that it wasn't a good time for me. Do you remember *that*?" He practically glared at me. I had never seen him look at me with such contempt.

Big, hot tears filled my eyes. I was so angry and hurt, I wanted to spit profanities at him...but that wasn't our way. Instead, I asked as calmly as I could, "So, what are you saying?"

He sighed and intentionally softened his demeanor. "I'm saying I can't go on a trip right now. I'm sorry."

I nodded, forcing the tears to stay inside.

"Okay," I said, then walked into our bedroom. I went

into our over-sized closet, sat down in the dark, and cried. And cried. For about thirty minutes, I cried. Joseph never came in looking for me. I don't think I'll ever forget how I felt in that moment. It was the only time I ever wondered if he truly loved me.

We talked very little over the next couple of days. My parents lived in San Antonio and were already looking forward to having the kids come for a visit. They had bought tickets to Fiesta Texas. The kids were excited, too, so I decided to go ahead and keep the plans I had already made for them. I didn't let anyone know that our trip had changed. I was still holding out that Joseph would come around. On Friday morning, before I headed out to San Antonio, I reminded him that I would be taking the kids and asked one more time about Fredericksburg.

"Alison, I can't take off work today," he said evenly, but firmly.

"I understand." I tried to hide my extreme disappointment. "Maybe we can have dinner tonight and get away for a little bit tomorrow. I made reservations at a vineyard."

He had been fixing his tie and stopped mid-motion. His back was to me and I saw him tense up then take a big breath. "I don't know why you can't hear me right now," he growled. "I have meetings today, into the night, and tomorrow. I can't go anywhere."

"Fine!" I shouted, and jumped off the bed, where I had been perched. "I'm sorry I wanted to see my husband on our anniversary! I'm sorry I thought you might even try to act like you cared!"

He turned to face me, "Alison, geez. Calm down, okay. You know I care."

"No. Actually, I don't."

He sighed and looked up at the ceiling. I felt like a child. "I'll try to wrap everything up by tomorrow afternoon and we can spend Saturday night and Sunday together, okay?"

"I have to pick the kids up on Sunday afternoon."

"What do you want from me, Alison?"

"Really? What do I want from you? You act as if you don't even like me anymore. You never touch me, or ask me about my life. You lose your temper and snap at me. You don't even care that it's our fifteenth wedding anniversary! I just want you to be my husband and act like you love me again." I looked at him, hoping for… something.

He rolled his eyes and sighed again. "You're being dramatic. You know I love you. You're my wife. You just ask for too much sometimes, Alison. You don't listen to me. I was clear from the start that I couldn't go away this weekend. If I could have, don't you think I would have planned something? I know it's our anniversary. I'm not stupid." He was done getting dressed. He walked into the kitchen, grabbed the travel mug of coffee I had prepared for him, and headed to the door. I followed like a sad puppy. When he got to the door, he turned around and gave me a perfunctory kiss on the cheek. "I'll be late tonight. You don't have to wait up."

"Happy anniversary," I said, pathetically.

"Yeah, happy anniversary." he replied absently.

When he closed the door, my heart dropped. I was angry, devastated, and wounded. I didn't have long to sulk though, because I had to get the kids up, make breakfast, and get on the road. I imagined my day stretching out before me, going to bed alone, and all the while feeling rejected by Joseph. It didn't sound like fun. While I waited for the kids to shower and pack, I called Janet and told her everything that had happened. She was incredibly sympathetic.

"Why don't you go by yourself?"

"I don't want to do that, but it might be better than sitting here alone all weekend. I didn't cancel in time, so I have to pay for the nights anyway."

"See? You might as well. Hey, Steve is off work today."

"Now you're just bragging," I teased.

"No, I mean maybe he could stay with the kids and I could come with you. I could use a break and I'll pay for half the room."

"Really? That would be so great, but you don't have to pay for anything."

"Well, I'll at least pay for your dinner. Let me talk to Steve and call you right back. This could be so much fun!"

I got off the phone and smiled. It was the first time I had smiled in a week. I wasn't sure yet if I'd go on my anniversary trip sans my husband, but I decided to pack a bag anyway. If Janet called me while I was driving to San Antonio, I at least would be ready and could take an alternate route to get there.

After I dropped Lauren and Paul off with my parents, I didn't know where to go. I still hadn't heard from Janet and nothing had changed with Joseph. It would have made more sense to just go home and hope that he would be able to take off a little early on Saturday so that we could at least have a nice anniversary dinner. I was still mad at him, though. I also knew that if I went home, with every passing hour I waited for him, I would get madder and madder. So, I decided that whether Janet called or not, I was going to Fredericksburg. I remember listening to the radio on the way over when our song, "Still the One" by Shania Twain, came on. I cried all the way through it. A part of me wondered if this wasn't the beginning of the end for Joseph and me. It wasn't that unusual for couples who had been together since they were teens, to have major problems, ultimately ending in divorce. Two couples we knew had just recently filed for divorce. We weren't extremely close to either of them, but we saw them at group functions, and in fact, Jenny, the wife in one of the couples, worked with Joseph. Suddenly I recalled hearing a rumor that her marriage was ending because of infidelity. Could it be? No, I shook the thought from my head. Besides, I heard it was her husband that had cheated. Suddenly, I recalled her and Joseph standing next to each other last weekend during all of Lauren and her daughter's soccer game. I was volunteering in the concessions and had been able to only catch glimpses of the game from afar. I hadn't really thought about Joseph and Jenny talking the whole time, until that moment. Just how good of friends were they? I tried to remember if she was working on this current project with him or not. Not that I was assuming anything just yet, but it might explain why they were talking to each other the whole game. For the next hour, I felt a mixture of fear, sadness, and anxiety. As I was driving past the LBJ Ranch, just fifteen minutes away from the bed and breakfast, Janet called to say she would be joining me. I thanked her, gave her directions, and said I'd see her soon. When I hung up, I let out a huge sigh of relief. The truth was that spending a couple of days alone terrified me. I had no idea what I would do besides obsess over mine and Joseph's fight. And now that I was worried about our marriage, and maybe even another woman, I knew I needed a friend with me for support and advice.

That trip marked the worst time in our marriage, but it was also one of the best times for me emotionally. I grew up and came into my own a little bit. The trip helped me discover that although I wanted Joseph, I didn't always need him. My emotions shouldn't be so tied to him, I should still maintain some independence. It was good for me. Janet and I had a wonderful time. I stayed both nights, and when I finally returned on Sunday afternoon after picking up the kids, Joseph was acting like a different man. I walked in to find a huge bouquet of flowers on the table, a beautifully written apology, along with a gift box, containing a lovely necklace. Joseph was cooking dinner for us all and was in great spirits. The kids were happy from their own mini-vacation and everyone was in a good mood. It was a memorable and fun family dinner.

It was also a good reminder to me that life could be bitter and sweet at the same time. Of course, what I'm going through now, being widowed, is worse than any fight or challenge we experienced, but I'm getting through it. The ugly, terrible reality of Joseph dying so young is not going to make my life ugly and terrible. Nine months ago, I doubted my ability to do anything. I didn't see how I would ever be happy again, and I thought I would be alone forever. But things are different now. I am beginning to believe in my own abilities, and I'm proud of my accomplishments. I can see a future, one where I can take care of myself, with or without a man in my life. I'm not saying everything is good yet or feels normal, but at least I can see glimpses of normal and happy up ahead.

CHAPTER 16

"I know it aches, how your heart it breaks. You can only take so much. Walk on." -Bono

My little grief book encouraged me to visualize and verbalize how I see myself, so I'm working on that. I am a writer and a runner. I am a mother and a widow. I enjoy cooking comfort food and watching old movies. My new favorite indulgence is making chocolate croissants. It took me five tries to get the recipe just right, but I did it. My chocolate croissants are the best. I am getting more joy from perfecting this recipe than seems normal, but I don't care. My book also told me to accept the things that make me happy and embrace them. So, to show off my new culinary achievements and to launch myself back into the social role of hostess, I invite Todd, Wendy, Denise, Christy, Kevin, and Jeremiah over to my house as sort of a celebratory milestone. During the week leading up to the party, I mostly think about what I will serve to eat and how nice it will be to see old friends. I want to be the perfect, happy hostess, my food to taste amazing, and my house to be warm and inviting. I picture lively music playing in the background and delicious smells coming from my kitchen. I'll walk around making witty conversation, looking adorable in my apron, and impressing everyone with my special croissants.

What I don't count on, just thirty minutes before everyone arrives, is opening a little used bathroom drawer and seeing Joseph's razor. It isn't one he even used. It's a vintage razor he purchased at an antique store in

Georgetown. I remember the day he bought it. It reminded him of his grandfather's razors. We had agreed that day to buy only things we loved but didn't need. I bought a stack of very old postcards from places I had never been, and probably would never go to, but it moved me to look at them. I don't even know where they are now. Seeing them would not invoke any emotional response in me, but seeing Joseph's razor brings on a sudden flood of tears. I sit on the edge of the bathtub and cry into my hands. When my tears finally subside, I raise my head and see my face in the bathroom mirror, my eyes, red and swollen. My guests will be arriving in minutes, and I'm not sure I can leave my bathroom. Ever.

However, the thought of a ruined dinner motivates me to get up and check on the food. My main course, calzones, will be done in five more minutes. I peek through the oven window and see that they are browning nicely. I straighten my shirt, smooth my hair, and reapply my lip stick. I am hoping that my pink berry lips will distract from my red-rimmed eyes. I wait for the doorbell. I can do this. I can have a life, hold a conversation, and even enjoy time with my friends.

The doorbell chimes at the same time as the oven timer. I vacillate between the kitchen and entryway, frozen for a moment by the simple decision of which to answer first. I choose the oven, and hurry over to the kitchen, calling out "just a sec!" over my shoulder to whoever is on the other side of the front door. The hot air hits my face as I open the oven and the enticing smell of sausage fills the kitchen. I breathe in deep. If only I could linger in a world that smells of sausage and chocolate, I think I would feel so much better about life. I place the hot pan on the stovetop and wonder if I can just blow off the dinner party, curl up on my couch, and eat all this food myself. The doorbell buzzes again, bringing me back to my senses. I walk over, breathe in deep, and open it.

"Hey, Denise! Sorry to keep you waiting."

"That's okay. How are you? Are you sure you want to do this?" she asks, pushing her way in and dropping her purse on the floor, before giving me a hug. Denise has been my close friend since we were teenagers, and although we haven't kept up as well as we could have over the years, our bond is strong. She has made it a point to be there on an ongoing basis for me, ever since Joseph has died. She is also the primary link connecting me to my old camp friends. I've seen Todd and Wendy frequently over the years, too, but our relationship is different from what Denise and I share.

"What do you mean? I'm fine. Of course, I want to do this. Besides, it's a little late to back out," I say, indicating behind her to the truck that just pulled into my drive. Wendy waves at me from the front seat.

"Okay. If you're sure. It just looks like you've been crying, and I don't want you to put pressure on yourself."

"You can tell I've been crying?" I hurry over to the hall mirror to asses myself. My eyes are a little red, but I don't think anyone else will notice.

"It's not bad. Don't worry." She pats me on the arm then turns to greet Wendy and Todd as they walk up the steps. "Hey guys! I'm so glad you came!"

I scowl behind her back. Who's the hostess anyway, and why does she think I can't handle this? So what if I've been crying? My husband died! Who wouldn't be crying? I move around her and give Wendy a hug.

"Hi. Welcome. Please come in–I'm so glad to see you guys!" I take Wendy's purse and lead *my* guest into the living room. The door-bell rings again. I hurry past Denise to get to it before she does. It's Christy and Kevin. I greet them quickly and leave them to talk with Denise while I go into the kitchen to finish getting things ready.

Todd follows me there.

"So," he begins.

"So?" I start pulling out plates and silverware.

"Is Jeremiah coming?"

"I think so. I invited him. Have you talked to him?"

"Nope." He rocks back on his heels with his hands in his pockets.

"No? I thought he was over at your house all the time."

"Not lately. I guess he's been busy. Or maybe he's just in a better place, ya know?" he says.

"Well, yeah. I guess he is, but still, he doesn't really like to be alone."

"Maybe he's not alone." Todd looks at me pointedly and shrugs.

I mumble a nonchalant response, then busy myself getting everything ready to set the table. What a fool I am! I haven't really considered that Jeremiah might be seeing someone else, probably that girl from Facebook. And why shouldn't he? He's been divorced for months now and I practically ignored him for most of those months. I told him I needed time and space to grieve before I was ready to move forward. I was stupid enough to think he needed that, too. He made it clear he was ready to date and wanted someone in his life. If it couldn't be me, why not someone else?

I send Todd out with a stack of plates, silverware, and napkins to set the table. He doesn't come back. I start getting out seven glasses to fill with tea or water, and seven more for wine. I can hear everyone talking just a few feet away in the living room. I want to join them but the wine needs opening. I wish for a moment that Joseph was there to do it for me. He always made opening the wine look incredibly easy, while I on the other hand, have been struggling for the last two minutes to just cut off the paper with the little knife attached to my old bottle opener. I'm so focused on my task that I don't notice that anyone has come into the kitchen.

"Hey there." Jeremiah's deep voice cuts through the silence.

He startles me and I accidentally drop the knife, nearly losing my grip on the bottle, too.

"Sorry, I didn't mean to scare you," he says, while chuckling.

I blush, hating myself for it. "Hi Jeremiah, I didn't know you were here." He retrieves the knife and hands it back to me.

"Just walked in. Denise said I should come and help you."

"Oh, she did?"

He indicates to the wine bottle still in my hands. "Can I open that for you?"

"Yes, please." I hand him the opener, and watch as he fumbles with it. I laugh and say, "Wow, you're as bad as I am."

He smiles. "I know, I'm terrible at it. Claire always opened the wine. I'm more of a beer bottle opener, myself."

"Joseph always opened the wine for me, too."

"You know what that means, don't you?" he says with a twinkle in his eye.

"What?"

"You're gonna have to be a beer drinker, like me."

"There's some in the fridge. Grab me one while you're at it. I'll ask one of my more sophisticated friends to open this," I say, carrying the wine and a few glasses into the dining room. He follows with two bottles of beer.

Within a few minutes, the table is set and my old camp friends are seated around it. I've known them all for most of my life, yet they aren't a daily part of it. We ate countless meals together as children, but now those meals are often five or more years apart. Yet, there is a special bond between us. Some more than others, of course. Todd, Wendy, and Denise actually knew Joseph and I when we were together as a young couple, and they're more familiar with me as a wife and mother. The idea of me as a teen camper is probably a distant memory. Christy's memories of me are all related to camp and reunion experiences. She met Joseph, but doesn't really have any personal memories of him. Jeremiah knew me as a child and teen, but also obviously knows me in a way no one else in the room does. He never knew Joseph, and has little, if any, memory of me as a wife and mother. He knows me as a friend, lover, and now a widow.

I'm very thankful to have a few friends I can talk to, laugh with, and who will be there for me as I move forward. If Janet and my kids were here, my circle would almost be complete. I say almost, because it will never really be complete, not without Joseph. Can memories and experiences be enough to fill that gap? I hope so. I need and want to feel whole again.

When we're through eating, we all stand up and carry our plates to the kitchen.

"Dinner was great, Alison!" Todd says loudly, while patting his stomach. "I am stuffed."

A chorus of praise from everyone echoes his sentiments. I breathe in deep, square my shoulders, and smile. I accomplished something!

We move out of the kitchen and wander out to the back porch. Several years back, Joseph and I had invested some money into making the back patio an outdoor living area. We bought big comfortable seating and arranged it around a fire-pit. We strung lights around the patio posts, and scattered potted plants all around the yard. A large bamboo ceiling fan keeps the air circulating, and built-in speakers allow for a nice distribution of music. It's the perfect place to relax, and we spent many hours outside enjoying it, but I haven't sat out here with anyone else since he died. Tonight the deep blue sky, lit up by the stars, is a beautiful backdrop to all the effort he and I put into the yard. Everyone compliments the patio and yard, but are unaware that it has any special meaning to me or reminds me of Joseph. It's how it should be, I guess. Most of my memories are intended for only me.

My friends find seating and naturally break into separate conversations. Christy and Wendy are discussing children. Todd, Kevin, and Denise are talking politics. I'm not interested in contributing to either conversation. Talking about children will only remind me of when Lauren and Paul were growing up and then I'll start thinking about Joseph again. After all, raising our kids was our biggest achievement. Talking about politics usually bores me and I hate to admit that I care very little about it. I usually just agreed with whatever Joseph said. Politics were very important to him. I look over at Jeremiah who is also on the outside of both conversations. He glances at me at the same time, and winks. I walk to him and say quietly, "Wanna help with dessert?" He nods and follows me into the kitchen.

There is a trick to making chocolate croissants. The dough has to be rolled out just right. If it is too thick, the inside won't cook all the way through, and raw dough mixed with chocolate isn't as good as you'd think. If the dough is too too thin, the chocolate seeps through the sides of the croissant when it cooks and makes a big mess. Since I already prepared my dough, and it is just waiting to be rolled out, I decide to let Jeremiah help me.

"Here," I say, handing him the mound of dough.

"What's this?" He stares at the lump in his hand as if

it's something he's never seen before.

"It's going to be the most delicious thing you've ever put in your mouth!"

He raises his eyebrows at me in a knowing manner, smiles, and says, "I don't know about that."

I blush, something I seems to be doing a lot of tonight. "Just roll the dough out, okay?"

I reach into a bag of flour and plop a large amount on the counter, spreading it thin with my hand. He lays the mound on top and I hand him a rolling pin. He looks at it and wrinkles his brows. I sigh and stifle a laugh. "Here, let me show you." I guide his hands over the handles. "It's like rolling out pizza dough, not too thin, not too thick. You've done that before, right?"

"I thought you were supposed to throw pizza dough into the air," he says.

I look at him with mock exasperation. "If you don't want to help, you could go back outside and talk about curfews and impeachments with the others."

He laughs. "No, no. I want to help. Let me stay, please!"

"Okay, then you need to behave. Roll the dough out and try to shape it like a rectangle instead of a circle."

He works with the dough while I prepare the chocolate filling. The best chocolate for the croissants, with the right amount of bitter-sweetness and melt-ability, only comes in slabs. I cut each piece precisely off the slab, so that they melt evenly in the croissants. I look over at Jeremiah and notice he's done a good job.

"Looks great," I say, moving over to him with my bowl of chocolate pieces. "Now we cut the dough into triangular strips, like this," I show him my first cut, then hand him the pizza cutter. "Now you do the rest."

"No problem," he says confidently, "I was made for this."

I steal a glance at his handsome profile and my stomach flips. "Yes, you were." He smiles and looks down.

"It's been nice seeing you tonight, Alison."

"Thank you, you too. I'm glad you came. I wasn't sure you would," I admit.

"Really, why?" He seems genuine, which surprises me.

"Because, I haven't been all that nice to you, and I wasn't sure you'd want to see me," I say, quietly.

He ignores my confession for a minute, and asks, "Is this right?" indicating to the strips he just cut.

"They're perfect. Now we add the chocolate and roll them up." We both carefully roll the croissants up, place them on the baking dish, and put them in the oven. When I turn back around, he's standing close and staring at me. I divert my eyes, waiting to hear the verdict of whether he wants to see me or not.

"You haven't been the best, I'll agree with you there, but you have been honest, and I respect that. You told me that you weren't ready to date, and I didn't want to listen. When I pushed too much, you pushed back. I can't blame you for that."

"I'm sure I sent you a lot of mixed signals though," I say, embarrassed that I had agreed to be physically intimate but couldn't handle simple companionship. If he had been the same with me, every friend I have would be telling me that he was a jerk, and I should forget about him.

"Yeah, you did. But I'm a grown up. I can understand some of it."

"I also wasn't there when you were going through your divorce and needed a friend."

"No, you weren't. I wish you had been, but I can understand that, too. I mean, you had a lot of your own issues to deal with, without adding my depression to your plate."

I try to think of another reason he might want to walk away from me, but I can't... or at least I don't want to.

"I'm sorry, Jeremiah. Can you forgive me?" I ask, moving to within hugging distance.

He reaches out and pulls me in. He's warm and comforting, and I sink into him.

"Of course," he says, pushing me to arms-length and smiling down at me. "Friends?"

Friends? Friends? I don't want to be just friends. The disappointment must be apparent on my face, but if so, he doesn't indicate anything.

"Friends," I say, trying to hide my emotions. We separate, and I busy myself with tidying up the kitchen. Jeremiah helps clear the few remaining items off the table and puts the leftovers in the refrigerator. There are three minutes left on the timer for the croissants. Three minutes I want to use to convince him that I'm worth another chance. I turn back toward him, moving in closer. I grab the cloth he's using to wipe the counter and throw it in the sink. He looks up, bemused.

"What's up?" He tilts his head inquisitively.

Instead of answering, I put my arms around his neck and kiss him on the lips.

He doesn't kiss me back.

Surprised and embarrassed, I pull away rather suddenly. I hear the back door open and voices carry inside. The timer goes off, and I turn to get the croissants out of the oven. The heat blasts me as I open the door and I am grateful, hoping it will hide my flushed face.

"That smells so good, Alison! What is it?" Christy walks in, followed by Wendy and Denise. As the three ladies gather around the island to see what I made, Jeremiah quietly slips out.

I divert my attention to Denise, who is offering to make coffee. The ladies help me set out dessert, and continue with the conversation they started outside. I'm silent, absorbed in my humiliation and at a complete loss as to what I should do next. Do I pretend that I didn't just kiss Jeremiah? Do I confront him and beg for a second chance? Do I return his rebuff by spurning his friendship? While I'm contemplating my next move, all the men join us in the kitchen. Croissants are quickly dispersed and coffee is poured. I busy myself, playing hostess and avoiding Jeremiah.

"These croissants are amazing, Alison!" Todd comments while reaching for another one.

"Thanks, Jeremiah actually made them," I say, looking his way to gauge his reaction.

He moves over to me and puts his arm around my shoulder. "No, no. I can't take any credit. Alison just told me what to do, and I obeyed. If I had made them they wouldn't be edible." He squeezes my shoulder and leaves his arm there. No one seems to notice or care, and the conversation continues as if nothing has happened. I can't look at him, I'm just too embarrassed. Why didn't he kiss me back, and what is he trying to tell me now?

We convene back out on the patio with coffee. I follow behind Jeremiah, feeling like a little puppy who's made a mess and wants to be back in his master's good graces. What am I doing? Just hours ago I was crying over one of Joseph's razors, and now I'm hoping desperately that Jeremiah will give me another chance. He sits down in a chair between Todd and Denise, so I have to sit across the circle from him.

The stars are shinning brightly and it really is a beautiful night, but I hardly care. Although my dinner party has been a big success, I feel terrible. I just want everyone to leave. Everyone that is, but Jeremiah. I need to talk to him, and find out if he gave up waiting for me. It might be he's already seeing someone else. As I watch him talking and laughing, I realize how much I don't want to lose him. He's funny, kind, and sensitive. Jeremiah is a good man, and I love being around him. He makes me feel excited and alive. If it wasn't for the guilt over Joseph, I would never have pushed him away. But am I ready now? It isn't fair to him to work toward building a relationship unless I know I'm ready to move on and truly love him for who he is, and not as a replacement for Joseph.

While I'm thinking about all of these things, I realize I'm staring at Jeremiah. He must feel my gaze because he turns and looks my way. We sit there looking at each other while everyone else continues talking and laughing all around us. He smiles faintly at me and subtly tips his head to the side. Tears that no one can see in the darkness, well up in my eyes. I can't stand it any longer. I excuse myself, and walk back inside, moving into my bedroom to compose myself before everyone walks back in. I'm just ready to call it a night and hope my guest feel the same. My back is turned to the door when I hear it open. I figure Denise followed me, but it isn't her.

"Alison...we should talk." I hear Jeremiah's deep, soft voice and lose it.

I turn toward him. "I'm sorry," I sob, "I don't know why I'm crying."

"I do," he says.

"You do?"

"You're crying because I was kind of a jerk out there. I'm sorry I brushed you off after you kissed me." He wraps his arms around me and squeezes.

"No, Jeremiah, you shouldn't be sorry. You didn't do anything wrong. I'm crying because I feel like a crazy person! You had every right to brush me off. I mean I'm the one who has been going back and forth. I don't blame you, I really don't." I look up at him, touching his cheek lightly. "I'm upset because I feel like I blew it with you and now it's probably too late. I don't even know if I'm ready to be in a relationship, but I know I don't want to lose you." I look pleadingly into his eyes, willing him to understand.

Jeremiah gently removes my hand from his face and holds it in his own. He kisses my folded fingers and says, "Will you go out on a date with me?"

"What?"

"A date. A real date. I think we should start over. Let's go out on dates that don't involve sex, travel, or dinner with friends. What do you think?"

I smile, unable to contain my relief. "I think that sounds great. I'd love to go out with you!"

CHAPTER 17

"No one ever told me that grief felt so like fear."
– C.S. Lewis

Jeremiah plans our special date for the next Friday night. I'm inexplicably nervous. It feels like a first date, despite our history and recent intimacy. I have butterflies all day. I carefully pick out my clothes and take extra time with my makeup. I still don't know if Jeremiah dated anyone else during the months I practically ignored him, but I do know that I'm ready to fight for him now. He is the only man alive that I want to be with. The negative side of that is that I'm not completely ready to share my whole heart with him. I can't give Jeremiah the parts of my heart that Joseph still holds onto. The truth is, I'll never be all his and I don't know if that's fair to him. A part of me will always be with Joseph and him with me. I wonder how my future with Jeremiah will look and if he'll understand that a portion of my heart is off-limits.

I think about all these things while I sit on the couch, waiting for the doorbell to ring. Our date is scheduled for 7 p.m. and I wait until 7:10 p.m. before I begin to panic. It's not like him to be late. I try to call his cell phone but immediately get his voicemail. Something is wrong! My hands shake as I send him a text. When he doesn't respond right away, I burst into tears, ruining my careful make up job.

At 7:20 p.m. the doorbell rings. I run to the door and fling it open. Jeremiah is standing there, looking apologetic.

"Oh my God, I was so worried! Are you okay?" I cry, wrapping my arms around his neck.

He gently pushes me away and makes me look at him. "Alison, are *you* okay?"

We move from the porch into the foyer, and I start crying again. Jeremiah leads me into the living room and has me sit next to him on the couch.

"What's going on? Why are you so upset?"

I sniff and wipe at my eyes. "I was just worried. You were late, and you didn't answer your phone."

He seems perplexed then sighs. "I'm really sorry to have worried you. I called and left you a message."

"You did?" I look down at my phone and see for the first time that I have a message. I feel like a fool. "I didn't see it, I'm sorry. What did it say?"

He wraps his arms around me, pulling me in close. I rest my head on his shoulder. "It said that I was going to be late because my phone was giving me problems and I was going to stop by AT&T to see about getting a new one."

"Oh," I say quietly, looking down at my hands. I'm so embarrassed.

"Yeah."

"I'm really, really sorry that I freaked out like that."

"I'm sorry that I upset you so much. I didn't think twenty minutes would be too big a deal."

"No, it's not your fault," I say, looking into his very patient and kind face. "It's just that when Joseph died, he was late getting home and I couldn't get a hold of him." I start crying again and he holds me close.

"Do you want to tell me about it?"

"Maybe. I think the worst part is that the last time I ever saw him, we were fighting...or at least, I was. I was angry with him."

"Why were you angry?" he asks, while brushing a

strand of hair off of my face.

"It was so dumb when I think back. I was mad because he had been ignoring me. He was working on an important presentation for days, and I should have been more understanding. It's just that it seemed like all he did lately was work and act stressed. I guess I was just fed up and we had a fight about it."

"That doesn't sound dumb. You just wanted to spend time with your husband, that's all."

"But it was his job. He was worried about getting replaced by someone younger." I sigh, remembering the many times he expressed concern about it. I always brushed it off, assuring him that his job was safe. I didn't really listen to him. "I went to bed mad and didn't tell him goodnight. He woke up early and left for work before I could say I was sorry, or goodbye, or anything." I turn to look at Jeremiah, wanting somehow to convey how much I regret that moment.

"It's okay, Alison, married couples fight. I'm sure Joseph wasn't upset with you. I'm sure he knew you were sorry," Jeremiah says.

"I did text him to apologize, but he never texted back. He called me though, twice. But I was at yoga the first time and in the shower the second time. I don't know why he didn't leave a message."

"So, did you call him back later?" he asks.

"No." I put my head in my hands covering my eyes. "I started working on my book right after my shower and I was so damn caught up in the chapter I was writing that I didn't call him back. I didn't want to be interrupted. I feel so selfish about that. He never called me during the day, I should have known something was wrong!"

Jeremiah squeezes my hand. "You couldn't have known."

"I should have known," I say, unwilling to waver on

that point. I should have known something was wrong.

"So what happened next?"

"Well, when I got done writing, I texted him again, said I was looking forward to seeing him soon. I figured I'd surprise him with his favorite dinner when he got home and I could make up for the fight. So, I went to the store and bought everything to make lasagna and apple crisp," I stare at the wall past Jeremiah and smile a little bit, remembering how much Joseph loved my lasagna. I know he would have walked in, smelled it cooking and given me a big kiss. Joseph appreciated a good meal.

"Everything was ready and waiting for him. The table was set and the food was out of the oven. It was all just waiting for him to come home. But he never did."

"How did you know something was wrong?"

"Well, I was frustrated that my dinner was getting cold, so I texted and called him. He never responded. I still didn't realize something might be wrong. I called his boss, thinking maybe he was with him, but he said that Joseph had left hours before because he felt sick. That's when I started to worry. Joseph never got sick. I called the hospital by our house, but he wasn't here. I thought maybe his car broke down or he had an accident so I went out looking for him. By now, it was hours past when he left the office. I couldn't find him so I pulled over in a parking lot and tried to call his brother to help me. That's when the police called and said they would send someone to get me."

I vividly remember the chapel at the hospital that I am taken into, how it looked and smelled, but I can't bring myself to tell Jeremiah about it. I can't tell him about the nervous doctor or the impatient police officer who carelessly blurted out that Joseph had died. I can't tell him how it took a minute for his words to sink in and hit my ears or how my vision narrowed and the room spun and spun until I passed out. I can't recount any more of it because I'm losing my ability to speak and think, my mouth is going numb, and my eyes burn from the tears. We sit there quietly for a few minutes. Jeremiah holding me, stroking my hair, with me staring at the wall, my head a jumble of thoughts and regrets. Finally, I'm able to speak. I know I must tell him the most important part.

"It was my fault that Joseph died."

"Alison, look at me," he pulls away and takes my hands in his. "It is not your fault that Joseph died. You can't own that anymore."

"But if I had just answered my phone! If I hadn't been so busy and wrapped up in my day, I would have known he felt bad. I would have known what time he left work and come to find him sooner. Did you know that he was still alive when the police found him? If someone had been there sooner, he would have lived."

"You can't know that for sure, Alison. The damage might have been irreversible no matter when he was found. And anyway, you can't change the past. It doesn't do any good to speculate what might have been. You're going to drive yourself crazy," he says.

We don't say anything for a few minutes. In my head I know he's right, but my heart doesn't like it. Feeling responsible for Joseph's death has kept me in my place as a widow. Letting that go is scary as it leads me one a step closer to letting Joseph go and moving on with my life.

"Do you think other people feel that way?" I ask.

"What way?"

"Well, like when someone you love dies...do they feel some sense of responsibility for the death?"

"I don't know. It seems like people die all the time and no one could have prevented it," he says.

"I mean, if someone dies in a car accident, wouldn't it

be normal to think that if they had left your house a few minutes earlier, maybe they wouldn't have been in an accident. You know what I mean? Like, what if I hadn't asked them a question that took thirty seconds to answer, or what if I had given them one more hug. Sometimes, it is literally seconds that save someone from being in a car accident," I say, matter of fact.

"That's true. But I don't think you can let yourself think like that. I mean, you can have a mental breakdown if you think every thing you do has huge consequences and the fate of everyone else depends on your actions," he says, while rubbing my hand.

"I know. Believe me, I know." I withdraw my hand gently and place it back in my own lap.

We sit there quietly for a few more minutes, contemplating.

"I just realized something important," I say.

He squeezes my hand. "What is it?"

"I need professional help. I need someone to help me through this. I've never gone through it before and it's overwhelming."

"That sounds like a good idea. I can ask around if you like."

"No, no, that's okay. I can find someone." Suddenly I feel a little better. I am hopeful that a professional counselor will be able to help me sort things out. I smile at Jeremiah. "Are you ready to go?"

Jeremiah considers me with reluctance. I can't blame him. It probably isn't easy dating someone whose emotions jump from one extreme to another. I smile again sweetly, and stand up.

"I'll be right back. I'm going to touch up my makeup," I say, as I walk back to my bedroom. All the crying has smeared off my mascara. I look in the mirror and notice a raccoon looking back at me. I sigh, and proceed to remove the black that encircles my eyes, then carefully reapply "luscious lashes." I half-expect Jeremiah to be gone when I come back out, but he is still seated in the same place, staring ahead at nothing. Poor guy.

He turns to me as I walk in, and shakes his head as if to clear his thoughts.

"You okay?" I ask hesitantly. I know I'm treading on thin ice.

"Yeah, I'm fine." He stands up. "It was just a roller coaster of emotions."

I look down and bite my lower lip. "I'm sorry, Jeremiah. I know I freaked out. I know I sound mentally unstable. But, I promise you, I'm not really as nutty as I seem."

He smiles and takes my hand in his, "I know you're not a nut. It's been a stressful time. For both of us."

"I don't know if I'm going to be very good company. Maybe we should do this another time?" I look down at my hands. I hate to be so unreliable, but the sudden flood of emotions I've just experienced has left me feeling like an empty well. I don't think I have anything left to give to him. It would be better to not go out at all, than to go out, and have a terrible time.

He squeezes my shoulders. "Not a chance, sweetie," he says, kissing me on the cheek. "I packed us an amazing picnic, which was quite a feat for me, and brought my grandmother's wedding quilt. We are going to see an outdoor musical at Zilker Hillside, and we are going to eat all the delicious food I brought. We're going to lounge on the blanket under the stars and let talented people entertain us. And, if I'm lucky, you are going to rest your head on my shoulder and let me hold your hand."

I can't help but smile at him and nod my consent. How can I turn this man down?

Thirty minutes later, we're spreading out our blanket

at Zilker Park, waiting for the 9:00 p.m. showing of *Bye, Bye, Birdie*.

Jeremiah opens the cooler he brought and pulls out two miniature bottles of wine, two plastic cups, and a chilled container containing sliced cheese and apples.

"Ooooh, classy," I say, with a grin.

"Just you wait," he replies, "I've got more. This is just the appetizer." He looks at me with a crinkle in his smiling eyes, and gives me a kiss, as he scoots in closer to me. "Feeling better?"

"Yes. I am definitely feeling better." I regard this kind, generous man beside me. "Lots better."

As we nibble on cheese and sip our wine, the show begins. I'm enthralled with the vibrant stage set, the animated young people, and the quick jerk of 1960's dance numbers. I don't notice when the blanket of stars rolls out above our heads or when Jeremiah lays out chilled bowls of pasta salad and refills my cup. I look down at the bowl he places in my hand and laugh. "How did that get there?" He just winks at me. I turn my attention back to the show and snuggle in closer to him, so that we're lightly touching. He kisses the top of my head and I breathe in deep, releasing my anxiety along with my breath, easing into complete serenity. I realize the euphoria I'm feeling is likely temporary and circumstantial, but nevertheless, I'm thankful for it.

Sometime during the performance, I move between Jeremiah's outstretched legs and lean on his strong body. His arms are wrapped around me and my hand has found his. When the final number ends, the audience erupts in applause. I don't move, even after the final curtain call, when the director thanks us all for coming out, nor when everyone gathers up their belongings and makes their way through the throngs and out of the park. When it is just the actors and their friends, and me and Jeremiah, I turn my body to look at him. He has sat patiently, waiting for my cue to leave. He looks down at me and raises his eyebrows as he gives me a small smile. "Did you like it?"

"I liked it, a lot. I mostly liked being here with you. Thank you for giving me exactly what I needed tonight." I lean forward and gently kiss his lips. He cups my face in his hands and kisses me back. When we part, he strokes my hair away from my face and rests his hand on the back of my neck.

"You are an amazing woman, Alison."

I blush, wondering how he can possibly feel that way. "I think you mean I'm an amazing pain." I smile to deflect my insecurities.

"No." He shakes his head and gazes seriously at me. "Just amazing."

We walk hand-in-hand back to his car, get in and start driving toward my home. I yawn loudly, not even trying to hide the extreme fatigue that suddenly overtakes me.

"Tired?" he asks, while resting his hand on my thigh.

"Very. I'm sorry."

"Why are you sorry? It's late. I'm tired too."

"I just didn't know what you had in mind after the show. I didn't know if you were expecting to come over to my house, but I think I'm just too tired," I say, apologetically.

He glances my direction and removes his hand from my leg. "Alison, I don't want you to think I expect to spend the night with you whenever we're together. I don't."

"No, I know. I just..." I trail off not sure what to say, because I did kind of think he expected that.

"In fact, I think it would be good for us to take it slower. You know, go out on dates and stuff."

"Dates? Is that what normal couples do?" I tease.

"I hear it is. I wouldn't really know."

"Um, about that..."

"About what?"

"Well, I was just wondering if you've been dating someone else? It's totally fine, if you have!" I add quickly.

He pauses and weighs his words. "I did go out a few times with a woman I met through a friend at work."

"Is she the one on Facebook? I mean, I just happened to see a picture of you... with someone." I fumble, not wanting to sound like I spied on him or was stalking him.

"Oh, that. Yeah, she posted a couple of pictures from our dates. I thought that was kind of strange."

"Well, I know it's not my business, and I don't have any claim on you. I just wanted to know if you were dating."

"Well, I'm not anymore, if that's what you want to know."

"Really?" I ask, trying to hide the relief in my voice.

"I'm a one-woman man, Alison. You should know that about me. And, as far as I'm concerned, you're the one woman I want to see."

"I'm glad," I say, smiling and leaning back into my seat.

"I only went out with her because of you anyway."

"What do mean, because of me?" Was he trying to make me jealous?

"Well, I know you said you needed some time, and I completely understood that. I didn't want to be a rebound guy to you. And, I started thinking, I didn't want you to be a rebound woman for me. I thought it might be healthier for us later if I tried dating someone else so I wouldn't ever have any doubts about that. I know you haven't dated anyone else, but if you feel you should, I understand. I'm looking to the future, Alison. I'm in no big rush, and I want you to take all the time and space you need to decide that I'm the man you want in your life."

"You seem pretty confident I'll decide you're the one for me." I turn to him, grinning. "Maybe I'll take you up on that and get on Match.com or something. You know, sow some wild oats before settling down again."

"If that's what you want to do, that's fine. Although, if you do want to date other men then I'd prefer to stay out of the picture until you're ready. I don't want to just be one of your guys."

I punch him in the arm. "I'm kidding! I am not joining Match.com, or any other dating site." I shiver just thinking about it. "I am barely ready to date you. I am definitely not ready for blind dates or anything."

"Well, if there is someone else you want to go out with..."

"Jeremiah, I promise you there is no one else that I want to date. You are the only other man I want to spend time with. I do think, though, that I want to take it slow. I am serious about seeing a therapist and just trying to work through some stuff. I don't want you to be my only sounding board."

We make it back to my house and Jeremiah turns off the engine. We unbuckle our seatbelts, but don't get out of the car.

"I don't mind being your sounding board, if that's what you need," he says, sweetly.

I smile at him and touch his face. "I know you don't. You are such a good man. However, that being said, I don't want you to see the inner workings of my crazy head right now. I need to talk to someone that I'm not trying to impress."

"You're trying to impress me?" he asks, with a glint in his eye.

I laugh. "I know. Hard to tell isn't it? That's my point exactly. I am barely making a good impression now. I don't need you thinking I'm more disturbed than I really am."

He smiles and lifts my fingers to his lips, kissing the tips.

"Okay. You see a therapist. We'll take it slow. I will be your full-time friend, and part-time boyfriend. You tell me when you're ready for more. Sound good?"

"Sounds great. Thank you. And, thank you for tonight. I had a wonderful time."

He walks me to my door and kisses me in a way that makes my knees buckle. As he steadies my crumpling body, I chastise him. "Stop kissing me like that. I can't take it slow when you kiss me like that. It's not fair."

"I make no promises," he teases. I smile and turn to walk inside. I notice that he waits to walk away until I'm inside and have locked the door.

I walk to my bedroom in a daze and get ready for bed. As I lay between the soft sheets, I think of Jeremiah's kiss until I fall into a peaceful, deep sleep.

CHAPTER 18

"Give sorrow words; the grief that does not speak whispers the o'er-fraught heart and bids it break." -William Shakespeare

I find my therapist through Yelp. It may not be the smartest way to find a person to share your deepest, darkest secrets with, or the person you expect to help heal your inner heart, but that's how I do it. She has good reviews and her prices are more reasonable than some of the others, although all of them seem overpriced to me, considering I have friends who are willing to listen to my problems for free. I remind myself that having someone listen to my problems isn't really the point, though. The point is to try and get through the worst event in my life intact, and without isolating everyone who cares about me. I'm hoping a professional therapist will help me to do that.

I make an appointment for the Wednesday after my date with Jeremiah. I want to get in a couple of sessions before I see him again. I also hope to wrap up the healing process in the next two months, before the big "death anniversary." When I mention this to my new therapist, she looks surprised and makes a note in her book. I realize she could have been writing anything, maybe she even just made a note about the anniversary date, but I doubt it. All I can think is that she's written about what a terrible widow I am because I'm putting a projected finishing date on my grief. She may be right. I know I will love Joseph for as long as I live, but I'm already so tired of being a grieving widow. I just want an end to the depressing role I'm in. When I mention this to her, she seems even more surprised.

"So, when you say "role," do you mean that you feel like a character playing a part?" she asks carefully.

"What? No. Yes. Maybe... I don't know."

"Alison, I want you to feel free to say whatever is on your mind here. I won't judge you. I am just here to help you make sense of what you're feeling so that you can make good choices about moving forward," she says, with a comforting smile.

I don't completely believe her, but it does sound good. "Okay. Well, in that case, yes. Sometimes, I do feel like I'm playing a part. The role of the grieving widow, except that I'm terrible at it. If I really were in a movie, they would have fired me."

"Why would they have fired you?" I can see she's trying not to smile.

"Well, I guess because I'm not authentic enough. You know, I'm not believable."

"But this is real for you, Alison. You really are a grieving widow. Why do you feel unauthentic?"

I think about it for a moment, but I can't come up with a good answer, I just feel what I feel. "I don't know. It just seems like there is a certain way to act if you're a good widow, and I feel like I'm acting like a bad widow."

We sit there in silence for a few minutes. She smiles in a friendly way, waiting patiently for me to speak. I wish she would say something. When I realize she's not going to talk for me, I think honestly about what I told her.

"I guess I'm feeling like I'm not as unhappy as I should be," I finally confess.

I look down at my hands. I can't believe what I just admitted aloud. I said I wasn't as unhappy as I should be. About my husband *dying*.

I feel I should clarify my comments. I should tell her that I *am* unhappy about him dying, in fact, I'm lonely, despondent, and miserable. But, I can't say anything. What is wrong with me? I look up at her, expecting horror, but instead, I see compassion and understanding. I start to cry. She passes me a box of tissues as my tears turn to sobs. She lets me cry for a while, and I'm thankful that she doesn't try to touch me. When I'm through, she surprises me by giving me a homework assignment. I am to make a list of all the things I liked about myself, before Joseph died, then make a list of all the things I like about myself now. We will discuss it at our next session in four days. I have four days to complete an impossibly hard task–to be honest with myself.

When I get home, all I can think about is my assignment. It feels like a very big deal to me; one that deserves proper attention. I take a long bath, thinking the whole time about what I will say. Nothing earth-shattering comes to mind. After my bath, I dress in my lounge pants and a super soft sweater. I bring my favorite blanket over to the couch, light my favorite candle, and make a cup of my favorite tea. I find a journal I have not written in yet and get my best pen out–the one I use for writing letters and cards. I also get out my Grief 101 book, in case I need a reference. I have no idea why I do all this, except it feels comforting to me and the task ahead makes me feel very uncomfortable. I sit there with everything all around me for twenty minutes before I have the courage to start my writing.

Things I liked about myself before Joseph died: Good mother, good wife, good friend, determined, creative, goal-oriented, consistent, friendly, and dependable.

I look back over my list and try really hard to think of

something else. These are good qualities and I'm proud of them all, but they seem so generic. I could say the same thing about most of my friends. It's sobering to realize that you can sum up your worth in nine generic attributes. I sigh and decide to move on, maybe I'll think of something else later. I don't want to return to therapy with such measly answers. I assume the next list will be more depressing as I'm certainly not a good wife, mother, or friend lately. I haven't made much headway in my new book, I'm often unfriendly and also not very dependable. I don't fit many of my old qualities at all. What am I? I don't want to write the next part with this mindset, so I get off the couch and stand to do a few yoga stretches. I close my eyes, and take deep breaths. I clear my mind and when I feel peace, I ask God for help– *How do you see me?*

Although, I'm sure God would be happy to answer me, what I hear in my heart and head is Joseph's voice. I sit back down and let the pen flow, knowing he is helping me.

Things I like about myself now: spontaneous, passionate, interesting, strong, open to new ideas, athletic, runner, resolved, smart, independent, and introspective.

I reread over the list several times, making sure the words are sincere and I can honestly accept them as mine. Reading them makes me smile, and I feel a sense of pride. I really am all these things, and many of them are not at all generic, but they're unique to me. I sit staring at the page for a while and when I compare the two lists, I see it. I see the whole point of this exercise. "Damn, she's good," I say aloud, picturing my smug little therapist sitting in her office.

I pull out a photo album and spend the next half-hour looking at pictures of Joseph and I. Pictures of us on our last vacation to the Grand Canyon, the kids college graduation, his best friend's birthday dinner, and of our last Christmas together. It was always me and Joseph. We were a team. When he died on that day, we died too. I understand that the memory of him, and us, will live on. I know that he's a part of me and always will be, but it's different now. I am no longer part of a couple. It's just me, and I'm beginning to see that just being me isn't so bad. I would do anything to have him alive again, but I wouldn't want to go back to being the same person I used to be. I have to believe that eventually I would have found this better version of myself. I want to believe Joseph would have helped me find her, but I don't know...

After a while of reminiscing, I put the albums away. I feel proud that I didn't cry over any pictures. This is a first for me. Looking at all the pictures reminds me of my children, and I realize that I haven't talked to Paul in a few days. I decide to call him. As the phone rings and I wait for him to answer, I picture my son's smiling face and am filled with warmth. I'm a blessed woman. Just when I think I'm going to have to leave a message, Paul answers, all out of breath, as if he ran to get his phone.

"Hi sweetie, it's Mom," I say, with a smile on my face.

"Mom! How are you?" he asks, seeming genuinely happy to talk to me. Maybe I should wait a few days between phone calls more often.

We talk for a while about his job situation and his new apartment. He tells me about a gig his band has coming up at the Lizard Lounge and I promise to go see them. It seems he hasn't given up on his band, after all, and I'm looking forward to hearing him play again. I wish I could ask Jeremiah to go with me. He loves live music and I think he would really like hearing Paul's band, but I know I won't ask him. Not yet. It isn't just that the kids' year time-line hasn't passed; it's also that I can't stand the thought of them being disappointed in me. Although I'm coming to terms with liking myself more and accepting the new me, I still feel like such a lousy widow. It seems wrong to have a boyfriend this soon. And, even though I can tell my best friends about it, and can even talk to Joseph about it, I just can't face my kids. They are so loyal to Joseph (as they should be), and I think they only see our relationship through the eyes of being our children. I don't expect them to understand the complexities of a twenty-four year marriage. Their ideals about it are so romanticized. I understand, because mine were too, at their age. However, I truly believe that if Joseph could send me a message from Heaven, he would be supportive of how I'm handling everything, including Jeremiah. I do think he would probably disapprove of me having sex with him, but I'm taking it slower now, so hopefully that would be okay. Anyway, what dead spouse would ever be fine with their loved one having sex with another person? Probably none. I can't help that; he'll have to get over it. I hope Heaven doesn't have an open viewing room or anything. I cringe imagining the Cloud of Witnesses all gathered around the giant "Earth TV" watching *Days of the Living*.

~~~

Four days later, I return to my therapist with my homework in tow. I'm very proud of my work and envision her stamping a big CURED across the front of it. I made an important discovery, after all. I'm not disappointed in my performance as a widow per se', I've been in denial about how I've changed since Joseph died, and I feel guilty for improving without him. That's the story I'm sticking to. However, when I mention all this to Dr. Yelp, she shoots me down.

"So, do you think Joseph would object to you

improving yourself?" she asks, resting her hand under her chin and leaning forward in her seat.

"What? No, I don't think so. I mean he always encouraged me to improve myself when he was alive."

"So, why do you think he would be upset?"

"Did I say he was upset?" I ask, feeling confused. "I don't know if he's upset. I mean he isn't here to tell me. He's dead." I say, stating the obvious on purpose.

"Yes, he is." She leans back in her chair and rests her hands in her lap.

I shift in my seat. I'm not sure about this one. I hate playing mental games, yet here I am playing games with my therapist, and it feels like she's winning.

"Can we talk about the homework you gave me? Because I felt like it helped me to discover some things," I say, hoping to gain some ground.

"Sure, we can talk about it. But, at some point we need to revisit why you feel uncomfortable talking about the fact that Joseph is dead."

I glare at her. This game is about to get messy. "I am not uncomfortable talking about it. We can talk about it all you want. As I have freely admitted, he is dead. I am not in denial. I am not afraid to say it. Joseph is dead. I don't think he would be upset that I have improved. He would want the best for me, but I feel a little bad that maybe, just maybe, I like myself better now."

"Now that he's dead?"

I take a deep breath and close my eyes.

"You seem aggravated," she says calmly.

I take a moment to collect my thoughts. "In dealing with Joseph's death, I feel that I have grown a lot. That growth has resulted in a stronger, more independent version of myself. I like feeling independent. I have always felt like I was under the kids' and Joseph's shadow before. I hardly knew myself." I say all this slowly and methodically. If she interrupts me I may walk out.

"I wish I had found this version of myself while Joseph was still living, but I don't think I would have. That is not his fault. I feel bad because I think most widows would be taking this time to grieve more, and I, on the other hand, have been discovering myself and liking it. That is not to say I don't miss him, or experience grief every day, because I do." I pause, looking directly at her. She remains quiet.

"That is all I have to say today."

Dr. Yelp nods her head and smiles sweetly. "I think we're out of time anyway. You can schedule your next appointment with my secretary."

I scowl and mumble unfriendly things under my breath as I wait for her secretary to get off the phone and schedule my next session. I debate leaving and never coming back, but despite my recent progress, I don't think I'm cured just yet. I'm giving Dr. Yelp one more chance simply because her exercise was so effective in helping me, even if she seems to have accidentally helped me. Finally, the woman gets off the phone and schedules me for a whole week later. I don't want to wait a week. I feel out of sorts as I leave the office. I don't want to go home yet, so I cross the road and go into a nearby shopping center to browse the stores. As I wander around I think about therapy. Before I saw Dr. Yelp, I was pretty determined to get through the grief on my own, and I obviously didn't give a ton of thought to my actions, as evidenced by the past nine months. Now I feel paralyzed, like I shouldn't move forward or do anything without first going through therapy. What if I do something that sets me back in my progress? What if she's right, and I'm unknowingly in denial about Joseph's death? What if I got the point of the list all wrong and because I missed the meaning, I'll never really see myself the right way?

My phone rings interrupting my reeling mind. It's Jeremiah.

"Hey you," he says. I instantly feel tension leaving my body, as I hear his voice.

"Hey yourself." I move over to a bench outside one of the stores and sit down. I sigh louder than I intend.

"Are you okay? Where are you?"

"Yeah, I'm fine. I just got out of therapy and it didn't go so well."

"I'm sorry. Do you want to talk about it?"

"I don't know. Can I do that? Is it allowed?"

Jeremiah laughs. "You can do whatever you want, Alison. It's your therapy."

"Oh, right. Of course you're right. See, I think my therapist forgot that."

"What do you mean?"

"Well, the first session, she seemed to get that and it went really well, but today it was like she was trying to annoy me or something. I don't know if I even want to go back."

"Well, you don't have to. That's the beauty of it. You're in control over who you talk to. But let me ask you something," he says.

"Sure, what?"

"Is it helping to talk to her? You don't want to quit for the wrong reasons."

"I know. It helped the first time, but not because of anything she said. It was because of what I realized. Although, I guess she helped me to realize stuff. Is that what therapy does? Teach you help yourself?"

"I'm not sure, but I would think that would be what you would want. To help yourself. Nobody knows you like you," he says.

I smile to myself, looking down and twisting my hair. Talking to Jeremiah almost always clears my mind enough to think straight. I think that he sees me better than anybody else right now.

"I can't wait for our date tomorrow," I say, changing the subject.

"Me, too. I've been looking forward to it all week. I gotta get back to work, but I'll see you tomorrow."

"See you tomorrow," I say with a smile. We hang up and I feel like a different person than I did just a few minutes ago. I continue walking, but now I'm swinging my purse, and holding my head high. I think I'll go buy a new outfit for my date tomorrow. After all I'm going out with Jeremiah, the most handsome, sexy, kind, and alive man I know right now.

CHAPTER 19

"I will not say, do not weep, for not all tears are an evil." -J.R.R. Tolkien

Even though therapy isn't entirely successful for me, I'm still making progress in my personal life. Jeremiah and I continue to see one another about once a week, and although I have romantic feelings for him, we're doing our best to focus on our friendship. Jeremiah is a great friend, but talking to him isn't the same as talking to a girlfriend. I need to confide in someone and am desperate for some best-friend time. So, when Denise asks me to go to the beach for the weekend with her, I enthusiastically agree.

"So, why me? Don't you usually take a man to the beach with you?" I tease.

The company Denise works for has a timeshare condo on Galveston Island and the employees all sign up for different weekends to use it. In the past Denise has taken whatever man she was dating. When her weekend actually came around this time, however, she had just broken up with her current boyfriend.

"Usually, but this time I want you with me. Besides, maybe I'll meet someone new while we're there!"

Denise changes boyfriends like most women change purses and never seems broken up by the break-ups. I don't understand how she can feel this way. Maybe I need to take a few lessons, I feel broken up by everything.

I wait for Friday to come like a child waiting to go to Disneyland. When it finally arrives, all I can think about is relaxing on the beach without a care in the world. Zac Brown's song, "Toes in the Sand" keeps running through my head. Luckily, it's just a four-hour drive to where we will be staying. Since we'll be going through Houston, Denise insists on driving. She still recalls a trip we had taken to Dallas, right after high school, when I was driving and very nearly killed us. After a terrifying brush with an eighteen-wheeler, I pulled off the highway, shaking and sobbing and refused to drive another mile the whole trip. That was twenty-five years ago. I assure her I am quite capable to drive in a big city now, but I guess the Dallas experience impacted her worse than I thought, because she adamantly refuses my services. Fine with me.

It is a beautiful day and Denise has a convertible that we put the top down on. I prop my feet up on the dash, don my cheap sunglasses, and spread my arms out, with my face touching the sun. I'm free! Denise looks over at me and laughs. "You really needed this, huh?"

"More than you know," I reply, with a sigh.

She smiles and cranks up the music. "Woo hoo!!" she shouts, pressing a little hard on the gas. My head jerks back and my hair starts flying. I look over at my crazy friend and howl with laughter. I can't help myself. I laugh for several minutes, full force, clutching at my stomach. Then, without warning, my shrieks turn to wails, and I'm sobbing uncontrollably. It takes Denise a minute to notice. She glances over and sees the anguish on my face, nearly running into the car that is slowing down in front of us.

"Alison! Are you okay? I thought you were laughing."

"I was," I sob, wiping at my eyes and smearing my mascara. The wind whips my hair every which way while violently slapping me in the face. I can't get my hair to cooperate in order to look at Denise. Every time I try to talk, a chunk of hair covers my eyes or mouth, threatening to blind or choke me. She signals to pull over and I almost protest, but instead, start laughing again. Denise glances over at me and I honestly have never seen such concern on her face. Poor thing. She has a crazy person in her car, and has agreed to take that crazy person on a trip.

She pulls over at a Starbucks and parks the car. Finally able to breathe, I push my hair back and take in several deep breaths. I avoid looking at Denise. Frankly, I'm embarrassed. I can feel her staring at me for a minute. She turns the car off and starts to get out.

"How about a coffee?" she asks, as if nothing strange has just happened.

I'm not sure adding caffeine to my system is a good idea, but follow her inside anyway. I trail behind and order after her, then go into the bathroom to assess myself in the mirror. I'm a complete mess. Black streaks run down my face (although I'm actually getting used to seeing this look on me over the last eleven months). My hair is sticking up and matted all over the place. My cheeks are pink from being slapped by my hair, and my eyes are red rimmed. I see something else, too. I see a nervous, scared person looking back at me. What just happened in the car? Why did I completely lose it? Just when I think I'm in control and have a handle on my life, something like this happens. Out of seemingly nowhere, I have a complete breakdown. It's terrifying.

I clean up as best as I can and rejoin Denise. She's sitting on a couch holding both our drinks. She smiles brightly when I walk up. "Hey! Ready to go? The beach is waiting!" I look at her and roll my eyes. "What?" she asks.

"You don't have to pretend I didn't just unleash a can of crazy on you," I say, sitting beside her and taking my latte from her hands.

"Well, I thought it might be better if I did pretend nothing happened. What the hell was that, Alison? Are you okay?" She furrows her brows and stares me down. Denise is the most blunt person I know, and it's one of the reasons I love her. I don't want her to sugar-coat my grief. I need her to stare me in the eyes and ask me the hard questions. Very few other people have the courage to do that. Most people seem afraid to upset a widow: as a result, it seems I'm rarely held accountable for my actions anymore. It's like getting old. Who questions what ninety-year old Aunt Beatrice does or says? She can do whatever she wants. She's earned that right. Well, I don't want to act like crazy, old Aunt Beatrice. I want to still fit in with the world and have friends who want to hang out with me. I want to contribute something positive to my relationships and not just be the person everyone feels pity for and therefore, treats me with kid gloves.

"I honestly don't know what happened, Denise, and I can't promise you it won't happen again. This seems to be who I am lately. I can't predict when insanity will overtake me. I wish I could promise you a drama-free, relaxing weekend, but my moods may jump from one extreme to another."

She stands up and turns back to me, holding out her hand to help me up. "It's about freakin' time you got unpredictable! Now we can have some fun." She smiles and wraps me in a hug.

We put the top up on the convertible (because wind in my face seems to trigger emotional schizophrenia), and get back on the road. I don't want to talk about my problems, or me, so I turn the conversation to Denise.

"So, what happened with the boyfriend who was supposed to go on this trip with you? What was his name?"

"Clint. He was nice and all, but just a little boring, I

guess. We never talked about anything interesting, ya know?"

I do know. "Joseph and I didn't talk about anything interesting either," I admit.

Denise makes a face at me. "Really? I'm surprised. I thought you two got along great."

"Oh, we did. I mean we hardly ever fought or anything, and we were happy, it's just..."

"It's just what?"

I think about how to say it so she'll understand. "It's just we didn't have a lot to say to each other that wasn't about the kids or his work. It wasn't always like that, but after a while....I don't know." I sigh and slump in my seat, putting my feet back on the dash.

"Go on..." She prompts by motioning with her hand.

"Well, the last couple of years we had gotten in a rut. He went to work, I did my thing, and when he got home, we usually would just have dinner, give the highlights of our day and watch TV."

"That does sound a bit boring."

"Yeah, but it wasn't always like that. I mean it was kind of nice knowing what to expect. We weren't grumpy with each other or rude. We just didn't do anything very exciting."

"Not like a spontaneous trip to New York?" She raises her eyebrows.

"No, nothing like that. I guess that's part of the reason I feel so guilty about seeing Jeremiah."

"And maybe part of the reason you love it so much, too?"

I think for a minute. "Yeah. My, whatever you want to call it, with him is definitely not boring."

Denise's phone rings and she takes the call. I look out the window and watch fields and cows zoom past, with an occasional ranch house in the mix. We're nearing

Houston and I'm feeling anxious to get there. I want to talk to Denise about all the thoughts I've been having lately, but I don't like opening up in the cramped car, trapped with my confessions. I want to be sitting on the beach where my betrayal and disclosures will be carried away on the wind and into the abyss of the open water. A place where I can drown my guilt with margaritas. Maybe Denise senses this because when she gets off the phone, she turns up the music and doesn't say another word about my boring marriage or scandalous trips.

The condo we're staying at is about two miles outside of Galveston along the shoreline. Before heading there, we drive slowly through the historic town with the top down. The warm air is fragrant with the scent of magnolia from the many trees lining the streets. The smell of beach and salt water, mixed with the magnolia, creates the perfect summer scent. I lean my head back and breathe it all in. Over a hundred years ago, the beautiful, prosperous town of Galveston had almost been completely destroyed by a raging hurricane. Although it never returned to the bustling hot spot and thriving economy it had once been, it still stood proud. A large seawall had been built to protect the city from another storm. It changed the look of the beach, but provided residents with a sense of security that was more important than aesthetics.

The city's history is a perfect example of my life; it will never be what it once was, but it can still be really good and worthwhile. However, I'm not sure I want the giant wall there. Sure, it provides protection and can be useful if there is ever another hurricane, but it keeps me at a distance from something I love...the ocean. I think about living my life safely, with a wall of protection to keep me from being hurt or damaged any further. Then I think of my life without the wall. I'm not sure I have a strong enough infrastructure to withstand another emotional blow, but being in a guarded relationship isn't what I want either. It's either going to be no relationship at all or dive in heart first.

We turn onto the road by the seawall and drive south toward the condo. The ocean slaps at the sand to my left and on my right, the street is lined with touristy restaurants, shops, and hotels. I keep my eyes on the water and smile into the breeze as the wind whips my hair behind me. I look over at Denise and see that she's dancing to the radio, swiveling her hips, and bobbing her shoulders. She glances over and catches me watching her. We both break out in a fit of laughter. I raise my arms high above me and whoop, throwing my head back to welcome the sun.

In no time at all, we arrive at the condo. There are four units in each of the six buildings, and ours faces the ocean. It has a small patio with two new lounge chairs pointing toward the beach. The interior has been recently remodeled in pale blues and greens, typical of so many of the other beach hotels and condos. It's nice, relaxing, and at the moment feels like a luxury vacation spot to me. I choose a bedroom while Denise reads over the instructions left by the owners. I plop my bag and myself on the bed. Through the window I see the rolls of the sand dunes, all topped with tall grass. Further out the ocean swells blue with white caps crashing against the shore. I close my eyes for a second. Jeremiah's face appears and then disappears. I concentrate on recapturing his image, and when I have the look I want in my head, I hold it there for a while. I see his handsome face and longing eyes as he gazes down at me the night we shared in New York. That's what I want to see–the look that turns my insides every which way.

Denise comes in and reclines next to me on the bed,

distracting me from my fantasy.

"It's pretty nice, I guess." She raises her arms to stretch, bumping the picture hanging on the wall above our heads. It falls down as we shriek and cover our faces. Luckily, it's a plastic frame and the glass doesn't break. I peek out from my sheltered face to see Denise doing the same thing. The large frame sits atop our arms. Our surprised and startled eyes crinkle at the same time. We snicker and break into a fit of laughter as we push the frame off us.

After a few minutes, we're taking deep, calming breaths and staring at the ceiling.

"So far on this trip, I have laughed more than all this last year combined," I admit.

"Well, that's good, right?"

"I guess. Except that I feel kind of like a nut job."

"What's wrong with that?"

"Really? Well, for starters, I don't want to be admitted to a mental hospital," I say dryly.

"Oh, that's no big deal. They're not as bad as TV makes them seem." Denise grins and I slap her with my pillow.

"Also," I emphasize, "I wouldn't mind being a normal person in a real relationship, and if this keeps up, I don't see that happening."

She sits up on her elbow, looking down at me. "What do you mean by 'normal' and 'real'?"

I sigh. I don't really know how to answer her question. I actually have thought about it. "Well, for instance, take my extreme emotions just in the last few hours...no sane person would want to take on that kind of drama in their relationship. Obviously, I'm talking about Jeremiah at the moment."

"Joseph took you on, and as far as I knew, he was happy to do it. Maybe, you're worth it."

"That doesn't really count, though. I mean, sure, I had moments of insanity when I was married–everyone does–but for the most part, I was pretty stable and normal when I was with him. I wasn't hard to live with or unpredictable in any way."

"Maybe Jeremiah likes unpredictable." Denise reclines back down on the bed and reaches for her toes with outstretched arms.

I look at her and smirk. "Maybe he'd like you then."

"Maybe. Are you hungry?"

"More like thirsty. I bought stuff for margaritas," I say, hoisting myself off the bed. I lean the picture against the wall and offer my hand to help Denise get up.

"Awesome. I'm all about a three o'clock buzz."

"Hey," I say, smiling, "it's five o'clock somewhere!"

"Oh, you are a beach girl aren't you? Well I'm hungry too, so while you make margaritas, I'll get out the chips and dip."

I'm suddenly energized having a plan. It's good to be away with a friend who doesn't seem at all bothered by my mood shifts and self-centered conversations.

I search every cabinet for a blender and finally find an old one above the refrigerator. I hope it has enough power to crush ice. I want a nice, blended, brain-freeze drink. After several attempts, I get pretty close to the right consistency and pour us both a margarita in tall glasses. I even salt the rims. Denise gets the snacks ready and heads out to the chairs facing the beach. When I join her with our drinks, she has her iPod playing and has laid out two huge beach towels over our chairs. She put the chips and dip on a table between us. I hand her the cold glass and sit down with a sigh of contentment.

"Thanks." She takes a sip and smiles. "Delicious. Maybe a little icy, but still...it hits the spot!"

"No kidding. I could lie here and drink these all day.

The blender was crap, so, sorry for the ice chunks."

I look out into the ocean. No matter how many times I've been to the beach, I'm always amazed at the vastness of the water. Being near the ocean makes me feel small, insignificant and strangely inspired. I close my eyes and let the balmy breeze blow over me. The heat pushes me further into my chair and acts like a weighted vest. There are no protective walls out here. We're susceptible to whatever the ocean wants to throw at us. I like it.

"Can I ask you something?" I venture.

"Of course. Shoot."

"Well, I was wondering about your relationships. You know, your boyfriends."

"What about them?" she asks, while looking over at me.

"Well, you seem to switch 'em out pretty often and I just can't relate to it. I'm not saying it's bad, at all. I just don't know how you do it, because I can't seem to get my head around dating. I feel like I'm going to go straight from a twenty-four-year marriage into another serious, long-term relationship."

"And that's not what you want?"

"I don't know."

"Well, no one is making you be in a serious relationship. Can't you tell Jeremiah you want to keep it casual?"

"I don't think so. I mean I've held him off for several months already. The thing is, if I am going to be with Jeremiah, I don't want it to be casual. He and I have definite 'falling in love' potential. We went for a couple of months without talking, and although it was okay for me because I was still trying to just deal with Joseph's death, it was hard thinking that he might be seeing someone else."

"Was he? Seeing someone else?"

"He went out with this woman a few times, but I don't think it was serious or anything."

"Did he tell you that?"

"I asked him. I saw her picture on his Facebook page. He said that he went out with her so I wouldn't be a rebound girl, or something like that."

"Hmmm. Did that upset you?"

"Well, I didn't show it. I mean, I didn't feel like I really had the right to be upset. I was the one who pushed him away and told him I wasn't ready. Me dealing with Joseph dying required more grief-time I think, than him dealing with his divorce."

"I've heard that divorce is a lot like a death though. Which is one reason I have never been married. I know I would probably get divorced eventually, and who needs that?"

I half-smile. Denise had been close to getting married once, but she found out that her fiancé had been cheating. I know it devastated her and I also suspect it's why she never lets herself get too close to anyone. Although she plays the care-free bachelorette well, there is deep pain and mistrust lurking in her heart. I don't want to be that way.

"I agree, divorce probably is a lot like dealing with a death, but Jeremiah and his wife separated over a year ago, so he's had some time to deal with it. Also, they were not doing well for the couple of years before they separated, so I think he saw it coming." I sigh, struggling with what I'm trying to say. "What I mean is, he never considered her the love of his life and he's had a lot more time to deal with it, so he's ready to date and even be serious with someone again. While I just don't think I've figured it out. Although I could see myself ending up with Jeremiah, and maybe even marrying him someday, I wonder if it's a mistake to jump into it so soon? Maybe I should date other people first, or maybe I should just be alone longer."

"That makes sense. Are you afraid you'll lose him though, if you wait?"

"Yeah, I am."

We both turn our heads to stare out at the ocean. I drink the rest of my margarita and know the buzz I'm seeking will require more alcohol. I get up. "Want another one?"

Denise gazes up at me, shielding her eyes with her hand. "You're already done? Going for drunk, huh?" She laughs and says, "I still have half of mine left, but you go ahead. I'll catch up later when we make the sangria."

I didn't know we had stuff for sangria, too. I smile a warm, content, lazy smile and slowly walk back inside.

When I get in, I check my phone and see that I have a text message from Jeremiah.

How's the water? Tell Denise I said to be good—she's a crazy one.

I smile and text him back. *I might be the bad influence this time. I intend to get very drunk and annoy the hell out of her.*

I hit send and refill my glass from the blender.

By the time I'm done, he's texted back. *Well, she probably has it coming. :) Be safe.*

I walk back outside, resume my spot, and tell Denise, "Jeremiah said for you to be good and if I annoy you, you have it coming. Oh, also, to be safe."

"Well, you can tell him to go to hell. Did he call you or something?"

"No, we just texted a bit." I sigh and say, "I like him. He's pretty great."

"Yeah, he's alright—one of the good ones."

"And, really cute, too," I can feel my buzz coming on, "and sexy."

She laughs. "Yeah, yeah, he's great. Superman and all.

If I didn't love you I'd be jealous as hell of you."

"Of me? Why? I'm a mess."

"Yeah, you are. But you're a mess that men seem to love. You had the perfect husband and now you have the perfect boyfriend who wants to be your next husband."

I think about what she's saying. A few months ago, having anyone tell me I was lucky would have sent me into a rage. How can I be lucky when my husband died at such a young age? But now, I can see why someone might say I was lucky or blessed, at least as far as everything else in my life is concerned. I sold my book, lost a lot of weight, reunited with my old boyfriend, and padded my bank account with life insurance money. Of course, none of it really eases the pain of losing Joseph. The hard work still has to be done. I still have to learn how to live this life without him, and I have to face everything that comes along, good or bad. I've spent a lot of time trying to be a better widow, but now I don't really care if I seem like a bad widow, I just want to be a good woman, living a good life.

"Do you think there is just one perfect person for everyone?" I ask her.

Denise looks over at me and makes a face. "You're asking *me* that?" She snorts and leans back in her chair, taking a long sip of her drink.

"Well?"

She sighs. "Okay, let me think… No. I do not think there is just one perfect person for everyone. I don't think anyone is perfect, and I think the sooner people realize that, the sooner they can get on enjoying life with many different someones."

I smile. I knew what her answer would be, but I enjoy challenging her with my different ideas about love. "I didn't say people were perfect. I said, perfect for someone else. I mean Joseph wasn't perfect, but he was perfect for me."

"Was he?"

I would normally take offense with her implication, but the margarita has dulled my emotions just enough so that instead, I contemplate her question.

"Well, yeah, I think Joseph was perfect for me, in the beginning at least."

"But not at the end?"

"I don't know. It's hard to say. People change so much as they grow older. When I was young I needed Joseph to be the one in charge of everything. As I got older, I resented it a bit. And now, I feel like I've changed since he died. If he came back I would stay married to him of course, but I don't know that he would be as perfect for the new me. Does that make sense?"

"Yep, it makes sense and proves my point," she says smugly.

"What? How does that prove your point?"

"I don't really think marriage is that great, precisely because of what you're saying. People change and their needs change. It's not natural to be stuck with the same person forever when you're both changing all the time. I say we should be together as long as it works, but when it stops working, you should have the freedom to find someone else who is more of what you need at that moment in your life."

"I disagree."

"I'm just confirming what you said."

"No, you're not. I said that I would stay married anyway, because there are so many benefits to staying with the one you love through all the changes. The goal is to change together and be sensitive to your partner's needs. You might have a couple of rough patches as you're both adjusting to the changes, but it's worth it."

"Maybe we should just agree to disagree?"

"Don't we always?" I say, laughing. I reach over and squeeze her hand. "I love that we don't have to agree to stay friends."

"We're just keeping it real." She smiles and pulls her sun hat over her eyes, leaning back farther in her chair. "But, let me ask you one more thing," she says.

"Sure. What is it?"

"Is Jeremiah perfect for the new you?"

I knew her question was coming, and I've already thought about it. "I don't know. I'm not sure anyone is perfect for me right now, mainly because I feel so lost and nutty at times. But I do know that Jeremiah gives me space to be who I need to be, to get through this time in my life. I think when the dust settles, so to speak, he'll still be good for me. He expects, and likes for me to be independent. He thinks I'm smart and values my opinion. He acts like I'm interesting."

"You are interesting!"

"Thanks. After Joseph died I realized how much I lived in his shadow. Not because he controlled me or anything, it's just that he and the kids had such big personalities that there didn't seem to be room for mine sometimes. When I'm with Jeremiah, I feel like my own person. I feel like there is all this possibility for me. I didn't really feel that before. If Joseph were still alive, I don't even think I would have noticed or been upset by it. I didn't realize it until I had to stand on my own."

"Well, I'm very sorry that Joseph died, but I am glad that you found a little more of yourself these last few months. Some people just lose themselves entirely when faced with extreme loss."

"There have been times when I felt very empty and lost, but honestly, I think Joseph has helped me find myself. He's watching out for me."

"I hope he's not watching all the time. He might not

like your sex therapy with Jeremiah."

"Shut up!" I swat at her arm. "It is not sex therapy, and besides, it has only been three times."

"Three? Girl, if you want to get better you have to go to therapy a lot more than that!"

I laugh, covering my face with my hands. "I'm terrible, I know. It was way too soon, but, my goodness, Denise, that man just does something to me!"

"I seem to recall you saying the same thing about him when we were seventeen."

"Aggghhh, I know." A slow smile spreads across my lips as a flash of our last time together displays in my mind. "It's even better now."

"Well, I would hope so. Our standards were pretty low back then, considering we had no idea what we were doing."

"Well, he definitely knows what he's doing now." I sigh, and finish off my second drink.

"So, don't get mad at me for asking, but is it better with Joseph or Jeremiah?"

I shake my head. "Nope. I'm not going there. I can't and don't compare. That's not fair to either of them. Sex is about so much more than the physical act and there are too many other things wrapped up in it for me to compare."

"Sex is about more than the physical part?" she asks with feigned seriousness.

"Of course. You know it is. For me, anyway. I've never been with someone that I didn't also love."

"You've only been with Jeremiah and Joseph."

"Exactly," I say, as I close my eyes. The warm breeze coming off the ocean is relaxing and soothing. The tequila has settled in and my buzz has morphed into a sleepy haze.

Some-time later, I open my eyes and notice that the

light has changed. I wonder how long I've been sleeping. I turn toward Denise, but she's gone. I hoist myself off the chair, stretch, and go back inside to see about dinner. The lights are on in the kitchen and the margarita ingredients are all still out and open on the counter. My call to Denise is answered with silence. I check both bedrooms and the bathroom. I walk out to the front, thinking maybe she took the car to go get something. The car is parked just as it had been. Perplexed, I go to the back again where we had been sitting. I think that maybe she walked down to the water, so I find my flip flops, put on my big sun hat, and head down to the beach. It's a longer walk than I originally thought, and less pleasant than I imagined it would be. The breeze has stopped and I'm met with little gnats and mosquitoes buzzing around my head and biting into my legs. The sand is soft and my feet sink into the hot, scratchy, surface making it hard to walk. The path is filled with dried seaweed, shell fragments and even some trash. In the ten minutes it takes to walk down to the groomed beach area, my relaxed, euphoric feelings has vanished. I'm frustrated that Denise left without telling me. I'm hungry and disappointed that dinner has not been started yet. I'm sweating and am starting to get a headache.

I scan the crowd. There are several families, set up under umbrellas and pop-up tents, and moms sitting in beach chairs directing dads while they help their kids navigate the waves. There are a few sets of bikini-clad girls walking side-by-side, giggling and looking to see who's watching them. I don't see Denise. I look further down the beach and see a larger group assembled under a big tent with several pick-ups with their tailgates down. I can faintly hear music coming from that direction and I think I see the blue of the sundress Denise is wearing.

I'm moderately frustrated with having to walk further

in the hot, soft sand, and with Denise for not leaving me a note, or a text, or something, telling me where she had gone. As I get closer, I can see that it's a fraternity party. The large sign displaying their Greek affiliation is draped over one of the tailgates. The majority of party-goers are probably between the ages of eighteen and twenty-three and are mostly male. In the middle of it all, dancing to the blaring truck radio, is Denise. She's holding a beer in each hand and has shed her sundress. Her too small bikini serves only to intensify the obvious age gap, and her desperation to appear younger. I have not seen her behave like this before, but am sure that it's a regular occurrence, given all of her wild stories and diverse dating adventures. I sigh, feeling suddenly sorry for my friend.

She spots me and calls out, "Hey, Alison! You woke up. Come dance with me!"

Several young men turned to stare, and two girls lean in to whisper to each other. One handsome, older man, smiles at me and holds out his hand to pull me in under the tent. I ignore him and walk over to Denise. Leaning in, I whisper loudly, "What are you doing here?"

She laughs and hands me one of her beers. I take it reluctantly. "Just dancing!" I can smell the alcohol on her breath and roll my eyes as she spins away from me. I wasn't asleep that long. I don't understand how she found this crew and got slightly drunk in such a short time.

"Come on," I said firmly, "let's go back to the condo and I'll make dinner."

"I'm not hungry." She stops dancing and is looking at me with innocent eyes.

I sigh. "Denise, come on. Let's just go back, please."

The older man saddles up next to her and says, "Let her stay. She's having fun. I'll bring her back later."

She smiles at me. "Yeah, let me stay. I'm having fun,

and he'll bring me back later." She raises her eyebrows up and down.

I can't believe Denise is behaving like a rebellious teenager. This is not how I envisioned our evening. I'm getting madder by the second.

"Can I speak to you alone?" I ask, while grabbing her arm and pulling her away from the loud music toward the water's edge.

She yanks her arm away and turns to me with a pout. "What's wrong? I'm just having some fun. What's the big deal?"

"The big deal is, I didn't know you had left or where you had gone. You're somehow drunk and hanging out with fraternity boys."

"You were sleeping so I walked down to the beach and that guy asked me to join them. I'm not drunk. I'm just having fun. Do you even know how to do that, Alison? Maybe you should try it."

I turn toward the ocean, look up, and take a big breath. "If you want to stay that's fine. I'm going back and making dinner. And hey—don't be stupid, okay? You don't know that guy."

"I know he's good looking and single."

I shake my head at her, disgusted and disappointed. "Just be careful," I say, before walking back to the condo. I'm so angry. But as I walk along, my anger dissipates into pity. Is this really what Denise's life is like? Random guys and parties? Part of me feels conflicted for leaving her. If I were a better friend, wouldn't I have stayed or tried harder to make her come with me? But the truth is she doesn't seem all that drunk. She's a forty-five year old woman who has been living the single life for a long time. If she wants to party with the college kids, who am I to make her leave? Grief caused me to do things that were impulsive, selfish, risky and even foolish. Isn't Denise also in a state of grief? Maybe not so obvious a loss as losing your long time husband, but hasn't she lost the dream of a happy marriage and a traditional life, too? Her life, like mine, is not turning out to be what she had planned for it to be. Who am I to judge how she deals with that? Still, her behavior is so risky. That man was acting awfully possessive of a woman he just met. She's a perfect target. Intoxicated, desperate for validation, barely clothed. I turn to look one more time and can faintly see that she is pushed up against the man, slow dancing. I walk faster back to the condo. I decide to drive the car over to the beach access road where the party is going on and fetch Denise. I'll never forgive myself if anything happens to her.

I finally make it back to the condo and decide to give her a few more minutes. Nothing bad is going to happen to her around so many people and if I give her more time, she might come away with me more willingly. I clean up the blender and the the rest of the food we got out. I'm no longer in the mood to stay in and cook. After I pick her up, I plan for us to go out to eat. Maybe that will even entice her more to leave with me. I change my clothes, taking off my swimsuit and replacing my cover-up with a cute sundress. I call Jeremiah and tell him what's going on. I want someone else to agree with me that Denise is misbehaving.

"Maybe you should just leave her there," he says.

This annoys me. "No, I don't think so. You didn't see this crowd. She was not only making a fool of herself, but also throwing herself at a stranger!"

"Okay. Well, it sounds like that's the idea. I mean she obviously isn't looking for a serious relationship."

"I know, Jeremiah. But that's so sad. I can't just sit back and watch her be so foolish. Who knows who this guy is? He made me nervous," I admit.

"If you're really worried, I don't know how much I like the idea of you going there and confronting him. I could be there in three or four hours. Do you want me to come down?"

I smile, touched by his chivalry. "No, of course not. You're sweet to offer though. There are a lot of people down on the beach. I'll be fine. I would just worry if she left with him somewhere. She left her phone here and she's obviously not thinking clearly."

"Okay. Text or call me when you have her back, okay?" He sounds concerned.

"I will. Bye," I say, squeezing me eyes shut, trying to picture him on the other end.

"Bye, Alison. I love you."

My eyes shoot open. I'm not expecting that, but it sends a warm trickle through my veins. He hangs up before I say anything, and I'm glad. I can't tell him I love him back, although I do.

I get in Denise's car, thankful that she left the keys on the counter, and head toward the beach access road. I park close to the party, but I can't see Denise. When I walk under the tent, several people turn to stare and I see one girl roll her eyes. Probably worried about another middle-aged woman coming to embarrass herself.

"Hi," I say hesitantly, "have you guys seen my friend who was here earlier?"

"The old lady in the bikini?" asks a very young college-aged kid.

I resent his old lady remark since she and I are the same age, but what can I say? "Yeah, her."

Another girl pipes up, "She left with Jack a few minutes ago."

Great. "Do you know where they went?"

"Nope," she says, losing interest. She turns toward her friend and ignores me.

I look around desperately. I could really kill Denise right now. I don't see her anywhere along the beach. "Look, does anyone know if they walked away or drove away? Anyone?" I ask loudly.

The young guy who said Denise is old, piped in. "They walked that way," he says, indicating toward our condo.

I can tell I'm not going to get any more information out of him, so I walk back to the car and think about what to do next. I'm really hungry. Denise is an idiot. She's probably back at our condo having sex with a stranger. I can't deal with her drama on an empty stomach. Besides, what will I do if they are there having consensual sex? Sit and wait for them to be done, then ask if they want to go have dinner? No way. We passed a pizza joint up the road on the way in, so I drive there and order a large pineapple and Canadian bacon deep dish pizza to go.

I text Denise, hoping she'll check her phone. *I'm getting pizza. Be back in about twenty minutes. Please be alone when I get there. I am mad at you.*

She replies almost immediately. *Sorry. Give me thirty minutes. LOL*

Well, at least I know she's alive. I'm fuming, but I try to get a handle on it. Denise has put up with a lot of my crazy emotions over the last eleven months, so I guess I'll have to put up with her crazy actions. This is who she is. I don't like it, but it's her.

While I wait for the pizza to be done, and for her escapades to end, I text Jeremiah back, telling him what is happening so far. His reply makes me blush and serves to lesson my aggravation.

Wish I was there. We'd need a lot more than thirty minutes.
Don't make it worse, I reply. *I'm already nauseatingly jealous. Jealous of what?*

Not jealous really. I mean I think it's gross what she is doing. But I'm jealous that it's not you and me at the condo.

Stop tempting me, woman. I'm not that far away.

Ha! Another time? Without Denise. Good night.

I smile, put my phone away, and check my watch. Thirty minutes has already passed. It will take me ten to get back to the condo. I eat a piece of pizza and then head back. That Jack guy better be gone when I get there.

Ten minutes later, I walk in the condo and hear the shower running. I pray she's alone. "Denise?" I call out.

"Be out in a minute!" she shouts over the sounds of the water. I don't hear a male voice or any giggling or groaning, so that's a good sign. I kick off my shoes, pour myself a glass of wine, carry the pizza over to the coffee table, and prop my feet up. Several minutes later I hear the water turn off, and eventually Denise emerges from the bathroom, with her pajamas on and a towel around her head.

"Hi," she says sheepishly.

I give her a look and shake my head.

"I know you're mad, but I don't really get why. I was just having a little fun," she says, walking over and getting a slice out of the pizza box. She sits down next to me, nudging my hip a little with hers.

"Well, your fun made for a crappy evening for me. I didn't know where you had gone. Then when I did find you, you had me worried to death that you were going to get carted away and raped by that guy!"

"What? You're making it worse than it was. He was harmless."

"How could I know that? How could you know that? You just met him! Geez, Denise! Did you actually sleep with him?"

"No—we didn't sleep," she says, grinning.

"Seriously?" I turn to her. "How could you have sex

with a complete stranger?"

"Hey, don't knock it until you've tried it, Alison. Might do you a lot of good."

I shake my head, "No. No way. That is not my thing."

"Fine. But maybe it is my thing. I don't tell you how to live, do I?" I can tell she's getting defensive and frustrated with me.

"Uh, yeah you do. You act like I'm a fool for believing in love and for wanting a committed relationship. You just told me I don't know how to have fun and I should sleep with a stranger!"

We're both silent for a few minutes. The tension is dissipating, but neither of us knows how to make up.

She speaks first. "Okay, maybe you're right. I'm sorry that I do that. I don't actually think you should sleep with a stranger. It's not as great as I say."

I feel bad for her. "Really? Was it at least a little good?" Despite my disapproval, I want her to be happy.

She smiles slightly. "Yeah, it was good. It was great, actually. The build-up and anticipation is awesome. It feels so wrong and risky, and that's awesome, too, but then it's over and it kind of sucks. So maybe it's not great."

"Geez, Denise. You sound like someone talking about getting high. Always looking to get that feeling back, but it can never last."

"I know. It's not like I do this all the time. And I'm not a sex addict, so please don't compare it to drugs, okay?"

"How many times have you done this?"

"What? Slept with someone I didn't know?" She thinks about it, silently counting to herself.

"Yeah, or someone you only went out with once."

"Oh, well that changes it. Hold on." She resumes counting in her head.

I shake my head and go to look through the movies left by the condo owners. Might as well watch something. I decide on a rom-com and put it into the DVD player. When I sit back down, she's done counting.

"Twenty-three. Not all strangers!" she clarifies.

"Oh my, God! How many strangers?" I am stupefied.

"Hmmm. Eight, I think."

I hold my breath a minute, afraid to say anything, knowing it will sound highly insulting.

"What? It's not that bad! We're talking over the course of twenty-three years! That averages out to only one casual sex fling a year! That is not bad, my friend. You just have no idea what the dating and single world is like."

I take a deep breath. Maybe I don't know what it's like, and I'm glad about that. I look for something positive to say. "So, you were twenty-one when you first had sex?"

"Yes, little Miss Virtue. I waited longer than you."

"I was already married!" I say defensively.

"I don't mean with Joseph! I mean when you were seventeen, at the camp-out with Jeremiah."

"Oh. Well, yeah, maybe that wasn't the most virtuous of behaviors, but come on—you remember Jeremiah that summer..." I fade out, thinking of that moment. Although the truth is, my memories of my first time aren't all that great, because they're always accompanied by memories of young heartache and sadness.

"Honestly, my best sex memories are of times with Joseph."

"Really?" Denise asks, perplexed. "I didn't think married sex would be that memorable."

I turn to face her. "Are you kidding? Married sex is the best."

"I doubt that," she says with a smirk.

"Denise, tell me...is it really that great with a guy you

barely know, who doesn't know you, what you like, don't like?"

She shrugs, not making eye contact. "It depends."

"When you're married, there is so much trust there. I think that's the key. Trust opens up all sorts of possibilities and you don't have any negative feelings after to taint it. You never have to wonder if he loves you, or will walk out on you, or if he has your best interest at heart. You just know."

Denise reaches for another slice of pizza and turns her attention to the movie. We fall silent for the rest of the evening and mumble our good-nights to each other before heading off to bed an hour later.

I stay awake for a least an hour before falling asleep. The evening did not go like I thought it would or even like it looked to be heading when we first arrived. I'm disappointed that Denise spoiled it with her selfish behavior, but I also feel immensely sorry for her. Even though I've suffered great loss, I'm still incredibly lucky to have experienced true love at all. Denise never had that. Or if she did, she was hurt so badly, that it counteracted any benefit from it. I was blessed. Joseph truly loved me and I truly loved him. Tears spill out of my eyes, streaming down my cheeks, wetting the pillow. I miss him so much. What we had was precious and rare. Even though I'm lucky to already have another man who says he loves me, I'm still so sad that I will never hold my sweet husband again. I cry myself to sleep .

I wake up the next morning with the sun spilling in through the blinds, the smell of bacon coming from the kitchen, and the Eagles blaring from the other room. It's 9:30 a.m. I stumble out of bed and walk into the kitchen. Denise is standing at the stove, swaying her hips and singing along to "Witchy Woman." I smile, quickly forgetting that I'm still mad at her.

"Hey there!" I shout over Don Henley.

Denise swings around, with a big smile on her face. "Oh! You're awake! I'm making breakfast."

"I can see that," I say grinning. "Where did we get bacon?" I sit at the bar stool overlooking the counter.

"I got up super early and drove to the store in town. I wanted to surprise you."

"Trying to make up for yesterday?"

"Noooo. I didn't do anything wrong yesterday. I am simply being a nice person, making breakfast for my oldest friend."

I smile. "Watch it with the oldest talk."

She lays a plate down in front of me filled with scrambled eggs, bacon, and a cinnamon roll.

"Viola!"

"Wow. Thank you so much. This looks great!"

Denise fills her plate and eats standing up across the kitchen island from me. "So, what should we do today?"

I'm really not sure. I have a sour taste about the beach after yesterday evening, but I know that will probably change if our time out there doesn't involve frat boys.

"I guess we could go walk along the beach after breakfast, then maybe go into town later. There are several old shops and antique stores and stuff. We could eat a late lunch on the Strand," I suggest.

"That sounds good. Let's do that," Denise quickly agrees. I still think she's being extra compliant to make up for last night.

The walk along the beach feels completely different from the previous day. The sun isn't yet blazing and the winds offer an almost cool breeze. The sand is warm-- not hot, and the bugs aren't biting. Most of all though, I'm not stressed out trying to find my friend. Instead, I'm walking beside her as we stroll along picking up shells and throwing them back in the ocean. We abandon our flip flops and walk near the water's edge allowing the waves to lap up on our ankles. We talk about our parents, my children, her job, my book plans, the president, God, and love. Denise admits to me that a lot of what I said the day before about love makes sense to her. She says that she doesn't think traditional relationships are for everyone, but she can see the merit of a long-term relationship. She even says that she really wishes she had someone who loved her the way I've been loved. This makes me sad for her, but also hopeful. I try to hug her, but she won't let me.

"Don't get all mushy on me. I don't want you to feel sorry for me. I like the way I live. I live on purpose, okay? I just think as I get older, the men appeal to me less and less and eventually being in love is the only thing that's going to make an older man look good."

I laugh. "You are so crazy! And probably right about that one."

Her phone buzzes, she looks down at the screen and grins. She laughs out-loud and texts, whoever it is, back quickly.

"Who's that?" I ask.

"No-one."

"Come on, who?"

It buzzes again and she repeats her actions. First a smile, laugh, and text.

I stop walking and just stare at her.

"What? Okay, okay. It was Jack."

"Jack? From last night?" I ask, incredulously.

"Yes, Jack from last night."

"I didn't think you exchanged numbers."

"Well, you didn't ask, did you? You just assumed I was slutting it up."

I clear my throat and give her a look.

"Okay, maybe I was slutting it up a bit...but I actually

liked him. And obviously he liked me too, because he got my number and actually called me."

"Texted you," I correct.

"He called earlier."

"Hmmm. What's he saying?"

"Hold on," she says, while sending another text. This one is longer.

"Well?" I say when she's done.

"I'm not going to tell you yet. I'm waiting on a couple more texts to come in."

I scowl at her and keep walking.

After a few minutes of us being silent and her sending and receiving texts, she's finally ready to tell me.

"Okay," she says while putting her phone away. "He wants to see me tonight. Go out for a nice dinner."

"Are you serious? You're ditching me?" I want to pinch her or something.

"No. Not ditching you. What kind of friend do you think I am?"

I roll my eyes. "Don't answer that!" she says. I stay silent, feeling disappointed yet again.

"I am a good friend," she assures me. "The four of us are all going together to a nice seafood restaurant tonight."

"Four of us?! I am not double dating with one of his friends. Forget it. You can go, I don't care, but I am not going."

"I really think you'll like him." She tries to convince me.

"What? Are you kidding me? No way!" I'm really fuming now. This will be the last trip I take with this woman.

"He's tall, good-looking, kind, sexy, considerate, and has a thing for widows."

"You are unbelievable! You don't even know the guy

you're going out with, so how could you know his friend?"

"Oh, it's not his friend. It's my friend."

I sigh, completely fed up with her. "Make sense, please," I implore.

"Seriously, I've known him since we were kids. You have, too. He's one of the good guys." She grins wildly as her words finally dawn on me.

"Jeremiah?"

She nods her head up and down, then does a little dance. "Yep! I invited him and he said yes! He'll be here around four!"

I shake my head. "You are unbelievable," I say, while trying to hide the smile that threatens to creep up and ruin my frustration with her.

Denise grins and resumes walking, swinging her arms happily. I fall in step, feeling lighter. I am excited to see Jeremiah, but I won't let her know that just yet.

~~~

Several hours later, Denise, Jack, Jeremiah and I are looking out over the ocean waiting for our food. Denise said Jack should pick the place and he chooses *The Spot*. Indoor seating is crowded so we're sweating it out on the huge patio. Jack and Denise are giggling about something, acting like they've spent more than an hour total in each other's company. I turn to Jeremiah, raise my eyebrows, and smile slightly. He reaches under the table and squeezes my hand.

"I have a surprise for you," he leans in and whispers.

"Is it a ride home?" I ask through gritted teeth. I'm being terrible I know, but Denise and Jack are making me feel nauseated.

"No." he squeezes my hand under the table and says,

"I got us a room."

"What?" I turn to look at him and shake my head back and forth in disbelief. "I don't know how Denise will feel about that," I say quietly.

We both look at Denise and Jack who are sitting so close, she's practically on his lap. He whispers in her ear and they both laugh. I'm guessing we'll be sharing our condo with Jack this evening. I make a face.

"I think she'll be okay with it. When she texted me about coming, she said that I could stay at the condo with ya'll and Jack. Personally, I'd prefer not to."

I grin up at him. "Good call."

Denise averts her attention from Jack. "I heard you guys," she says, sticking out her tongue. "I didn't want you to stay with me anyway, so there!"

We both laugh. Once I know that I won't be spending the entire evening with Jack, I start enjoying the dinner more. The food is good, the view is nice and best of all, I'm with Jeremiah. He has a way of making most situations feel relaxed and fun. He doesn't have the same prejudices about Jack as I do, and so he asks him some questions about himself. Turns out that Jack is the uncle of one of the frat boys I met the day before. He has recently gone through a divorce and has also just lost his job. He's visiting his nephew for a few days while he interviews for a job in Houston. As he talks, I can see the pain in his eyes, and I start feeling some compassion for him. Although I'm not thrilled at the way he acted with Denise the night before, I can see that he's also hurting and going through his own life transition. In his defense, he did call Denise back and seems very interested in her tonight. Maybe he isn't the kind of person I pegged him to be. I wonder if all people do irrational, impulsive things when their lives are a mess? I feel suddenly ashamed at how judgmental I've been towards him. And, even though I still can't condone what Denise did the night before since I think her actions are irresponsible and dangerous, I do hope that maybe she and Jack can contribute something positive to each other's lives.

After dinner, Jeremiah drives me over to the condo to get my things. I'm not sure how the next day will go, so I pack up my whole bag, just in case. When Denise and Jack walk in, she sees my bag and frowns.

"Aren't you coming back?"

"Yeah, I don't know. I mean, what's the plan?" I ask, feeling a bit exasperated.

"Well, Jack has to leave pretty early tomorrow, and you and I weren't planning to leave until after lunch, right? Are you still riding home with me?" she asks hopefully.

I look up at Jeremiah and he shrugs. I look to Denise and her shoulders fall. I sigh and drop my bag on the floor. Jeremiah reaches down to pick it up.

"How about you meet us at the hotel around ten. I'll buy you both breakfast and then you two can hit the shops for a bit before heading home. I have to leave before lunch, so Alison will ride back with you. Sound good? Everyone happy?"

"Sounds good," I say.

Denise smiles at him. "Yes. Thank you. You really are one of the good ones."

When we got in the car, I turn to him. "You are amazing. How do you always fix everything?" I'm astonished at his ability to swoop in and say and do the perfect thing in any situation.

"I don't always fix everything, Alison. I make a mess at plenty of things. I just want you to have a good weekend, and having Denise be upset with you, would have worried you all night. I want you to be happy. I want our time together to be as stress-free as possible."

"That's what I mean, though. You always fix things for me. The two trips I've taken this year, you've shown up and turned a bad situation into a fairy tale."

"Fairy tale? A hotel in Galveston? You're expectations are too low, I think," he says with a grin.

I sigh and lean back in my seat. "You have no idea. If you hadn't shown up, Denise still would have gone out with Jack, would have still brought him back to the condo. I would have had a terrible night. So, yes, in comparison, going to a nice hotel with you instead, is a fairy tale."

"I'm surprised at Denise. I thought she was more sensible," he admits.

"Nope," I say quickly, and then think better of it. She's one of my best friends and I don't want him thinking less of her than she deserves. "Denise is sensible, most of the time. However, when she goes on vacation or out to party, she really goes all out, ya know? The rest of the time though, she works hard, takes care of herself, and helps a lot with her parents, who are pretty sick. It's as if she's a responsible adult and amazing friend for three hundred and fifty days a year and the other fifteen she acts like a 'girl gone wild.' Since I've been married and raising kids though, I didn't see the other side very often. I kind of forgot how she gets."

"Oh. Well, I guess if it works for you, it's fine with me. In this case, I'm glad she called me and I'm glad she brought Jack back to the condo. Now I get you all to myself."

He reaches over and squeezes my knee. I tense up and tell myself to relax. I want to be with Jeremiah. I trust him implicitly. I care for him more than I want to admit, but it's still so hard for me to completely let go with him. Every time he touches me in an intimate way, I feel a stab of guilt. I'm constantly telling myself I'm not cheating.

It's been months since Jeremiah and I spent the night together, and even though it should be easier now than it was before, it actually feels harder. When he came to New York, I was feeling very impulsive and even irrational. Nothing in my life made sense, and if I'm honest with myself, I can see that I used Jeremiah as a distraction. He allowed me to forget for a weekend that I was a devastated widow. Now, I am more sure of myself. I know who I am and what I'm capable of doing and feeling. I know that I'll be okay, and as a result, my decisions feel more rational and less impulsive. Now, I am consciously making the decision to be with Jeremiah, and therefore, I will need to live with the implications of being intimate with him. He doesn't deserve a fickle and distanced girlfriend. He deserves a woman who loves and respects him. Giving him not only my body, but my emotions and heart as well, ups the ante for both of us. Am I ready to admit love for another man?

By the time we arrive at the hotel it's after seven. The sun is just beginning it's descent from the sky. Pink and orange bands of color displayed over the shimmering water and white crashing waves is stunning. I suggest we go down to the beach to watch the sunset before going up to our room. Jeremiah checks us in at the front desk and asks to have our bags taken up for us. We walk across the street to the beach, remove our shoes, and stop at the waters edge. The waves wash over our feet and my toes sink into the sand.

"It's beautiful, isn't it?" I breathe in deep and exhale slowly.

Jeremiah looks at me and squeezes my hand. "You're beautiful."

I smile and lean over to kiss him. "You are so special to me. Have I told you that?" I gaze up at him affectionately. He looks down for a second. I see a slow smile spread over his lips. I realize at that moment that I have not done a good job of assuring him of how much he means to me. "Hey," I say, while pulling him closer, "I am so thankful that you are in my life. I don't know what I would have done without you these past few months."

He turns to face me and wraps his arms around my waist. I look up in to his eyes, and am lost in them. This man moves me so much. I want to stay in his arms forever, but I know that at any minute that can change. I know that I still have too many moments when I want to be left alone, with only my memories of Joseph. I hope he'll understand when those moments come and won't be hurt by them. Because even though I'm not over Joseph, and will likely never be over Joseph, I am now ready to be a bigger part of Jeremiah's life. He kisses me softly and passionately, as the sun disappears into the ocean behind us. I swell with satisfaction, peaceful and content in his embrace.

Once in our room, I decide to take a shower in order to wash off the sand and sea from my body. When I'm done, Jeremiah slips in after me. The shower and the singing start almost simultaneously. I chuckle, turn down the bed, and crawl in naked, waiting for him to come out of the bathroom. The few minutes I have to wait only increases my desire for him. When the bathroom door finally opens, a waft of warm steam precedes Jeremiah. He steps out with a towel around his waist, and when he sees that I am already in bed, drops the towel. Apparently, waiting has increased his desire, too.

I smile, pull the sheets down on his side, then pat the mattress for him to join me. He shakes his head while moving in closer. "Woman, you amaze me."

I bite my bottom lip and bat my eyelashes playfully. "Come show me," I say, without shame.

His eyes get a little bigger and he smiles. "Yes, ma'am."

He dims the light and climbs in beside me.

The next morning we stay in bed long after we wake up, ignoring the clatter from the hall as other guest scramble to check out or make it to the early hotel breakfast. Jeremiah gets up once to pull back the curtains so we can look at the ocean. He comes back and wraps his arms around me. I rest my head on his chest, and start running my fingers over his abdomen and arms. We talk about nothing and everything. He tells me stories of his childhood and recounts funny situations at his job. I tell him of my parental frustrations and joys, and mull over a plot idea for my new book. We laugh and I cry once, but even during the tender, sad moments, Joseph does not make a reappearance. For this, I think, we are both grateful.

Eventually we have to pull ourselves out of bed to meet Denise for the breakfast Jeremiah promised. When we arrive at the hotel restaurant for the Sunday breakfast buffet, Denise is already waiting. I'm surprised to see her looking happy and refreshed. She isn't surprised to see the same look on me.

"Jeremiah, I knew you were just what Alison needed. Look how great she looks!" she says, generous and warm with her compliment. I smile and thank her. I feel bad for thinking she couldn't possibly be made happy by Jack.

Once we have our food, I ask her about her night. "How did it go with Jack? Are you going to see him again?"

"We had a great time. He has another interview in Austin next week, so I think he's going to call when he's in town. We'll see." she shrugs her shoulders. I couldn't be so flippant with my romantic life, but since it seems to work for her, I decide to stop judging.

"Well, it turned out to be a good weekend after all. I had my doubts on Friday night," I say.

"You didn't need to worry–I took care of you, didn't I?" she asks. "I invited Mr. Wonderful, here." She points to Jeremiah, who shrugs and smiles. "I should get brownie points for that."

"Yep, brownie points indeed," I say, with a wink at him.

After breakfast, I kiss Jeremiah goodbye in front of the hotel while we wait for the valet to bring around his car.

"Thank you for being so wonderful." I wrap my arms around his neck and look into his eyes.

"No problem." He grins. "Thank you for an amazing night and for being so pretty."

"No problem." I kiss him on the lips. It's hard to pull away from him.

His car arrives and we part. He tells Denise goodbye and gives her a hug, then he waves and winks at me. "See you soon."

Denise turns to me. "He's a keeper. You know that, right?" We start walking to her car that is parked in the garage.

I sigh. "Yes, Mom. I know."

"I just wanted to make sure, because it would be really wrong to lose him just because you're grieving over Joseph."

I look at her dumbfounded. "Just because I'm grieving over my husband of twenty-four years who hasn't even been dead for a year yet? It would be wrong to lose the new boyfriend? Are you for real?" I try to keep my tone light. If I'm not careful, I'll unleash all of my frustration and disbelief at her cavalier and shallow ideas of love.

"I'm just saying..." We reach her car and she opens the doors.

"Yeah, I know what you're saying. I don't really want

to talk about it, but you don't need to worry. Jeremiah and I have talked plenty about Joseph, and whether I'm ready to be in another relationship. And even though it is none of your business, and you probably won't appreciate the gravity of it, I told him how special he was to me, yesterday."

"Are we going to the Strand?" she asks, as we pull out of the garage.

"Sure." I try really hard to quell my rising frustration with her. I'm looking forward to walking and shopping around the historic district and I don't want to argue with Denise while we do it. The sky is filling up with dark clouds and rain looks imminent. Hopefully it's not an indication of the rest of our trip.

"So... told him he was special, huh?" she asks.

"Yes."

"That's pretty lame, Alison. Jeremiah is an amazing man and he's not going to stay single forever. You might need to up the ante from 'you're so special' to 'I love you.'"

"I thought you didn't think love *was* so special," I counter.

She shrugs. I sulk. She's right, of course. I do love him. I'm just afraid to say it. After his confession on the phone though, I don't have too much time to return the sentiment, before he starts to feel slighted. I stay silent on the way over to the Strand thinking of how I might feel when I actually do tell Jeremiah that I love him. Will it be okay with Joseph? I don't want to have to say those three little words with a disclaimer. Surely Jeremiah will understand that by me loving him, it doesn't necessarily mean I'm over Joseph.

We make it to the Strand area in just a few minutes, find a good parking spot, and start shopping. As I thumb through the rack at a little boutique store, I ask Denise (the worst possible person to give advice about love), some advice about love.

"So...do you really think Jeremiah would start to see someone else just because I didn't tell him I loved him?" I ask, my insecurity obvious.

"What do you think about this dress?" she says, ignoring my question and holding up a short, trendy dress that is way too young for her.

"It's fine," I lie. "So, do you?"

"Well, he did see someone when you told him you needed space last month," she replies matter-of-fact.

"I mean, Jeremiah told me that they just went out on a couple of dates, but I don't think it was serious or anything."

She shrugs. "It probably wasn't. I'm just saying, it's not like he doesn't have any options."

We walk out of the store and into rain. I pop open the umbrella I have in my bag and we both crowd under it. "Let's go over there," I say, pointing across the street to a fine arts store. Once inside, I continue with our conversation.

"I know he has options. I promise you, I am aware. He could do a lot better than a frumpy, emotionally compromised, widow, like me."

"Hey, you're not frumpy anymore." She smiles and hugs my shoulders.

"Thanks."

"There are a lot of single women out there, and you're competing with all of them. Jeremiah doesn't have kids, he's handsome, has a decent job, and is good in bed, I'm assuming."

I think back to last night and smile. "Why would you assume?"

"Because you haven't told me very much and if he was crap, you would have said."

"Hmmm–that's true, I guess." I stop walking to look at a glass sculpture. It's beautiful blown glass with shades of green, blue, and purple, crashing waves beating against brown glass rocks. "This is so pretty," I say, lightly touching it.

"Yeah, it is. Stop changing the subject. When are you going to tell him and seal the deal?"

"Seal the deal? I don't necessarily think me telling him I love him will seal the deal. I think me being consistent and non-nutty might do the job better."

"Well, yeah, that too." She winks at me and nudges me playfully. "Hey, look, it stopped raining."

Suddenly I want to go home. "Do you wanna head out soon?"

Denise looks at her watch and nods. "Yeah, I think so. Do you wanna drive?"

"Me? Are you sure you trust me? I am emotionally compromised, ya know."

"I know, but I am so tired. Jack and I–"

"No, please stop, my food's not settled yet. I can't hear about your hook-up this early."

She punches me in the arm as we leave the store, "Shut-up!"

We laugh all the way back to the car.

CHAPTER 20

"There is something you must always remember. You are braver than you believe, stronger than you seem, and smarter than you think. "– Winnie the Pooh

After Joseph died, I received a steady stream of cards and messages conveying sorrow, comfort, condolences, and prayers. The sentiments poured in for about two weeks. During those first two weeks, if I happened to see someone I knew, he or she always approached me with a heartfelt hug, penetrating stare, and firm shoulder squeeze. I heard a lot of "I'm so sorry," "Please let me know if I can do anything," "It was such a shock to us all. He seemed so healthy," and "I'll be praying for you."

After about two weeks, it seemed people were at a loss for words. I think it's a common misconception that the initial grief abates after a couple of weeks. Maybe they thought I should be getting used to Joseph's death. After all, everyone else has gotten used to it and moved on. Not that people really expected me to be over Joseph's death just two weeks postmortem, but I really think it is hard for people to know what to say in the way of condolence and encouragement past a certain time. What I discovered is that most people will just avoid you altogether. If they can't avoid you, they ask a knowing, "How are you doing?" while lowering their voice and squinting just a bit. I don't blame them, really. I never knew what to say to people who had experienced tragic loss either.

Death and grief stumps us all. But Being on the receiving end really stinks when people you need in your life start to drift away. I want people to be okay with things feeling awkward until the time is right for it to feel better. I don't expect any magic words or helpful sentiments from anyone. I just want people to sit with me, and if I need to be quiet, I want them to be okay with it. If I need to talk about celebrity gossip or something equally shallow, I'm hoping they won't judge me for not talking about something other than Joseph's death or my grief. If I suddenly let a tear slip out, I need them to not freak-out or feel the need to hug me. It is never *normal* to be a griever, and the sooner people stop expecting things to be normal, the better it will be. Just let me be a crazy person, if that is what it takes for me to get through the day. Janet and Denise are good about letting me still be me, and not reducing me to a grieving widow. I cherish their friendships. I'm finding that Jeremiah is also good at letting me experience difficult emotions, without it changing how he feels about me. At least I hope it isn't changing how he feels about me. The poor guy got involved with me at the wrong time, that's for sure.

My kids can certainly identify with what I'm feeling and experiencing, but they also have certain expectations about what they need from me. I can't just be a griever around them because I'm still their mother and they need me to comfort them. Their emotional needs come before mine, and that's how it should be.

I am now only weeks away from the year anniversary when we lost Joseph, the dreaded "Death Anniversary." My dear, sweet husband has been dead for eleven months, two weeks, and one day. Not a single day has gone by that I don't think about him or miss him terribly. However, I am feeling stronger than I imagined I would be at this point. Eleven months ago, I couldn't even conceive that I would laugh again, love again, or dream again. Now, I almost felt like a real person. Almost. I still have days where I burst into tears at the slightest provocation, scream, shout, and hit the walls. I still have days when I am so easily bothered that I want to strangle any person I came into contact with, but thankfully, those days are becoming rare. I don't always have a handle on things, particularly regarding my career or my relationship with Jeremiah, but I'm doing pretty well. I've come to terms with loving him and have even told him that I love him, but I also know that I don't love him with my whole heart, and maybe I never will. That's okay.

I accidentally, or maybe not so accidentally, sign up for my first half-marathon to be run on the anniversary of Joseph's death. When I register on-line, it doesn't even occur to me that it's the same day, I'm just excited that I'll actually be able to run most of it. When I receive my registration packet in the mail, I slip on the t-shirt, look in the mirror and right below the name of the marathon is the date of the event. In my mind all I see are the words DEATH ANNIVERSARY in bold, screen-printed letters across my chest. My face falls and I feel a little sick inside. How did I not recognize this before now? I sit down on my bed and try to realistically decide if I should still participate. I've always heard that the first anniversary is the hardest, and this day has played a prominent marker in what I perceived as the timeline for my grief process. Although, I'm not sure why. The kids asked me not to date until the year passed, but clearly I did not acquiesce to their request. I not only dated, but also slept with, traveled with, fought with, and made up with a man they didn't even know about. And even though they are somewhat adamant about the timeline they laid out for my grief and the use of what they call "death money," apparently these rules don't apply to them. Both have already dipped into the funds that they so ardently refused to spend before the year mark. Lauren went on a trip with her new friends, and Paul bought an expensive guitar he doesn't really need. I'm not judging though. I bought a pretty dress at Saks 5th Avenue that I don't need.

I think of Joseph and ask him aloud if I should run the race. It's not the first time I've asked for his advice, although it's becoming less frequent with each passing month. I close my eyes, lean back on my bed, and breathe in deeply as I try to clear my mind. I think of not running in the marathon, but then an image pops in my head. I'm looking sad and forlorn, and all my friends and family are surrounding me with pity on their faces. I don't like that picture so I then imagine myself running, pushing myself to physical exhaustion, achieving more than I previously had thought possible, and crossing the finish line as my friends and family stand there waiting and cheering me on. I smile. The choice is clear. I know what Joseph would want me to do.

Over the next two weeks, I continue to train hard, pushing myself even in the middle of the hot day, as I work to get used to running such a long distance. I send out an email to my friends and children. In the email, I acknowledge the anniversary of Joseph's death and say, that in honor of his life, our life together, and the life I have ahead of me, I will be running a half-marathon on the year anniversary of his death. I ask them to come and support me and suggest we all remember and honor Joseph together after the race by going to his favorite restaurant. I'm not sure if I should invite Jeremiah. I want him to be there, but I don't know if it's appropriate. At the last minute I decide to include him. He is, after all, in my life, and I want him to remain in my life. It will be the first time that he and my children will be together, and although I'm slightly nervous about that, it will need to happen eventually.

On the morning of the race, I oversleep. I need to be up at 5 a.m. so that I can be at the starting line by 8 a.m. There's a lot to do before a big run. I have to properly hydrate, eat a good breakfast, stretch well, and allow time for any unexpected mental breakdown about the death anniversary. My eyes shoot open at 6:30 a.m. and without having to even look at the clock, I know I'm late. I jump out of bed, dress quickly, eat some oatmeal, and drink a large glass of water. I barely have time to pack a bag of necessities as I run out the door. There is no time for contemplation or grief.

When I arrive at the registration table, I'm surprised to see Lauren and Paul already there. They catch sight of me approaching and both start waving frantically with big grins on their faces. I am so taken aback that I stop dead in my tracks. They hurry over and embrace me in a group hug.

"We're so proud of you, Mom!" says Lauren.

"Yeah, we really are," Paul says, giving me a kiss on the cheek.

"Wow, you guys. Thanks so much. I can't believe you're already here. I didn't even know if you were coming or not."

Lauren's smile fades and she looks hurt. I don't mean to offend her, but really, my kids have not been very involved in my life lately.

Paul squeezes me around the shoulders. "Of course we'd be here, Mom. We love you. We're really proud of you."

Lauren wipes at a tear threatening to drop from the corner of her eye. "It's been a really rough year, but you have been such a rock, Mom. I don't know how I would have handled Dad's death if you had not been so strong. I know you've had a lot going on, too, and we haven't been all that involved, but I hope you know that we really love you."

I am so touched by her words I have to wipe at my own tears. I was definitely not expecting this from my kids. I realize how much I need to hear what they're saying and how much I need their support.

"Thank you, Sweetie. I love you both so much, You two are my world. I'm so proud of you both, and I know your dad is, too. We could have all faltered this year, but we didn't. We're stronger than we thought we'd be and we're going to be okay. I know we'll always miss Dad and always want him here, and those feelings won't ever change. But, he wouldn't have wanted his death to ruin our lives. I know he is smiling down on us right now."

At that moment we all look up into the sky. I laugh. "We'll maybe he's not in the clouds, but still, watching us from somewhere else." They both smile.

"Alison!"

I turned, recognizing Jeremiah's call. He's approaching with a big smile and a bouquet of flowers. I cringe a little. I have not yet told the kids about him and now it will be obvious that he's more than a friend. Well, like most things this year, I'm just going to have to go with it. It's time that I'm honest about my feelings for Jeremiah. I shouldn't have to hide my feelings from my children. I'll be putting their supportive declarations to the test. Let's see how they handle me having a new boyfriend.

"Jeremiah!" I smile and hug him, aware that my kids are staring at us. "These are my kids, Paul and Lauren." I turn to face them. "Kids, this is my friend, Jeremiah."

To their credit, they both smile warmly and shake his hand, "Nice to meet you," they say in unison.

"Jeremiah and I have known each other since we were

kids and have recently gotten back in touch." I realize that I need to shut up. I don't want to open the door for too many questions. We can talk about who he is after the race.

Paul nods. "Cool," he says. Lauren just smiles.

"Hey, I think they want all the runners to report to the front area," Jeremiah says. He gives me another hug, "Good luck!"

"Thanks!" I jog away from them, hoping it will go okay. I see Denise and Janet approaching and wave. I'm glad that they will distract my kids from asking him too many questions.

As I walk past the first group of runners, the obviously more experienced participants, I start to get nervous. These people look serious. Most of them have no body fat, and have defined muscles. They are focused—stretching and breathing with purpose. My group, further down the pack, is a little more relaxed. Thank goodness. They all still look incredibly fit, but at least those in my group are smiling and making small talk with each other. I feel like an impostor. I have to remind myself that I have every right to be here. I have consistently been clocking between fifty-nine and sixty-three minutes on my practice 10K runs. I can hold my own. It doesn't matter that I'm a new runner or still have body fat. It doesn't matter that I started running to escape emotional despair, or that today is the one-year anniversary of my husband's death. What matters is that I'm moving forward with my life. I'm accomplishing something and pushing myself further than I ever realized possible. That is what matters.

The loudspeaker announces the race is about to start. I find a place next to another woman about my age, and we tentatively smile at one another. I take a big breath and release it slowly. I close my eyes for a second and think of Joseph. I capture an image of his face smiling at me. He winks, the horn blasts, I'm moving. We all start off slowly at first, but as other runners find their space, I find mine, as well. I pass my cheerleaders early on, I look over through the blur of runners and see Lauren, Paul, Jeremiah (still holding the flowers), Denise, Janet, and Joseph's brother. They all smile and wave enthusiastically. I wave back. My heart swells with love and thankfulness. I am truly blessed.

I run a good race, crossing the finish line with a time of two hours and thirty minutes. My friends and family are there cheering me on as I cross the line with three other women. My face is red, my breathing labored, and my heart is pounding. I am so happy! I hear Joseph in my head, telling me, "Good job, Honey!" I start feeling pats on the back and hear audible voices congratulating me with praise. "You did it!" and, "Way to go, Mom!" and, "You're amazing Alison!" and, "We're so proud of you!"

After many sweaty hugs, encouraging words and praises, I thank everyone for coming out to support me. I invite them all to meet the kids and me for lunch at The Salt Lick, Joseph's favorite restaurant, for lunch. After lunch the kids and I will visit the cemetery, alone. We plan to part ways for a couple of hours so I can go home and get cleaned up. Everyone leaves but Jeremiah, who walks me to my car. He finally hands me the flowers and I thank him.

"I'm really so very proud of you, Alison," he says, while kissing me on the cheek.

"Thank you. I feel great. It means so much to me to have you all here. Did you get to talk to Paul and Lauren?"

"I did. They were very friendly. I don't think they know much about us, though. Am I right?"

I bow my head and grimace. "No. Sorry, but I haven't told them about you. They were pretty set on their timeline of me not dating until a year had passed from Joseph's death. I know it's not up to them, but..."

He gently lifts my chin to look at him. "Hey, no worries. You should tell them when you're ready. I don't even have kids. I would never tell you how to handle this situation with them. I think you are a great mother and I trust you to tell them when you think is best."

I smile at him. "Thank you."

"I think though, that they knew something was up. Lauren kept looking at my flowers and Paul grilled me for a few minutes about what I did for a living, how I knew you, and basically what my future plans were."

I laugh. That sounds about right. I tell Jeremiah goodbye (thankfully, he decides not to meet us at lunch), and get in my car to drive home.

I am so elated, I don't even know how to express myself. How can I be so happy and victorious on this day—the anniversary of the worst day of my life? But, really, what is an anniversary, anyway? It only has meaning because of an arbitrary method of timekeeping. Life isn't a wheel that leads us back to the same day again and again. It is rather, continuous in motion, leading us forward to each new day. We never need to go backwards. I will always have trouble with this date if I choose to acknowledge it as something negative and sad to revisit every 365 days. Why would I do that? I decide that this will be the last "Death Anniversary" I recognize. I will honor, celebrate, and express my love for Joseph any day that I want, without giving thought to appropriate times or designated days. Joseph and I shared a wonderful, beautiful life, and we created two amazing children. We loved each other more than many couples had, and every memory was something to be cherished and valued. However, I still have a life to live. If I've learned anything from Joseph's sudden departure, it's that you can't count on life giving you another day. You have to embrace every day, every relationship, and every dream as completely as you possibly can. The good and the bad; all of it is valuable and worthwhile. I believe this world is but a fleeting moment in time and our souls are eternal and will live on long after our bodies fail. How will the afterlife look? I don't know. How will I handle one day having the souls of two men in Heaven that I loved? Who will I be with and really, does it matter? I don't know that, either. What I do know is that right now I have to live my life with love, grace, joy, and forgiveness. I have to treasure every single moment and experience I have left. The rest is out of my control and in much bigger, more capable, hands.

A couple of hours later, I pull into the gravel parking lot leading up to The Salt Lick. I've showered, put on clean clothes, and am now breathing normally. I'm a little apprehensive though. Running in the race filled my body with endorphins and when it was over, I felt like I was on a cloud, invincible and immune to anything negative happening the rest of the day. But now, now I'm remembering what this day really signifies. Even though I feel I have a handle on Joseph's death and this day is just a marker that he left us one year earlier, the kids might not feel the same. The rest of our afternoon could turn out to be harder than the race.

I get out of my car and am greeted with perhaps the best smell in the world –Texas barbecue. As I approach the outdoor wait-stand, I see Paul and Lauren, my brother and sister-in-law, nephew, Joseph's best friend, Todd, Denise, and Janet. I smile. They all see me at once and wave in unison. My heart swells. Twelve months ago I would not have said I was blessed, but today I feel it with complete assurance and conviction. I hope the kids feel a sense of God's goodness and His blessings in our lives.

Feeling blessed when you've lost someone you love dearly, is hard medicine to swallow. But I believe it is so important to recognize all the good, before you can really release all the bad.

"Hi, Mom." Paul gives me a hug and kiss on the cheek.

"Hi, Sweetie." I hug him first, and then Lauren.

As I hug her, Paul embraces us both in a group hug. "I love my girls," he says.

There is an apparent pause, as we all recognize the familiar phrase Joseph said countless times about Lauren and me. I smile at him and squeeze his hand. "I love you, too." Lauren doesn't say anything, but I notice the tears she's trying to hold back. I squeeze her hand, too. I want to say so much to them, but decide I will wait until just the three of us visit the cemetery.

I turn my attention from my children and greet the rest of our party, who are waiting patiently a few feet away. Soon, our table is called and we all file into the main dining room. The atmosphere is busy and noisy, punctuated with shrieks from children, and laughter from big parties of people already in the room. It's robust, fragrant, and lively. I am so glad. The last thing I want is a somber meal. Although I know we aren't at a party, I do feel slightly celebratory. We're not celebrating Joseph's death, of course, but I feel a sense of accomplishment that we've survived the first year of his death. None of us is worse off, like I thought we'd be. We've all not only survived, but in some ways, thrived.

We order Family Style. It's all you can eat ribs, brisket, sausage, and sides. I feel a slight pang on my heartstrings, remembering how much Joseph loved this place. He was not a big man and I rarely saw him overeat, but when we came here, the man could put it away. He was a bottomless pit when it came to ribs. I look around the table and can tell that a few other people are thinking the same thing. If you have ever eaten at the Salt Lick with Joseph you can't help but remember his appetite here. He was over-the-top fanatical about telling you how good the food tasted. I smile to myself, and suddenly feel the tightness in my chest that often accompanies my thoughts of him. But, that's okay, I remind myself. I'm allowed to feel things and remember things about him. I'm allowed to miss him and want him back. I can do all those things and still get on with my life. It's okay to still live and love.

When the plates of food are laid down in the middle of the table, Paul clinks his glass. "I'd like to make a toast, to Dad," he says, picking up a rib and holding it on the air. "Please, pick up your rib," he instructs us. Several people chuckle, but we all obey, picking up sticky, messy ribs and holding them in the air. "To Joseph. Still the best dad, husband, and man that I have ever known. May he have all the ribs he could ever want to eat in Heaven." He takes a big bite.

"To Joseph," we all reply in unison, and bite into our own ribs. I smile and nod at Paul. Lauren leans her head on his shoulder for a minute. As we continue to eat, we take turns sharing funny or special stories about Joseph. I am so proud and happy to honor him in such a way. He deserves all the praise in the world, but as stories are being shared, I notice they all are slightly inflated. There is an element of a tall tale to them and I wonder about that. Why do people feel the need to make the dead sound better than they were? Why do we make our memories of them more amazing or special than they really were? Isn't it okay to admit that Joseph had faults, too? That he was human? It's the aspects of our humanity, both positive and negative, that make us who we are, and that should not be something we forget. I'm not going to bring the subject up, because I'm okay with only thinking of his good qualities on this special day, but I can't help but remember that some of these stories are missing some important facts. The kind words and hugs often came after an argument or some rather harsh words. The fun trip with his friends came at the expense of an important family event and had even caused some real pain for Lauren, on one such occasion. The special father/son camping trip, took extreme persuasion on my part. In addition, those generous gifts he often gave, put us in a financial hole many times and caused a fight between he and I. Joseph wasn't perfect. If others want to remember him as perfect, I'll let them, but I need to remember that he had faults, just like all humans do. And, I loved him anyway.

We eat and reminisce until we're all completely stuffed. The waitress has cleared the big plates and brought the ticket (which I pick up). We all sit at the table for a while longer. It's hard to know how to end our time together. It's true that the first year is the hardest, but it seems we're all in a pretty good place right now. We miss Joseph and we honor him today, but our life will need to continue. And today our extended friends and family have other things to do, and so do we. They will likely remember this day as special, but will not be greatly affected by it. The kids and I, on the other hand, are not yet done. We're going to the cemetery and that trip requires a certain amount of deference. It can not be done flippantly or with brevity. I think we're all dreading it a bit, and are not eager to leave the comfort of Joseph's favorite restaurant, and the support of friends. Still, the day must go on. I take the lead, stand up, and thank everyone for coming. I tell them they all meant so much to Joseph, and that they have been invaluable to the kids and I this past year. I promise to call if we need anything and with that, we part ways.

Lauren and Paul ride with me over to the cemetery. It is just down the road in Dripping Springs. Joseph's grandparents had purchased four plots many years ago when the town was not so large and people lived near their families forever. Both grandparents and his father were buried there. His father was an only child, but we all assumed that Joseph's mother would use the plot. However, when Joseph died, she insisted that we bury him there with his father. She had remarried and said she would be buried next to her new husband or would be cremated. We pull up to the cemetery and I feel peace wash over me. Unlike most people, cemeteries do not bother me. I love them. Especially the old, historic ones, like this one, with unique headstones and statues. There is so much history in a cemetery. Joseph and I used to seek out really old cemeteries in small towns. He loved history, I loved stories, and the headstones were brimming with both. Today though, I'm not planning to wander around imagining the lives that used to be. Today I will be focused only on Joseph and our children. We all carry something for him by our sides as we walk the short distance from the car to his plot. His grave is near a giant oak and the grass surrounding it is plush and soft. This makes me feel better. We walk up and stand around the four graves lined up next to each other, then move over to Joseph's. Lauren kneels down where his feet would be.

"Hi, Daddy," she whispers. "I miss you. I brought this for you." She pulls a small frog statue out of her bag and, leaning forward, places it next to his headstone. "It reminded me of that time we went to the pond at Grandpa's and you helped me catch my first frog." She looks up at me and I see a tear fall off her cheek. I smile and nod to her. Paul kneels down beside her. He squeezes her hand.

"Hi, Dad," he says, clearing his throat. "I really miss

you. I feel you with me a lot, so I know you already know what's going on in my life." He wipes at his eyes and I feel like my heart is being squeezed. I don't know why it's so hard for me to see my son cry, but it is. He reaches into his jeans pocket and pulls out something small and silver. I can't tell what it is. He moves forward on his knees and digs a small hole in the ground next to the headstone. He pushes the silver piece in and covers it back up with dirt. "I love you, Dad," I hear him whisper.

Paul stands up and helps Lauren to her feet. He leans in and says something to her. I can't hear it. "We'll give you some privacy, Mom," he says, and then they both give me a hug and walk away. I watch them for a minute, and then turn to the grave-site.

"Well, Joseph, I think they're doing pretty good. They seem like it anyway. I know they miss you terribly, but I've been surprised at how well they're handling things." I sit down in the grass and pull at a weed. I'm not expecting it to be so natural and easy to talk to a plot of grass. I've been dreading it, but it feels nice to talk to Joseph like this. And even though I know his spirit doesn't hang around the cemetery waiting for visitors, I still feel really close to him here. "I miss you, too. A lot. I guess you know what's been going on with me. But, just in case...my book is being published! Soon, in just a couple of weeks, actually. I had to change it some, but I think you'd still like it. I'm excited. I wish you were here to celebrate with me. I could never have done it without you. I know that."

"I also ran my first big race today, which I know you know, because I could feel you cheering me on the whole time. I know you know about Jeremiah. I don't really want to talk about it, except to say that I love you the most, and always will."

I look over at the kids, now walking through the plots, readings headstones. "I brought you something. We all did. It was Lauren's idea." I pull a small bag out of my purse and open it. I take a black rock out and hold it in my hand, caressing the smooth stone. "These represent my grief. And I'm leaving them here." I pull them out one by one and lay them in a heart formation on top of his grave. I make the outline, then fill in the middle, creating a black, rock heart. "Sorry. I didn't mean for it to look so dramatic." I smile and chuckle a little.

"I will always miss you, Joseph. I will always feel sadness that we didn't grow old together. But, I am choosing to leave my grief here. When I can't take it anymore and I feel overcome with it, I will come here to share it with you. I can't take it home with me, though. I just can't. I hope you understand that." I wipe at a tear sliding down my face. "I feel like you do. Goodbye, Joseph. I love you."

I stand up and close my eyes for a minute, breathing in the air around me, and savoring the feel of the breeze touching my skin.

I'm ready to live.

90461500R00132

Made in the USA
Lexington, KY
11 June 2018